Saving Thomas

by

Scott Kauffman

Saving Thomas

Cover Art by *The Wild Rose Press*

The Wild Rose Press, Inc.
PO Box 708
Adams Basin, NY 14410-0708
Visit us at www.thewildrosepress.com

Publishing History
First Edition, 2022
Trade Paperback ISBN 978-1-5092-3863-7
Digital ISBN 978-1-5092-3864-4

Published in the United States of America

"When this lets up, we'll go back to change."

"Don't be silly. This is a dream come true."

"Getting soaked in a bucket drencher, to say nothing of hypothermia, is your dream come true?"

"Where's your romance, Michaels?"

"Romance?"

"Yes, romance. R-O-M—"

"That's all right. I think I remember."

"Good. There may be hope for you yet."

"Me? What about for you?"

"All my life I've wanted to get caught in a rainstorm on the streets of Paris on a summer evening."

"But aren't you hungry?"

"R-O-M-A—"

"Okay, okay. I get the picture."

"We can go back to that bistro we passed, with those heavy wooden chairs, and sit outside. They'll be ecstatic for any business they can get on a slow evening."

So we watched the rain for a few minutes more as it slowed to a drizzle. Clem stood in front of me under the arched doorway, me breathing in deep the jasmine scent of her wet ringlet hair. She was right. This was indeed a dream come true. A moment in time. A moment like so many others in my life I had let slip by. If it rained until morning with us standing there, I would be one happy guy. But did I really want her in my life come morning? And the morning after? Did she want me? Was there even anything left in me to give? Was there anything anyone would want? Had Helen been right?

Dedication

As always, for Elizabeth

Chapter 1

"Freeze, you two!"

You better believe I froze. Froze as only a nine-year-old can freeze when he looks down a gun barrel as wide as his thumb, held on him by a grinning railroad dick working for Union Pacific. All of me froze. All of me except my bladder. I peed my pants.

"Hands up. Both of you. Get 'em up where I can see 'em."

Thomas Thoreaux raised his from the door of the Kansas & Southern freight car he had just slid open. I raised mine. Red dawn breaking over Laramie. October 1955 and we had been on our way to winter in the orange groves above San Diego. The railroad dick snapped open a sheaf of papers pulled from the pocket of his deer-hunter vest. Studied it before holding it up to Thoreaux, his grin all the wider.

"Well. I'm waiting on you to tell me why these two desperados ain't you. Why this here reward ain't mine."

Thoreaux looked at me with the same forlorn eyes as had our cocker spaniel after she'd been run over in front of our house.

"End of the line, Jeremy. I'm sorry, but it's the end of the line for us."

****

That line began the May before, when Thoreaux found me on his front porch, rocking in one of four

1

hand-carved chairs as carrot-vested robins hopped about his uncut grass with breakfast bloodworms wiggling from their beaks. I can only guess what he must have thought on that Ohio spring morning when he saw me bundled up in my red-checked coat and matching hunter's cap. He stood back in the shadow of his screen door, Greek New Testament in hand, but did not come out. He never came out. Not in daytime anyway. Not when one of our village gossips might spot him when no one had spotted him in years, and buzz a beeline for his telephone.

"Jeremy? What's wrong, boy?"

"You gotta get me out of there. You gotta."

Partly out of habit and partly not certain what to do with a pre-adolescent refugee, Thoreaux made hot chocolate for us on his Buckmeister wood stove, taking it same as me—sweetened with a fistful of marshmallows. He listened with his white head bowed while we sat at the table in a kitchen tanged by his rotating band of brigand cats.

"You want to live here? With me?"

"Sure. Why not?"

"Because for one, somebody would see you and turn us in to Constable Durkin."

"What about out in your barn?"

"What are you going to do when the snow starts flying in November?"

"Well, there's California."

"But I don't own a car, Jeremy."

By then, after everything that winter, I was in tears.

"Don't make me go back! Please. You know what it's like there. I know you know. Please don't make me go back."

For a long time he sat looking into the dark of his cocoa cup. Looking the way I felt as I lay in bed on the night after they took Mom away.

"Do you know what's the worst feeling in the world, Jeremy?"

"N-no, sir."

"To know you let someone down. To have betrayed them. It eats away at you. Hollows you out until there's nothing left. Nothing of the person you once were or the person you wanted to be. Do you understand what I'm saying, son?"

"I-I think so."

He smiled. Those forlorn eyes holding secrets I did not yet know looked into my own.

"Maybe we could. Maybe we could make it. Maybe you're giving me a chance. A chance to right old wrongs. Make a fresh start."

The oak legs of Thoreaux's chair screeched across a hardwood floor splotched with kitchen grease.

"Come along. We need to find you some clothes suitable for vagabonding. We're going on an adventure."

"Really?" I shot out of my chair ahead of him.

Up in his bat-infested attic we searched through a stack of mothballed trunks until he found the backwoods clothes he wore as a boy in Quebec. He packed a raggedy knapsack for himself, stuffing some sort of ankle wallet (from his old newspaper days, he claimed) with ten- and twenty-dollar bills he took from a wall safe hidden in his second-story study behind the mantel clock. While he thumbed out the bills, I found a pile of yellowing letters webbed with spider silk, stacked in his bay window. Like all nine-year-old boys, consumed by an insatiable curiosity of all things *arachnid*.

"What are these, sir?"

He looked at them with a face I lacked the years to read.

"Do you remember what I said in the kitchen? About righting old wrongs?"

"Yes, sir."

"Mine begin with those."

"With th—"

"Come on now, Jeremy. We've still lots to do."

"But we're getting out of here? We really are?"

"We really are. Tonight."

Midnight found us on the other side of the village where the Penn Central bent in a sharp curve as it swung through Hoover's Woods. Because the train ran slower than molasses in March, it posed little problem for Thoreaux to boost me into the open freight-car door and swing up after me with the agility of someone well versed in living the hobo life. Or some sort of outlaw life.

It took a long time for the pounding of my heart to slow. But slow it did, and I did sleep, his arm draped around my shoulder as steel wheels on steel rails clacked beneath us. Their song, promising freedom and adventure, I love as much now as I did that night. And oh, what an adventure we had.

****

With our troubles soon miles behind us, we enjoyed a more pleasant life than you might suppose. Our day began when whatever train we'd hopped pulled into the yard. We would jump down and walk about until we came to a mom-and-pop grocery store, where

Thoreaux packed his knapsack with our day's provisions. Cheese and crackers and dried fruit and maybe some beef jerky. Saw to it I drank a pint of milk and brushed my teeth twice a day. When we got back to the yard, he picked out a promising freight car for our next leg west. Some evenings we came upon a hobo campfire. Went shares with our fellow low-budget travelers. Listened to tall tales of lost love and high adventure and hardships endured and priceless opportunities blundered away on a reckless throw of spin-and-toss. Songs from their long-ago childhoods and roadhouses of youth remembered got sung. Often a bottle passed hand to hand. Once when Thoreaux had his head turned to the tramp beside him, I sneaked my first taste of moonshine corn. I mean to tell you, my voice went hoarse and eyes watered as the blazing liquor burned all the way down to the pit of my stomach, but the bearded bum across the fire winked at me in our cabal of cahoots. Me, I was no longer a boy but a man accepted among other men.

More fun than I ever had camping out, before or since. To pass the time between towns, Thoreaux taught me the rudiments of gin rummy or told tale after tale of derring-do. Of Resistance fighters dynamiting Nazi trains, then hiding out in barns and under hayricks. Crossing snow-drifted mountain passes into Spain as they guided to safety scores of allied pilots downed by German Messerschmitts. His stories sounded so real. As if he had been there to see it all.

"How do you know this, sir?"

"Oh, you hear all kinds of stories when you're a newspaperman, Jeremy. All kinds. You'll learn what I mean when you get to be one."

"But I'm a newspaperman now. With my grandfather."

"Well, so you are. So you are."

Now and again, though, a murk of melancholy crept into those forlorn eyes. Once—but only once—he told me war was not all bravery, not all glory. Intrigue and betrayal was all too common. Heartbreak from those the partisans had come to trust. The deaths of heroes, too many heroes. Sons. Fathers and mothers. Even lovers. For a long time he sat in silence on a wheat-chaff floor, staring at the opposite wall as staccato slats of light and dark slit between board cracks.

"What do you mean, sir?"

"Not just now. I'll tell you some other time. But not just now, Jeremy."

But some other time would be a long time coming. The next morning our train pulled into the Union Pacific yard at Laramie.

****

All sitting in Judge Biltmore's packed courtroom on that frosted Ohio morning edged forward in their seats as my small voice gave up its reluctant testimony. This troubling lesson for a fledgling teller of tales to reflect on: Words have power, the stories they tell, consequences. Consequences that toll on for years. For decades.

When I stepped down from giving my testimony, I returned to where my mother and grandmother sat in the front row of the courtroom gallery. I was too shamed at my betrayal—at my failure to tell Constable Durkin and Judge Biltmore to buzz off—to look anywhere but down at my shoes. Thoreaux had been right. The worst feeling in the world is to know you betrayed another. Now I understood my Sunday school lesson for why Judas met the fate he did.

"Defendant will rise."

With young Lawyer Kauffman beside him, Thoreaux stood at second counsel's table as Judge Biltmore, with the self-righteous satisfaction of a true townie hypocrite, sentenced him to serve a term of three to five years in Lucasville Penitentiary. The courtroom still echoed from the sharp report of his gavel when Durkin hurried up behind him with handcuffs clinking. The two passed between the courtroom bar and gallery, Thoreaux's hands now cuffed. He side-glanced me for half a broken heartbeat, but Durkin yanked him back around, seeming to have forgotten it was Thoreaux who made his reputation for him, seventeen years before, that had now risen to the level of legend in the county.

"Don't be eyeballing the young'un. You done enough to him already."

But I saw anyway. Saw hurt and betrayal reflected in those forlorn eyes. Saw what I feared would be an utter refusal to ever forgive that even eighteen years later haunted me. Haunted me to search as Thoreaux had searched that May morning for a chance to right old wrongs. If not to make things right for him, then, as he had for me, to make them right for another.

A fool's errand if ever there was one. For words have power, and the stories they tell have consequences. Consequences that toll on for years. For decades.

Chapter 2

And toll on they did. For, unlikely as it may seem, Thomas Thoreaux's story arose anew one drizzly Thursday as the bell tower of our Maritime Sailors Chapel chronicled the eleventh hour. A thick soup of Oregon fog boiled in over the banks of the Willamette, and I walked the murderous streets of Portland's skid row with my poncho hood slung over my head against the cold and mist despite that making it harder to see. Harder to hear the askew footsteps of a war-wound limp stalk up behind me.

"You picked one damn damp night of it to talk, young Jeremy."

A rasping, sandpaper voice hinting of France and two packs a day for forty years. Erec Renard beside me. His lizard-green eye—his good one—weary and wary as only that of a one-eyed man too long on the run can look, his disconcerting left failing to keep symmetry. Watchman's cap tugged low to bushy eyebrows. Wisp of a weasel mustache greased an upper lip. A five-o'clock-shadow darkened his loose-skinned jowls that together with his tobacco-colored workman's trousers and coat that hung off a skeletal frame gave him the look of a recent deceased who had slipped off a misplaced cancer-ward gurney. Oil-stained, worn-heeled boots. He grinned at me through the drizzle, his good eye taking in the bandage taped above my left eyebrow.

"Talking when you should have been listening, hey, college boy?"

"Me? Not this college boy. Only a critic exercising his inalienable right to take extreme umbrage at what I wrote. Professional hazard common to reporters who pursue their trade with too much zeal. Forget it."

"Forget nothing." Renard turned his head and spat. "Let's walk, you and I," and set off at a brisk pace despite his limp.

We had talked a half-dozen times. Always on the phone. Telling me not much but a little. For thirty years after shipping out of the Port of Marseilles, he had worked as a longshoreman on the dog-eat-dog docks of Brooklyn where he saw plenty of what fun-and-giggle games mob goons played. "Worse even than the bastard *Boche*," he'd claimed.

Doug Rago, who last month our Local elected its new president in what Renard told me was as blatant a fixed election as he ever saw, once served as vice president of the International back in Brooklyn. What more, Renard would not say. Even over a payphone where I heard his quarters dropping. Not say until his edgy voice called me out of the blue earlier that evening when I was wrapping up at my desk. He wanted to talk. I demanded we meet.

"So how much time can you spare tonight?"

"Consider yourself lucky I give you any. You should not have demanded I come. Do you not know the risk? Risky as anything since the war. And to come to the docks! Where on every corner eyes watch. Where ears listen at every door. The more the two of us are seen together, the more danger you place me in. Why not meet out of town? Astoria maybe. Maybe this weekend."

Something—someone—I suspect had gotten to Erec Renard since we last spoke and was why he had called me earlier that evening. It had taken me months of payphone tête-à-tête to build enough trust for him to get over his paranoia and agree to a face-to-face. Understandable. In the war he fought alongside the *Maquis*. The Resistance. There, he told me, trusting got your back stood up against a cold garden wall of the village inn.

"Why this rush to meet—the docks of all places— on this wretched curse of a night?"

"My editor and I had a talk right before you called," I said badgering the truth because after what I had learned in the last five months this was one story I was not about to let slip through my fingers. Perhaps be *the* story to get me noticed at the *New York Times*. Unless some other paper broke it first, and sooner or later they would. "There're other stories bubbling in the caldron he wants stirred, and he's fast losing his appetite for this one. He's telling me it's time to fish or cut bait."

"Yes, but you cut bait with me hooked at the end of your line, it is me they fish from the river."

"He says either I hand him copy before Sunday deadline or he'll find something else for me to dirty my hands in. So talk. Tell me what's going on with the Local so I can do your joes some good. Maybe do you some good too."

"What do you mean by do me some—"

But at the soft grumble of a car engine rumbling up behind us, Renard spun on his heels, agile as any

Béarnaise dancer, so he stood behind me looking over my shoulder back the way we had come, me his human shield between him and a black Mercedes. Windows tinted three shades too dark to be street-legal. Not only way too slick a set of wheels for these rat-hole streets but the common conduit of choice favored by union flunkies as they went about their knee-capping rounds. Its headlight beams slowed but kept going as an earless cat, sleek with wet and yellow eyes gleaming, skated up over the curb before disappearing down the steps into a derelict hotel catering to heroin-head pimps with their ravenous wolf packs of street hustlers well down on the last of their luck and varicose legs. Renard breathed a whiskey-stale breath on the back of my neck, and we set out again, his good eye now darting into every doorway and up every darkened alley.

"All right. I've told you too much to turn back now. It will be me they finish if I do not tell you the rest."

The rest was how back in Brooklyn this Rago answered to Anthony Salerno of the Genovese family. Very ugly how those Genoveses did business. Ugly but patient. They knew how to bide their time. For years when they had to. Then, with their flock ripe for the plucking, with all of their political ducklings lined up, they got their guy elected.

"Like what they just pulled off here, putting in Rago. Nothing but a stooge for them. A real stooge."

"You sound peeved, Renard. Were you expecting them to put you in? Isn't that what Salerno promised when he moved you out here?"

Renard's glare burned through the drizzle. Nothing like hitting a nerve to yank out the truth.

"Do you want to hear me out or not? Say the word, college boy, just say the word, and I leave you standing in the rain."

"Leave me in the rain, and Rago leaves you floating in the river. Now tell me how they got him in."

Renard shot me another one-eyed look but kept walking. I had him hooked, and he damn well knew it.

The get-in was mere child's play. They got to the flunkies counting the votes. First with money, but if money failed, then by other means. Photographs of their kids swinging on the playground. Daughters walking home from school. Alone or sometimes talking to some grinning goon seeming lost and asking directions. He smirked at my forehead.

"A baseball bat over an eye has been known to work magic."

Certainly grabbed my attention.

"So these goons get their guy into office. Then what? I've heard about that shakedown scam called the Shape."

"*Bah*, the Shape. More mere child's play."

Pocket change when they had so many more lucrative means to score. Say deposit Local funds with a friendly bank. One with loan officers who displayed adorable children's photographs on their desks. The bank then loaned the funds to businesses already being bilked. Loans paid back at pennies on the dollar. If that.

"What kind of slime-ball business would ever do business with these goons? Doesn't sound healthy."

"What kind?" Renard held out a hand. "Look around you, college boy. These kind. My kind."

We had reached Clay Street's treacherous tenderloin district. Rows of raunchy strip clubs plying an admirable trade by keeping longshoremen entertained and boys blessed with pimples educated before getting their pockets picked bone clean inside of bars with eardrum-blasting jukeboxes.

"And the price tag?"

"A big payoff to the Local. Passed along—or what of it Rago doesn't pocket—up to Salerno."

"Couldn't be you're miffed at missing out on pocketing some of that payoff?"

Renard again side-eyed me but held his tongue. He had to. Had heard it in his voice ever since he called me that afternoon. For reasons he cared not to disclose, his life depended on getting this story out there. His story.

"So why call me? Portland P.D. has a racketeering squad. Pretty effective one, too."

"Portland P.D. effective? Do you joke me?" and again he turned his head and spat. "Useless. Utterly useless."

Useless, Renard claimed, because in the last election Rago made quite generous campaign contributions to the district attorney and a handful of our judges—Harper. Rawlins. Crowl. They were just his easy marks. Easy because they had suffered embarrassing pecuniary reverses on their weekends visiting our tribal casinos. Losses prearranged. Lost weekends with wives left at home. Company of young ladies also prearranged. Compromising photographs taken. Easy marks for now. Rago would pick up more judges, more crooked politicians, but before he got serious he was going after our pressmen to control what got read. Already, he stirred unrest within their union.

"You need to watch your back, college boy."

Renard must have thought he needed to as well, as

his good eye seemed to have picked out something ahead, and he hurried across the street, with me trailing behind, without saying what it was and not wanting me to ask.

"So is what I tell you good enough? Or do you need it gift wrapped with a pretty bow?"

"Maybe."

Maybe it was good enough, but if Renard was leery of me, I was twice as leery of him. First rule Henry taught me about any copy you dredge up is when a source slimes out of the sewer they are looking to hand you no favors. They're looking for one and likely one posing a serious risk to your health if not your career.

"Maybe? What do you mean maybe? Maybe what, college boy?"

"Tell me why you lost your job."

"Because I quit. Something better came along, and what is it to you?"

"Just figuring your motive for talking to me. You said yourself you're slinging your neck in the noose by taking a long walk on a rainy night."

"You let me worry about my neck."

"And if you're not working, how are you making ends meet?"

"I'm a thirty-year man. Thirty-year men have their pension."

"I thought you said you landed something better."

"Leave my neck and my livelihood to me. Answer my question. Is what I tell you good enough for your paper, or must I peddle my wares elsewhere?"

"It's okay. I guess."

"Okay? You guess? Okay you guess only?"

"Yes, only." Sure, I could convince my editor to

risk a first installment. Give our readers an overview. Tease them with a bouncy shimmy and shake, but Henry had eyeballed that strip club before. He was going to demand, before we ran it, that our next card feature a cast made up of the down-and-dirty details tying Rago to the rackets. Something to give our readers a real eyeful. Grab some national notice. Down-and-dirty details. Like maybe photos of our district attorney and judges at those casinos in the compromising company of young ladies.

"Think you can manage to pilfer a portfolio of those?"

A pack of feral dogs on the other side of Clay Street raised their noses from a row of spilled trashcans as we passed.

Renard nodded.

"All right. I get you your something else. For next week. My touch I have not lost, but you have enough so you run Sunday?"

Talk about antsy. What was so important about Sunday? How much hot water was Renard in with the boys? Would he even be alive next week?

"Yeah. I think so."

We had stopped beneath a streetlamp. For a moment his jaundiced face studied mine before he reached a hand into his workmen's pocket and slipped a coin into my left palm.

"To seal our bargain of collaboration. A custom of my country from the war. For while I want to trust you, I am not certain. Sometimes, though, a man must make his best guess. Take his chances and hope lady luck smiles down on him. Now wait here five minutes. No, ten."

"Wait? Wait for what, Renard?"

"For me to disappear. So I see you do not follow."

"I'm not going to follow you.

It's wet and getting wetter, and I need to get back to the paper if I'm going to write this up and get it in my editor's basket before he heads home tomorrow, if we were going to make a Sunday deadline.

"You will not follow me because this I not allow you. You will dry out. I promise."

This guy was so paranoid there had to be some truth in what he had told me. How much? That was the question.

"All right, Renard. Ten minutes. Thank you for coming out."

"No, thank you," and shoved his waterfront-callused hand into mine. "Do us some good, young Jeremy. Dazzle the world with the magic of your words. You have the touch. This have I seen. Were this not so, never would I have called."

"So when will I hear from you?"

"Soon. You will hear from me soon."

His "soon," though, sounded a little too much like "Don't hold your breath, college boy."

"How about a number where I can get hold of you if something pops?"

But Renard had already turned his back on me, raised hand bidding me farewell. Or dismissal. As he limped off into the foggy drizzle, I wondered if he had not just played me like a kazoo. An oozing oily something I could not quite put my reporter's finger on. Renard was right. Trusting *could* get you dead. Or at least kill my career. Leave me with egg on my face and out of a job with not even some weekly cowboy rag over in Pendleton willing to roll the dice on me, let alone the *Times*.

Renard's coin warmed my hand. On one side an eagle's talons grasped a wreath wrapped around a swastika. Minted in 1939. I recalled enough of my college German to make out it was a Nazi coin. A Nazi coin? Why seal our bargain of collaboration with a coin minted by the Nazis on the eve of World War II? Or was he telling me in his happy-go-lucky way with what devil I had struck my bargain. Told me I'd better think long and hard about the cost before breaking it. Two blocks down, Renard had all but slipped off into the fog. Something about him familiar, but familiar from where? My boxcar adventure with Thoreaux where we had come across so many down-and-out characters? Maybe.

So there under a streetlamp I waited for my promised ten minutes to tick away. The bell tower at our Maritime Sailors Chapel again tolled. Tolled on a drizzly night when, as unlikely as it seems, Thomas Thoreaux's story and my own rose anew out of a dodgy pact bargained with the Devil incarnate.

Chapter 3

Pact with the devil incarnate or not, to get Renard's story down straight while fresh in my head, I wrote it up back in the City Room on my Selectric just the way Renard had spun it. Proofed it, then blue-penciled down to erase all trace of my source.

As I typed up the sanitized version, beads of sooty rain streaked down our floor-to-ceiling windows looking out on the rodent-eyed lights that winked from a dozen boom derricks sprouting from the Portland docks. Out where Rago's bloodsucker rackets leeched off blue-collar joes who if they wanted to put food on the table had little choice but to give in to a labor swindle called the Shape. A cattle call the Local boys ran from the front steps of our Knights of Columbus Hall at six o'clock each morning, Sundays not excluded. Where dockhands pushed and shoved one another to grab the eye of a crooked hiring boss. Say, with a toothpick wedged behind an ear. Or maybe a shot of Jack bought the evening before across the street at the Port-of-Call. All for the privilege of forking over a quarter of his paycheck while keeping mum about whatever high-jinks he witnessed as he put in a twelve-hour day.

A story oozing right under my nose. Yet one I had known nothing of until my editor waltzed back to my desk with a propaganda press piece put out by the Local

18

in hand. Their new president, the release said, was Doug Rago. Out of New York. Which to Henry smelled, and he wasn't talking asters.

"Local means local, Michaels. What's he going to know about what's going down here? Has to be a story stinking up some dog-pissed alley."

Somewhere. All I needed to do was bloodhound enough trashcans until I sniffed it out.

Easier said than done, but along about quitting time I had hit a string of raunchy bars bordering the docks. Barkeeps often make swell leads. Sandy, the saloon jockey setting up at the Port-of-Call, seemed more than a little loquacious. Nothing we could print other than to add some color, but he said he had heard plenty of malcontents badmouthing into their beers about fixed elections. I chatted him up for a couple of hours—Sandy the one who wised me up about the Shape—keeping my voice an octave too loud.

I hoped maybe one of his malcontents might find an excuse to bend my ear when I hit the head, which I did more often that evening than my bladder demanded. I should have, though, been keeping track as to who came and who went. Should have because, when I finally stumbled out to my Jeep near midnight, wondering how to explain to Henry the size of my bar tab when I turned in my expense account, some kind soul had slashed all four tires. And a baseball bat had slugged for the fences when I stood from eying the damage.

"You need to be finding something else to write about, Michaels. Ladies' basement bingo over at Our Lady's, maybe. Be a lot fewer headaches for you."

****

Having now paid my school-of-hard-knocks dues and then some, I was invested in seeing this story published. So I typed on into the early hours, working my way to almost three o'clock when I wrapped up, City Room dark save for the green glow cast by my banker's lamp. Fortunately for me, Helen had flown out early that morning for a pharmaceutical confab in San Francisco and was not coming back until tomorrow afternoon, because Renard's story had to hit the street as soon as I could knock it out.

But before I handed my copy to Henry, I wanted to confirm what Renard had told me about Rago's alleged leveraged buyout of our district attorney and three judges. Campaign contributions got reported down in Salem to the Secretary of State. I could check those out when I came in again later that day, but I figured they had to have been made. Anyone savvy enough to have survived five years in the Resistance could not be so stupid as to lie about a fact so easily verified. Stupidity, however, can be a relative state of mind.

As I proofed my second draft to be dead certain I had edited out anything pointing to Renard, so I could give it one last read over with a less muddled head when I got back later that morning, the cleaning crew trudged in.

"Hard at it again, huh, Mr. Michaels?"

I had not bothered to learn their high-turnover names, but he must have been in his fifties. Two fingers on his right hand were missing, and he had not troubled to shave for a couple of days. Probably not showered either, because even two desks away the smell of something like over-ripe onions drifted my way.

"Have story, will write."

"What're you working on so late this time?"

"Corruption we got brewing down on the docks."

"That so?"

From my wastebasket he fished out the crumpled first draft.

"Hmmm."

"Do you always read other people's trash?"

"Just yours."

"I'll be more careful what I toss."

"Don't on my account. Your stuff's got some real meat on it is all. Something to appeal to us rubbished to the lowly proletariat, you know?"

"Proletariat?"

"From my one year at City College. Before they kicked my keister to the curb."

He read for a minute before he glared up at me. As if he'd caught me exposing myself to his teenage daughter.

"I always took you to be a friend of the working joe, Mr. Michaels."

"I like to think of myself *as* a working joe."

He let my wrinkled first draft drift into the trash before placing the wastebasket on a corner of my desk.

"Show me your fingernails."

"What?"

"Come on. Show 'em to me."

I held my hands out, palms down. Once more a sixth-grade delinquent about to get his knuckles ruler-whacked by Sister Windle for the commission of some cardinal sin or another. Like getting Carol Reash to notice me by shooting spitballs at the back of her head.

"Don't want to insult you none, Mr. Michaels, but you ain't no workingman."

" Why aren't I?"

"Number one, you talk too much like a book. Two, your nails look better than my old lady's when she sashays off to Saturday night bingo at Our Lady's. If your nails ain't broken, if you ain't got some monkey grease under 'em, you're not no working joe. Not in your bones you ain't."

"Isn't it what's in his heart that counts?"

"Us joes works with our hands, not our hearts."

"Why doesn't he work with his heart too?"

"'Cause his heart's been done busted, broken, and tossed out with the trash a long time ago. Besides, I just read your story."

"You don't think it's going to help your joes?"

"Maybe in some la-la land you're tap dancing in your head. But not in their wallets it ain't."

"I like to think it's going to protect working joes from getting hustled."

"It's a free country. Big fish like you get to think whatever you wants when it helps you sleep at night."

"I hear Rago's out to organize our pressmen."

"More power to him. Then maybe he'll work his way downstream to us littler fish."

"You're not afraid of the grift that'll come with him?"

"Not me. What's a little grift if we got more jack jingling our pockets? If my pockets is jingling, I can stand a little grift."

I switched off my banker's lamp. Same old story of the haves pillaging the have-nots, and the have-nots peeved as hell over it. My lost dogs and stray cats of the world. My Beths. The joes and janes I liked to think I came in there for every day.

"Well, time for this no-more working joe to hit the bricks. Got a dog that'll want fed, and it's been one long day."

"Mine's gonna be a damn sight longer."

"Don't doubt it for a minute. You take care."

At the door leading from the City Room, I patted my pockets to be certain I had my keys and glanced back for anything left behind. Wastebasket still on a corner of my desk. The cheesed-off at the world news groupie had moved on to the next, emptying its wastebasket into the trashcan he wheeled behind him. I should have thought more about what I was seeing, about the missing two fingers of his right hand, about my trashcan oddly sitting where it was, but I was muddle-headed from a lack of sleep and headed out to the elevator.

Chapter 4

Next afternoon as I was hanging up after being left to dangle on hold for half of forever with the Secretary of State and not getting through because of another round of state budget cuts, our teletype broke out in a clacking burst of magpie chatter, having been on the fritz since late morning when I'd staggered sleepy-eyed into the office. As the wunderkind repair kid squatting beside it packed up his tools, Henry was also hanging up back in his glass-walled office. He stepped into the doorway where for a moment he watched the teletype make up for lost hours with a vengeance before he walked over and started to read even as it spat out line after line.

Something had caught his gimlet eye. Some plane crash maybe? Maybe an earthquake of Biblical proportions south of us in the hedonist paradise called California? He glanced over his shoulder to where I sat behind my desk, one of twenty scattered helter-skelter around the open office with only me and five other ink slingers slouched behind them, with the rest of the guys and Katie out. Maybe working their sundry beats, but as we made up a motley crew of sojourners for truth, just as likely sleeping it off with newly acquired acquaintances.

Henry ripped the sheet from the teletype and began buzzing a slow beeline for my desk through the curls of cigarette smoke, head down as he read. No doubt about it now. That something was headed my way. Now don't get me wrong. Henry's all right. My journalism advisor at Ohio University for the one year he snagged a sabbatical. Gave me my job here when I came out after Beth died. Straight-laced for a former college prof. Salt-and-pepper goatee and thinning hair over the collar gone. Now the same stale-blue tie stained with ketchup and mustard day in, day out. Same poly blue suit he bought off the rack at Sears during their spring clearance when they give away everything not nailed to the floor. Pretty easygoing with the rest of us.

That morning when I showed up in Levis and a chambray shirt—but at least wearing my one tie and a canvas sport coat—Henry did not so much as bat an eyelash. Well, when chances are you'll be talking to dopers and a hodge-podge of back-alley burghers sometime during your workday, you don't want to look like some narc freshly minted out of the police academy. And while Grandfather Hardy taught me half the nuts and bolts of everything I know about the newspaper business when I worked for him at the *Oracle*, Henry taught me the other half. The half about digging deeper. About forever being curious. About asking questions. He could ask some tough ones and had a sharp ear tuned for any trace of bull pucky he heard lurking in your answer. Mine especially.

"Jeremy? You hail from Hanna, Ohio, right?"

Already I hated where we were headed.

"Yes, sir?"

"Then you must know a Thomas Thoreaux."

I guess I flinched.

"I'll take that as a yes."

"S-some," I dissembled. "I k-know him some. From a long, long time ago. Just some, though. Why?"

"Queen Elizabeth's bestowing a knighthood upon Mr. Thoreaux. Soon to be Sir Thomas, I guess."

"Queen Elizabeth of England?"

Henry's eyes rose over the top of the teletype.

"No, Michaels. Of Botswana. Of course Queen Elizabeth of England."

"Impossible. That's impossible, Henry."

"Well, that's what Associated Press is claiming." He again scanned the teletype. "I didn't think Americans could get made knights of the realm. I thought the most they could be was like honorary knights."

"He came out of Canada. Likely a dual citizen. I think if you're a citizen of any Commonwealth country the Queen can make you a full-fledged knight and dispense with the honorary."

"I thought you said you only knew him some."

"I do only know him some, but he was sort of friends with my grandfather. My dead grandfather. Why is she making him a knight of any kind?"

"For services extraordinaire rendered during World War II to the Commonwealth."

"What kind of services?"

"Still classified, it says."

I leaned back in my chair, dumb end of a dull pencil bouncing off my desk. "Wouldn't that make for one humdinger of a story."

"Glad to hear you say so." Henry folded the teletype before handing it to me. "How'd you like to hustle back to get it for us?"

"Fat chance."

"What makes you say so? You said you know him."

"I said I knew him. Some. Knew as in the past tense. I know who he is. From a long, *long* time ago."

"Knew's still the same as know."

"Not in his case it's not."

"Why isn't it?"

"Because Thomas Thoreaux was the village hermit. Lived in this tumbledown house that had to be a hundred years old, with desiccated cat carcasses strung from his ceiling."

"Cut it out, Michaels. You're embellishing. Again. He doesn't have cat carcasses strung from his ceiling."

"No one knows what's in there because no one's been inside for the last umpteen years. No one's so much as seen this guy."

"Oh, come on. Someone must've seen him."

"Not even Noony the nosy mailman has seen him. My grandfather was his cousin and best friend, and long before he died Thoreaux stopped opening his door even for him."

"How do they know this coot's alive?"

"Someone now and again spots a candle burning in his window."

"A candle?"

"No electricity."

"So no telephone."

"Now you're catching on, Henry. No telephone, no television, and no radio. I told you he's the village hermit. So no sense in me going back."

"What about groceries? Even hermits have to eat, unless he's making meals off those cats you claim he's got strung from his ceiling."

"Boy from Crawford's makes deliveries on his back porch."

"Sweet Jesus."

"Yeah. No kidding sweet Jesus."

"No, I mean sweet Jesus this is one hell of a story. One that's got Pulitzer written all over it."

"So does our longshoremen exposé, and we're the only ones working it. For now. By tonight, if Thoreaux doesn't unload rock salt on them with his antique ten-gauge, the three networks will be camping out in his yard. Along with the *New York Times*, *Washington Post*, and *Chicago Tribune*."

"Will this Thoreaux even talk to them?"

"Not a snowball's chance, Henry."

"But he might to the hometown lad made good. Seeing how your grandfather was his best friend."

"I repeat. Not a snowball's chance. Besides, last night I finally hooked my source, who pulled together some of those loose strings for our longshoremen exposé you've been carping after me for months to pull together before we go to press on it."

"So what's the problem with your flying out for a few days?"

"Because I only pulled together *some* of those loose strings. There's still plenty more needlework to thread."

"So do it when you get back."

"Because I have a lot—I mean a lot—more needlework to thread from a jumpy source who could go rabbit at the drop of my sorcerer's hat if I'm not here to pick up my phone. Haven't you always told me to strike while the iron's hot?"

"This knighthood story's hotter. Americans—even

ones with dual citizenship—don't get knighted every other day, especially for services rendered but still classified. This could finally be the big one to get us both noticed in New York."

"So could our longshoremen exposé. Why don't you send Collins?"

"Because Collins grew up on the south side of Chicago. A bull stung on its butt by a nest of hornets set loose in a china shop has more finesse than he does."

"Okay, but what about our exposé?"

"Did you get enough for a first installment?"

"Bare bones," I said handing it to him. "Barely bare bones. Was getting ready to walk it in once you hung up the horn, but we need to put some real meat on this if we're going to do any good."

Henry read my copy, head nodding as he flipped the first page.

"For it to hit home, wouldn't we want to run our follow-up in the next couple of days? A week at most, if we wanted to hit these bastards where they live?"

Henry's arched eyebrows rose over the page.

"You sure on your facts?"

"Sure I'm sure. You taught me better than that."

"Sure enough to survive a libel suit?"

"More than enough. Why?"

"Because not only are you implicating a union official who has shown little hesitancy about spilling the blood of innocents, let alone those he sees as a threat, but doing so now with the aid and comfort of our district attorney and three judges. Implicating them by name, no less."

Whatever qualms I harbored about Renard's credibility, if I wasn't going back to Hanna, I had to convince Henry how hot a story we had here and how much more work it needed by me staying where I was.

"Sure I'm sure."

Except with me not yet having gotten through to the Secretary of State's office I should have been a little less than sure. But my gut was screaming that, if nothing else, on this Renard could be trusted if only in his own self-interest. If he was lying, his name would come out in any libel suit, and he would soon find himself sound asleep with the salmon run.

"All right. I'm trusting you on this."

"You won't be sorry."

"If I am, so will you. If this blows up in our faces, not only can the two of us forget about ever getting to New York in this life, but we'll both be out of our jobs here."

"I know, I know, but it won't blow up on us."

"Let's hope not, because this is good, Michaels."

"Thank you.

"Good enough the rest can wait until you get back. Come see me tomorrow morning. First thing when you get in."

"But what about—"

Henry stood shaking his head at me.

"You know, Jeremy, the only guy in this room you're fooling is yourself."

"Fooling?"

"Yes, fooling. You've been working for me for what now, two years?"

"Going on. More or less."

"And in that time you haven't taken a single day off. Not one. Nicholson down in Security snitched to me you even came in last Christmas. *Early* last

Christmas. Like at the crack of dawn, and still here when he left. Gave me the dickens for being such a scrooge."

"I like my work."

"Commendable, but Christmas is rumored to be a day some of us consider spending with family."

"What little family I had was all back in Ohio, and they're all gone now, except for a cousin and her cabal of hooligans, so what's the point?"

"That is the point. To go see whoever you have left while you still have time. They even have these contraptions called jets so you can get there in less than half a day. You'd see one now and again, if you ever bothered to look up from your typewriter. You're a busy guy."

"Try to stay that way."

"Busy so you don't give yourself too much time to think."

"I fall into a lot less trouble not thinking too much, Henry."

"I'm surprised Helen puts up with your shenanigans."

"Yeah, me too. She's a sweet girl."

"A sweet girl with a big heart."

"How'd you know?"

"I know the type. But even a sweet girl with a heart big as the world will walk out if you give her reason."

"Reason? What reason?"

"When was the last time you so much as took home a bouquet of roses?"

"Why do I need to take home roses when my back yard is full of them?"

"Because, unlike yours, store-bought ones don't

come with dung beetles."

"My roses don't have dung beetles."

"My point is even if you no longer have much family back there, you do have unfinished business you need to face up to and come to terms with if you're ever going to move on. You've got your ghosts. So first thing tomorrow."

"But—"

"First thing."

"Sure, Henry. First thing."

And he walked back to his office, where he lifted a six-inch stack of stories from his in-box in need of editing before we punched deadline. For a long minute, I studied the boom derricks rising from the Port of Portland. No way in hell was I going back. That was one door I was not about to walk through. Because Henry was dead-on right. On its other side—ghosts. One in particular.

****

One ghost from that Saturday evening before Valentine's Day—a tissue-clutching Beth seated beside me. She wore her let-out communion dress she had changed into in the doorway behind the old Lucky Strike bowling alley, a seedy small-town honey trap on the wrong side of the tracks, where girls desperate at whatever costs to trade up from their abusive homes for an at-best tenuous paycheck-to-paycheck future preyed upon hormone-crazed boys, and where we had hooked up that summer to initiate our backseat trysts. When we pulled out of its parking lot, a half dozen of her girlfriends herded in my rearview mirror. Waved us off in the winter drizzle as if expecting a bride's bouquet to sail out her car window for one of them to snare in her (be careful what you wish for) good fortune. Me having gone back and forth for days before I decided for me not to make a mad dash for the freedom offered by the California border would always be the road not taken. Pocketed in my wrinkled white shirt I had not even bothered to noose with one of my dead father's paisley neckties, a gold-plated brass ring bought two hours before at Walmart that had set me back all of six bucks. Her arm circling mine trembled as we crossed the girders murmuring their portents of Weirton Bridge into West Virginia. Aka Hillbilly Heaven. Where the local yokels defined a virgin as any girl amply fleet-footed to outrun her brothers and where she was permitted to marry without parental consent at the ripe age of fourteen, though rumors ran rampant through the village of a desperate few who had managed to beg birth certificates from older cousins with families now of their own who understood all too well the predicament of the younger.

Sonny, if the little darlin's toes can touch the street when she's sitting on the curb, she's...

Beth stayed behind while I finished my final college semester, graduating in June swollen-bellied from Hanna High. I graduated cum laude on the same sweltering Saturday afternoon, with only my beaming grandfather, fanning himself with his Panama hat, seated in the audience. I couldn't blame the others for finding excuses to be elsewhere and didn't want them hanging around anyway. Never even asked them to make the drive down to Athens. For who would want to celebrate a commencement into the dystopian life I saw stretching before me?

When finally I did find my errant way home,

taking a full alcohol-numbed week to put my college life out of its broken-leg misery, we swept out the rat droppings from the decades-vacant apartment upstairs from the *Oracle* offices and set in to await our bundle of joy. A girl. I knew she would be a girl. Had to be a girl. For only a girl could so totally bitch up a guy's life once and for all and forever.

Beth duck-waddled around our apartment all summer, bulging big as a beer keg and, having escaped the family lunatic asylum, smiling. Often she sewed baby clothes as she sat in a church-sale rocker while she hummed some love song picked up off of WHOT before they switched to talk radio, back when they were still a rock-and-roll station.

Love can make you happy.

You better believe that unlike Beth I did not smile, and I certainly did not sing but rolled out of our less than conjugal bed well before first light and did not trudge up those creaking steps again until long after dark. Found any excuse no matter how lame to dally, and when I did go back up said next to nothing. Grunted a porcine reply if spoken to. Beth but smiled, shaking her head at my barnyard antics. Swelled ever larger.

Grandfather Hardy tried to talk some sense into my pig-lard head. "You're not the first male member of this family to sew his oats on the early side of spring. She's a good girl at heart, Jeremy. I see that. Why can't you? Give her half a chance. Coming from that family of inbreds, she probably never set eyes on one before in her life. Give her half a chance, and if you can't see it in your heart to give her a chance, remember—that's a part of you she carries inside of her."

As he did so often, my grandfather hammered that nail square on the head: But because I loathed myself, how could I not loathe what Beth carried inside her?

June passed. July stretched on and on without end, but by August my anger—my self-loathing—had abated. On one cricket-chirped night, I put an ear to her swollenness and listened as she held me, the two of us happy, Beth maybe for the first time ever. Me definitely for the first time since Mom got straightjacketed away. A mere scarecrow when I ran breathless up to her window in the October frost when she came home a year later, her once lush auburn hair now a stubble of course winter straw. A zombie, straight out of central casting for the Creature Feature, who looked at me with unknowing, electroshock eyes. And my plans no matter how rash for making good my escape in May took root.

Happiness is an illusion I learned that summer. Always too short and always tenuous. Ours lasted no longer than until one September morning when Beth stumbled down the back steps into the *Oracle* newsroom, nightgown blood-soaked and heart always frail as gossamer rendered. Likely she had inherited the family skitzo gene, fueled in the hospital by her snake-handling mother telling her that losing the child was God's judgment for our sin. Drove her the rest of the way down that dead-end road. Solace from guilt she found in drink. Drove dead drunk in broad daylight. Her scream out to the world, to me, for help. For forgiveness. Sucking for breath in the depths of my own guilt, I only screamed back. Three days for her first offense followed quickly by two weeks for the second and even more quickly by a full month when Judge Biltmore thundered down from his bench he would pack her off lickity-split to the Marysville Reformatory for Wayward Women for as long as he could pack her off and then some if she ever stood before him again. She completed a month in rehab, but only two days out and Constable Durkin's siren screamed behind her, followed by the sirens of six county deputies screaming behind him. God's own judgment must have screamed in her head as she crashed her mother's crucifix-strung Impala into the concrete abutment of Mill Creek Bridge. Less than a dozen steps from where we'd parked the Christmas before, where our miscarried child had been conceived.

Had to be going ninety easily, Jeremy. At least ninety. Why couldn't you have kept her hands off them damn keys?

Her mother's stolen Impala was a smoldering hulk by the time I arrived on scene and throwing off heat you could feel as far as a hundred feet away, so it surprised me to read in her autopsy report the coroner determined Beth had been driving with a blood-alcohol level of well over four times the legal limit. He also determined she was once more with child.

So on one fine, Indian-summer afternoon two weeks before Christmas, as four grizzled gravediggers smelling of whiskey and workmen's sweat roped her casket into the brown autumn earth, followed by clods of clay thudding off the polished rosewood—thudding that even now will waken me from a tossing sleep—I made Beth a promise. Somehow make it right. Somehow right my wrong just as Thoreaux had tried to right his so many Mays before. Promised to give what solace I could give to the lost dogs and stray cats of the world. Her world. Stories giving voice to the working joes and janes from her side of the tracks. That was what my longshoremen's exposé was all about. Giving voice. But giving what solace, what voice I could was here. Not back in Hanna. Back in Hanna lay only ghosts I was not about to resurrect. But to convince Henry not to send me back, I had to squeeze more from Renard. If I could find him.

Chapter 5

My best—my only—hope for finding Renard was how I found him the first go-round. Or how he found me. Father Connor was wrapping up a meagerly attended Mass early Wednesday evening when I slipped into the back pew of our Maritime Seaman's Chapel. No longer listed in the genteel annals of the Portland Historic Society, the Chapel opened in 1852 to an outbreak of considerable civic-pride boosterism, paid for by the captains of sleek clipper ships out of their exorbitant profits earned in the China opium trade. On its walls of seasoned juniper timbers that yet carried the memory of brine from oceans sailed long ago were carved scores of the names and dates of demise for the members of their ill-fated crews. Some washed overboard in chance encounters with tropical typhoons in the Strait of Singapore. Others had had their brains bludgeoned out in alleys behind Shanghai brothels in discords concerning the amorous favors of Mandarin beauties hinted by their wily proprietors to be of royal descent from the Dynasty of Dao Xi. Still others, if fortunate enough to have made it home at all, had succumbed in the Jesuit asylum south in Salem at the ripe old age of forty-four to the frothing deliriums brought on by what gentlemen of the day referred to as the French Disease and their ladies referred to not at all, not even in their softest whispers when alone among themselves, as if for them to mention it by name would be a summons for its visitation.

"I'm sorry, Jeremy, but I don't have a number for Erec. He may not have one. No idea of where he even hangs his hat. Not what you would call one of our regulars. Was he any help to you?"

"Indeed."

"Good. This Rago must be stopped at all costs."

He saw what Rago did in Brooklyn and did not want to see it replayed here. Too many bodies without hands washing up along the Hudson. Father Connor said he would again make his rounds. Leave word with our bartenders, a description with some of the shopkeepers, but likely it would be some days if not weeks before he ran him to earth.

On my drive back to the paper, I checked in with the detectives over at the Pearl District Division. They mostly seemed jazzed—at least those not on Rago's payroll seemed jazzed—that someone was finally taking an interest in his sundry shenanigans, Matt Lemons being one of those who was not.

"You know what we're doing for you, Michaels?"

"No. What?"

"Making sure your funeral procession has got a full police escort. One at least a mile long, with lights flashing, and the motorcycle boys in white gloves riding their hogs, and K-9 units sporting bulletproof vests. The works. The complete works. And your wake? Saints preserve me. I'm giving myself a hangover just thinking about your wake."

I made a dozen phone calls from the paper to anyone and everyone I could think of who could help me spin out my next installment. All evening someone, most likely Helen, kept ringing my phone. Something had been bothering her for the last few weeks, but I was in no mood to deal with her distractions. By morning I had to have my next installment in play if I wanted to convince Henry not to send me back to Hanna. Out of desperation I even went back to the docks, hitting the bars, but I remained *persona non grata*. No one would so much as look my way, let alone talk to me.

I considered on my drive home the possibility of telling Henry to stuff it. That I was not going back to Hanna and he could damn well trashcan me if he wanted, but I hated to let the guy down. Not after he took a flyer on me when I was dangling at the end of a short rope. Plus I saw him as my ticket to New York, either taking me with him or giving me a glowing letter of recommendation. New York. Hotshot reporter for the *New York Times* maybe. One more barren accolade to hang on my wall to hide behind. Or try to. Cutting myself off from the living to keep myself cut off from the dead. Sacrificing consciousness for conscience. Sacrificing those I cared for most and who cared for me. Or tried to whenever I gave them half a chance.

****

Though it must have been close to one o'clock when my Jeep pulled into the driveway, Helen had the house lit up like she was throwing a party. A going-away party, as it turned out, and not one thrown for my benefit. Or maybe it was. She stood at the front door locking up, her back to the street and wearing the navy blue dress with yellow trim she wore when she traveled for Merck Pharmaceutical. Helen stooped to slide what turned out to be her keys under the doormat before she started down the walk for the driveway with a suitcase in each hand. Looking straight ahead. If you were to guess from the steadfastness of her step the two of us no longer inhabited the same solar system, you would not be far from wrong.

When I met her halfway, I reached for the larger of the suitcases. I knew I had been tuning her out, but for the life of me I could not remember Helen saying anything about going back out on the road so soon, after she only came home that afternoon. And what planes left Portland at this hour?

"Here, I've got it, hon," but she yanked it from my fingers, damn near pulling them out of their sockets.

"No! No, you don't. Not anymore you don't."

The back of her Peugeot was packed to the top of the seat with clothes still on their hangers. She swung open the lid of an almost-full car trunk, the slam when she dropped it echoing down the street. A dog barked some houses away, and Sophocles ran up to my living room window, where he looked out with his tongue lolling the way it did when he saw he was about to get left behind, big bobtail paws resting on the sill. Oh, boy.

"Is it your mother?" I stalled, rubbing my knuckles.

"No, it's not my mother. My mother's fine. *I'm* the one with the problem."

"Problem? What problem, hon?"

But Helen only sidestepped around me to the driver's door, snapping open her purse.

"Where're you going?"

"What's it look like? I'm leaving."

"But it's late."

"Yeah, no kidding it's late. It's been late since the morning after I moved in."

"Well, when are you coming back?"

Helen rolled her eyes, not so much as looking at me, shaking her head as she fumbled with the keys. Finally, she did look at me. Blue eyes sharp as icicles and twice as cold.

"Jeremy. Don't be so goddamn dense. I'm leaving you. For good and forever."

"Now, wait a minute. Come back inside. Let's talk this out. Tell me what's bothering you. Tell me what I did or what you think I did or what I didn't do."

"Oh, Jeremy. That's rich. That's really rich. We have been talking this out. At least I have. Trying to, but it's like a one-way conversation with the bedroom curtains. You, on the other hand, have not only *not* been talking, you've *not* been listening."

"That's not fair. I have been listening."

"If you've been listening, it's with your ears wedged where it's anatomically impossible for them to be."

"Now, that's really not fair. I *have* been listening."

"Where were you tonight?"

"At the paper. Working on my longshoremen's exposé I told you about."

"I tried calling. Like umpteen gazillion times. Half the time your phone was busy and the other half you weren't picking up."

"Oh. That was you?"

"Who else would be calling you at this time of the goddamn night?"

"Well. It might've been Collins. Collins might've been trying to call. He may be taking over a story I'm hoping to take a flyer on."

"So why didn't you pick up no matter who it was?"

"Because I had to have my follow-ups in play before Henry gets in later this morning, and I didn't need the distraction."

"Distraction! So now I've become a distraction?"

"You know what I mean."

"I'm afraid I know all too well what you mean, and that's your problem. Your whole problem in a nutshell."

"Problem? What problem?"

"Your stories are your problem. Your stories that get all of your attention. Leaving zilch for me. Your stories are who you are, and you bury yourself inside them as an excuse not to connect. So you don't connect to me."

"We connect."

"We connect?"

"Of course we connect. Now come back inside. I'll make coffee, and we can talk this out. Please."

"Do you recall us having plans this evening?"

"Plans?"

"Dinner plans."

"For this even…"

I closed my eyes. Drizzle dripped down my face.

"And you were just about to wish me happy birthday, weren't you?"

I bit into my lower lip.

"Ah, I see a glimmer of comprehension begin to creep into your face."

Maybe now, she said, I saw her point. She had kept calling to tell me she had to keep pushing back our dinner reservation. One left up to her to make because I claimed I was too busy with my story. The last time she called, Roseau's told her they had stopped serving. That it was too late.

"They were right, too. It was. And is."

I think I nodded. I don't recall saying anything. What could I say? She was spot on.

"I can't take the disappointments anymore, Jeremy. Your letting me down. Time after time after time. Your lack of attention. The loneliness. Loneliness even when you're here. Your inability to give of yourself. I can't. I won't. This is no life."

"Let you down? How do I let you down? Besides tonight, I mean."

"Let me count the many, many ways. How about your hours? How about hardly ever seeing you? Not even on weekends, and when I do see you, you're always distracted with whatever story is your flavor of the week. When I try to talk about us, about where we should be going as a couple, you tune me out. Push me away. We never talk."

"We talk."

"We talk?"

"Yeah. We talk."

"What did we talk about the night before I left?"

"The night before you left?"

"Yes. The night before I left, Jeremy. Night before last. As in forty-eight hours ago. What did we talk about the night before last?"

I looked up to the house, Sophocles still at the living room window, head a little askew. Even he saw I was digging my own grave deeper.

"We watched television. I got home late—"

"You got home late *again*. You're always getting home late."

"I got home late again, and we watched television.

We didn't talk about much of anything, I don't think, unless it was about whatever was on. Did we?"

"*I* tried talking about us going out this weekend to replace those shabby old gray curtains you have hanging in the bedroom."

"Was this during the big chase scene?"

"No. This was during the commercial for Hunt's tomato ketchup."

"Aren't we out of ketchup?"

"No. You've made sure we have a lifetime supply of ketchup in the cupboard, and don't even get me started about your ketchup fetish, even putting it on your goddamn oatmeal, and what did you talk about?"

"I think I fell asleep, didn't I? Right after the big chase scene."

"No. You did not fall asleep. You talked about having to work on your goddamn longshoremen's story this weekend. Again."

I let go a long breath.

"Helen, I'm sorry. Really. I'm really, really sorry for being such a jerk. We'll go shopping for curtains this weekend. Now, please come inside. Please. Don't leave."

"Sorry, Jeremy, no dice. Toss after toss I've gambled on you, and toss after toss I crapped out. Big time. So goodbye, and better luck with the rest of your life."

A police car pulled in behind Helen. Likely a neighbor with an open bedroom window had called us in. Maybe Widow Thompson. Self-appointed mayor of Bernard Street. I didn't think we were being all that loud, but maybe we were. The patrolman gave me the once-over as he rolled down his window.

"Everything okay here, miss?"

"Yes, thank you, Officer. Just saying our farewells," and slid with ballerina grace into the Peugeot, slamming the door on me. On us. The patrolman gave me the once-over once more before he shifted into reverse. As she backed to the street, the white beams of her headlights bounced off my garage door she had helped me paint the summer before. I stood with my hands in my pockets, she not so much as glancing goodbye in the mirror, but I knew she was crying. She cried so easily. Over anything. Even some stupid commercial for kitten food. But what if I had run down the street, yelling and screaming after her at the top of my lungs, not caring if the stupid cop came back, waving my arms like a lunatic. Yes, like a lunatic in love. Would she have come back? Last Christmas I had watched Alistair Slim playing old Ebenezer Scrooge watch as Belle walked away. *Go after her*, I had screamed at him from the couch, startling poor Sophocles. *Don't be a fool. Go after her, man.* He didn't, and neither did I, only stood watching her red taillights grow fainter until they disappeared into the drizzly night.

Can't blame her for not looking back. She was right. I had let her down. Even after promising Beth never again to let another down, I had. If alone I now was again, alone I deserved to be.

****

A slate-gray dawn cracked the drawn curtains as my hand reached out, but instead of sleek pajama silk found only Sophocles' matted coat. Should have made time last weekend for us to visit Ginger the Gypsy Mutt Groomer. Lead-pencil drizzle outside my window, but the clouds coming over the Pacific Coast Range had that falling apart look they get when they might break up near noon and give us a half-decent afternoon.

I went into the bathroom with its turn-of-the-century clawed tub and pull-chain W.C., shaved and showered, then into the kitchen, where I poured a cup of goat's milk over a bowl of blueberries and granola. As I spooned up breakfast, I wandered the house in boxers and T-shirt.

She didn't leave me so much as a note, but everything where it was yesterday. Only the clothes she brought six months before were gone. Everything else was never taken out of storage. As though she knew she was up against Las Vegas odds, as if this roll of the dice hadn't any real chance of paying off, so why bother. Shortest romance I'd ever had. Though it was only my second.

Sophocles sat in the doorway when I returned to the kitchen, slobbered bowl hanging from his mouth. Nothing bashful about bobtails. I fed him before returning to my bedroom and into its walk-in closet where I found a fresh chambray shirt and a worn pair of khakis and my tan chukkas and knotted my one blue knit tie. Sophocles by then had finished breakfast and stood on his hind legs looking out the backdoor window. As the drizzle looked like it might let up for all of fifteen minutes, we went out into our back yard, where he went on a sniffari around my rose beds before treeing a red squirrel up a sycamore where it sat on a branch giving us hell.

Back inside, I turned on the classical radio station he seemed to like, because whatever he's doing or not doing, his head shoots up when I turn it off. Mozart or maybe Brahms. I refilled his water bowl before going out into the garage where I climbed into my Jeep. Probably could get Widow Thompson's nephew to look after Soph for a couple of days, because after Beth and now Helen I could not let Henry down no matter how much I didn't want to go back.

Maybe my going back would all work out for the best. Nothing like a change of scenery and a new story to clear out the cobwebs while putting my disarrayed life back into some sort of order. Again. Plus I would still have Henry in my corner to get me to New York. He could run the opener while I was gone, which would only be for a couple of days. Then I could finish up the exposé when I returned. Give Father Conner a chance to track down Renard for me.

Sometimes to run away from your problems *is* a good way out. Sometimes, however, is not the same as always. Not always, especially when not only do the ghosts of your past await you but the ghosts of those of another. A past buried for thirty years now about to get resurrected.

Chapter 6

Morning broke in Hanna bright and sunny. And raucous. Calico Pete and her renegade crew of eight meowed in every nook and cranny of Katie's bedroom. Her note said they had asserted their squatter's rights to her garage with a cat's customary doggedness after her former next-door neighbors—the husband previously employed by a now shuttered steel mill—lost their house in foreclosure and been forced to move in with a mother-in-law who took extreme umbrage with cat dander. One cute-as-a-button gray kitten, its chest blotched by a white tuxedo bib, for some odd reason took a liking to me. Followed me around as I dressed and wantonly attacked the shoelaces of my chukka boots, all the while wanting his little ears scratched. Now, how would Sophocles take to a kitten meandering our digs? Probably pretty good. Once I came home to find him beneath our backyard sycamore, sitting guard beside a baby squirrel that had fallen from its nest. Oregon crows can wreak havoc with adolescent wildlife no matter whether it's squirrels or sparrows. Soph, however, had a hard time grasping the mother of his new best buddy was not about to cease scolding him and come down off her branch to the rescue until he came inside. Which is where I had to drag all ninety pounds of him by the collar and let him stand watch looking out our kitchen door window on his two hind legs.

Chicago thunderstorms had delayed my flight out of O'Hare the day before, so it was late Sunday before the plane touched down in Cleveland. My cousin Katie was gone on her annual month-long vacation to Virginia Beach, her two hooligans mercifully in tow. So with the nearest motel over twenty miles up Route 457, I didn't need to air out Grandfather's old bungalow Katie and I were hanging on to while we waited for real estate prices to crawl back—a prospect less likely with each passing year, given the mothballing of the last of Youngstown's steel mills that Hanna depended upon.

Pete and her mewing band followed me into the garage after I finished dressing, where I fed and watered them before setting out, the newsroom of my grandfather's old paper seeming like the second best place for me to start snooping so I could burn rubber out of there. Though I had to admit, now that I was there, my curiosity was whetted more than a little with exactly what it was Thoreaux had done for the Queen to find him worthy of knighthood.

The *Oracle* housed its offices in an Art Deco eyesore put up in a last-gasp orgiastic breath at the end of the Roaring Twenties, financed by bootlegger gin and finished mere weeks before Wall Street plunged into its self-drudged abyss. About the same time as old Van Griffin stroked the final touches to his Taj Mahal, my grandfather withdrew his life savings from the soon to be bankrupt Union Bank, which he buried on a moonless midnight in his rose garden inside a Mason jar sealed with paraffin. Not six months later, he slapped cash down on the literal barrelhead out front when the sheriff auctioned off the *Oracle* with him the only bidder. Given a quarter of the village men devoted what were once their workdays to counting their ribs as they griped to one another about that damned Dutch socialist who now occupied the White House while they slouched in a line three blocks long for whatever relief Shawnee County chose to hand out that week, a gutsy move by my grandfather. His lifelong dream of breeding a Midwest clone of what William Randolph Hearst did in California ended, however, when I fled to Portland. A week before a heart attack claimed him, he handed the keys and his broken dreams over to Clémence Mercier, whose mother was a distant cousin of his and Thomas Thoreaux's and had moved to Hanna from the French village of Ribeauville at the end of World War II.

Inside the *Oracle's* twin twelve-foot-tall doors of nouveau stained glass, my grandfather's refugee tabby napped at the far end of a walnut counter that squared the center of what passed for a newsroom in small-town Ohio. Dust motes danced in the summer sunlight flooding in through its high Palladian windows, while down in the basement their ancient Mergenthaler linotype clanged as it had ever since I could remember, with breaths of hot-lead steam seeping through the rough-cut floorboards.

Back in an office behind the counter that, like Henry's, had a window for a front wall, Clem sat taking notes. Heels of her Wolverine boots hooked on the brass brace beneath my grandfather's swivel chair at his rolltop desk, telephone receiver wedged between ear and shoulder beneath her tangle of black hair that fell in ringlets. I indulged myself with a long nostalgic look. All through high school, I'd suffered from this humongous crush on Clem, one of those girls I would have loved to ask to a show but could only manage to mumble a couple of sometimes barely coherent words when we passed in the hall, and then only if she spoke to me first. Otherwise I did not dare look up. Not with her surrounded by that clique of giggling girlfriends I was certain had to be giggling about what a dweeb I was.

A little girl sat outside the door to Clem's office, playing with a stack of alphabet blocks. She glanced up. Pouted. No doubt deciding whether she should let go with her best banshee wail, but must have decided I was hardly worth the trouble and went back to stacking her blocks. Don't know what it is, but I have always had this certain magic with women.

Clem lowered the telephone receiver, wheeling back her chair.

"What are you building, honey? What?"

How Norman Rockwell. A smiling mother taking pride in her daughter. Smiling, that is, until she noticed me. More of my magic with women.

"So who you got down in the basement running the linotype, Clem?"

"Oh. Managed to drag Jess Walters back in."

"How'd you talk him out of retirement?"

"Didn't take much talking."

Clem said Jess had claimed watching reruns of the *Newlywed Game* was getting right tiresome. Way too tame. Suggested they needed to come up with a game show where the contestants had been married for ten years or better. Maybe served hard time for when their spats got out of hand. That, he said, would have more real-dollar entertainment value than all this mush.

"Told him I knew of couples who didn't need ten years to commence being entertaining."

Knew from hard-earned experience. Bad form to speak ill of the dead, but Chris had been a blue-ribbon jerk.

"I see you've kept General Pershing on the payroll."

"Oh, yeah. Our first-rate mouser. Got to keep him downstairs, though."

"Oh? How come?"

"Mixes it up with my three Persians. Or rather they with him. They can have their issues with men when they get to feeling moody."

"Three?"

"My three little sweeties."

"A real cat hater, huh?"

"I'm thinking of getting three more."

I suggested she talk to Katie.

"I will. So something I can help you with, Jeremy?"

Whatever her skills at running a small-town newspaper, subtlety, let alone diplomacy, did not play much of a part in Clem's repertoire. Grandfather had taught her well.

"So with all this excitement Thoreaux's garnering, you must be keeping Jess busy on overtime."

Clem's chair shot back from her desk. Taller now than what I remembered. Eyes black as blast-furnace coal. Still tough as nails. Not easily snowed and, like Henry, a keen ear for bull pucky.

"What do *you* know about all the excitement Thoreaux's been garnering?"

"Just what the A.P. wired out. You heard anything

more?"

"Wish to God I had. Talk about a publisher's dream." Clem said her circulation had picked up some, but snagging the story behind the story would bring in scads of local advertisers and maybe allow her to pay off that drawerful of bills that had been gathering dust since the day after she took over. Put an end to Elmer Cole pestering her every Friday for a payment on the note she owed to Hanna Bank and Trust, before he headed out to Whispering Pines for his golf game. "The lecherous bastard."

The smile I recently had come to associate with a collection of pool sharks calling the Port-of-Call home and possessing a special penchant for plucking pigeons crept across Clem's face. Now, if I stood in her boots and knew, would I rush to publish? Or would I dribble out the drama in drips and drabs for as long as I could dribble it out, to pump up my circulation even more, if no one else had a snowball's chance of finding out? No one else until I walked into her newsroom.

"You must think it has some potential, or you wouldn't be here. What's it been, now? Two years since your mother's funeral?"

"Year and a half. She passed six months after I cut out. My editor sent me to dig up the why of it all."

"Well, luck of the Irish to you."

"Have you talked to him?"

"Don't be funny."

"You've tried knocking, of course."

"Until my knuckles left bloodstains on his door. Gave myself laryngitis for a week from shouting."

"Well, I'll likely get the same result, but I need to start somewhere."

"Good hunting."

That pool-shark smile again. Something she was setting me up for. A pigeon about to be plucked.

"Anything else new with him since I beat it out of Dodge?"

"Not a whisper. If he'd spoken to anyone, the whole village would've heard about it by dinner."

"Still no telephone?"

"Hasn't put electricity in yet, Jeremy."

"Does he even know about the knighthood?"

"With the half-dozen news crews camped out on his lawn, he has to know something's up. And he gets mail. Takes a subscription to the *Oracle* your grandfather paid for before he passed."

"And still a mystery." I nodded back to her office. "How old's your little one?"

Her pool-shark smile softened.

"Aimée was three in April."

"She's a cutie."

"Thank you."

"Going to grow up to be a heartbreaker like her mom?"

"Likely the other way. That's how the world runs. As you of all people know."

"Clem, I never—"

But her telephone rang, and she turned to answer. "Sorry. I need to pick that up. Leads have a habit of crawling out of nowhere."

She raised the telephone, and I turned to go. No sense in hanging out here. She had as little interest in any lame excuse I had to offer now as she did then. Clem and Beth had been BFFs, Clem one of those half-dozen girls herding in my rearview mirror as we pulled out of the Lucky Strike parking lot on that Saturday before Valentine's Day. She took Beth's death hard. Real hard. Dropped sobbing to her knees at the internment. You would have supposed she had been the one who'd handed Beth the car keys. Icy as Oregon rain in winter ever since. With Thoreaux's knighthood the biggest story to hit Hanna since Judge Biltmore's arrest for soliciting an undercover vice officer in a Youngstown alley outside the oft-raided Park Burlesque (or, as he claimed, lost his way and only asking directions to the Brown Derby five miles on the other side of town), if Clem had any leads she was saving them for the *Oracle*. Couldn't much blame her.

"He what?"

The yowl of her voice spun me around, Clem dropping the phone from her ear and cupping a hand over the mouthpiece.

"Was there something else, Jeremy?"

"No. Thanks for the update," and closed her doors behind me. Set out with more than a little reluctance to confront another of those ghosts from a problematical past I once hoped I'd left far behind.

Chapter 7

When I turned up the lane leading back to Thoreaux's tumbledown house, my heart sank to my shoes and kept heading south to that special journalistic purgatory set aside for those hacks of my profession who commit the cardinal sin of allowing themselves to be out-scooped. A pudgy reporter for ABC News, along with one of his roadies, was sliding a tent into the back of their news van—a tent that looked as if Calico Pete and her crew had clawed it to ribbons. I recognized him from his evening broadcasts. Hotshot newbie ABC brought up to New York from its affiliate in Atlanta after his coverage of Hurricane Christine last October. Steven something or maybe somebody Stanley.

They slammed shut the van's twin rear doors, antenna already collapsed on the roof. The roadie circled around to the driver's side, flat of his hand slapping the side of his head as though clearing out an ear after stepping from the shower. Newbie had started to climb in on the passenger side when I caught up with him.

"So you must've scooped your story."

"No way, dude."

"But you're packing up."

"Damn straight we're packing up. Packing up, packing it in, and getting the hell out before somebody loses an eyeball."

"Why? What happened?"

"Crazy coot fired an M-80 into our tent at the crack of dawn is what happened. Exploded an inch over our heads."

I fought back a smile. The more things change…

"Had to be a slingshot. Had to be. Maybe out of an upstairs window, because I'll tell you what, dude, I flew out of that tent, or what was left of it, and there wasn't nobody standing around. I mean not nobody."

"An M-80, you say?"

"Had to be. Five-hundred-dollar tent, too. My ears are still ringing."

Newbie turned inside the van. "Kyle. Your ears ringing?"

"What?" Kyle said, still slapping the side of his head. "What?"

"Kyle's ears are still ringing too."

"So did you talk to him?"

"Talk to him? We never even saw the bastard." This time Newbie shouted into the van. "Did we, Kyle?"

"What?"

"How long've you been camped out?"

"Friday afternoon."

"You two the only ones here?"

"No. Only last ones to pack it in. Everyone else gone ten minutes after the bombardment."

"You talk to Constable Durkin?"

"That cracker. Wanted to know if we had the geezer's consent to be camping out on his lawn."

"And of course, how could you get the geezer's consent if he wouldn't even come to his door?"

"That's what I said. To which Crackerhead tells me

the fair citizens of this hick town have got themselves some sort of a Constitutional right to chase off any and all criminal trespassers by whatever means. Goddamn townie cracker."

I did my best to imitate Clem's pool-shark smile.

"Sure am sorry about you leaving without your story."

Newbie said he was too, but they had their guy over in London checking it out. He would turn something up if there was anything to be turned up. Ex-FBI and all. Newbie's guess was the story would wind up in France somewhere.

"But we'll see." Newbie slapped the dashboard. "Let's roll, Kyle. If you push 'er, we can be back in the city by evening."

"Suits me to a T. We'll be a whole lot safer on the mean streets of the Big Apple in the dead of night than out here in broad daylight with the loonies from the boonies."

"Amen to that, Brother Kyle. Amen to that. Now put the pedal to the metal and let 'er roll."

Roll they did, driveway gravel spinning off their wheels and pelting my trouser legs. With a warm glow in my now resuscitated heart, I watched as the van turned out of Thoreaux's lane onto Court Street, then turned myself to the story at hand.

****

All that remained of the original Thoreaux homestead was a decrepit three-story clapboard farmhouse that towered into a thicket of leaves. Once upon a time white in color. Likely last painted by Jacque Thoreaux himself soon after he purchased the premises at one of dozens of Depression foreclosures in

Shawnee County that year. Old-time porch out front where he could rock on sweltering summer evenings, shaded by ash and oak, and watch creep by a world run ever deeper into the despair of bankruptcy. Hand-adzed cedar shakes shingled his roof, and in its center, atop a cupola infested with dozens of cooing pigeons, perched an obstinate weathercock, rusted to flinty orange, that refused to tell true even in the severest winter gales. Beneath the roof eaves hung cone upon cone of buzzing wasp nests. Rain spouting corroded with dozens of holes the size of half-dollars fed into a bottomless black cistern at its south corner, where our village delinquents speculated the bodies of no less than a dozen runaways drowned by Thoreaux's own gnarled hands rested in a watery grave. Dark-paned windows tinted to near black made it impossible for them to spy what acts of moral turpitude transpired inside at night, even if they could suck up their juvenile courage to draw near, while every frame missed at least one of its eight panes, shattered by their slingshots. Lawn gone to seed with grass reaching to my knees. Grass I had once cut.

Three or four times each summer, Grandfather Hardy took me with him when he loaded up a reel push mower into the back of his 1940 Ford pickup after the one summer where dozens of complaints resulted in what the *Oracle* branded a vigilante-cowed meeting of village council. They ordered out Jay Groaner's park crew, then mailed a bill to Thoreaux. A bill unpaid for over a year even after second, third, and fourth demands went out. Constable Durkin was finally ordered to hold Thoreaux in the village jail for thirty days, which considerably goaded Durkin, who goaded easily anyway, as it conflicted with his afternoon euchre games upstairs in Shorty Stevens's pool hall where he supplemented his meager constable's pay, but it proved to be the last time anyone in the village claimed to have caught even a brief glimpse of Thoreaux. Whispers in the years to come circulated how he had mutated into a frothing-mouthed hunchback worthy to play Quasimodo, should the Hanna Players ever stage a revival production of *The Hunchback of Norte Dame*. In back, his mammoth barn, its clapboards spooned and sprung from their wall studs, they too now wind-scoured down to bleak gray. The perfect Hollywood haunted house. Complete with its own ghost.

****

Only those in the village who knew nothing claimed to know much about Thomas Thoreaux. What little I knew came from Grandfather Hardy, who only let slip the tiniest of tidbits on the rarest of rare occasions when he sat by his fireplace on snow-driven nights with a second Irish in hand.

Thomas Thoreaux was born Thomas Hardy in Hamburg to German Anabaptist parents. His mother's people came out of the village of Ribeauville in Alsace Lorraine, a province of France until seized by Germany in 1870 at the end of the Franco-Prussian War. Both parents worked at the sprawling Blohm & Voss shipyards, he as an arc welder, she for the plant manager as typist, but she wrote in her own letters with growing alarm at the surging Teutonic militarism she saw in much of the correspondence going out. With the outbreak of fighting, the German Ambulance Corps drafted her pacifist husband, who later died at the Somme one sunny morning when a British eighteen-pounder vaporized him in a puff of pink mist. A week after the Armistice, she and Thomas fled—first to Cornwall by British cruiser, arranged by a cousin who worked inside the British Secret Service Bureau, then on to Canada. There she married Jacque Thoreaux, who ran a lumber mill in upper Quebec, and for his own safety the boy's last name changed when Jacque adopted him. After the Royal Canadian Mounted Police discovered a woodsman's tomahawk buried in the back of the skull of an Amsterdam purchasing agent they suspected of being an operative for Hitler's resuscitated Abwehr, the family moved to Hanna, in the spring of 1933, where a cousin of Thoreaux's dead father, namely my grandfather, ran a small-town newspaper.

****

I walked up the loose-board steps of Thoreaux's porch and knocked, an upper corner of its rusted door screen curled over. Odor of must and mold. Wood rot and decay. I knocked again, this time with more ardency.

"Mr. Thoreaux? Mr. Thoreaux, sir? It's me. Jeremy Michaels. Samuel Hardy's grandson. Mr. Thoreaux?"

I waited and knocked and called out again. Nothing. Not a sound. Nothing but a breeze rustling leaves. An overhead caw of malevolent crows. I looked in the front picture window, hands to my temples to cut the early-morning glare. Just enough light to make out the shadowy inside. A high-ceilinged wainscoted parlor with long tresses of paint peeling off the walls. Two-foot-tall stacks of magazines and newspapers piled between a couch and easy chair. The last refuge of a man utterly estranged from the world. Something Thoreaux and I shared. For him, I could only guess since when. For me, I had no need to guess but knew. Knew to the exact afternoon.

****

Angry October afternoon. Horse clouds of gray wisp galloped across a gray sky. Spits of sleet stung my eyes shut. Whispering branches of bare-bone white birches. Ankle-deep leaves carpeted the frost-heaved sidewalk, slippery beneath the smooth soles of my almost new Buster Browns, leaves so full of color only the Saturday before when I helped Dad rake the dead ones into a pile we set on fire in our fall custom of farewell. Dad, always taciturn, more so. A gusting wind cut through my red-checkered coat. Cliques of kids. Girls and boys. Some older, some younger, only me walking alone. Mercifully short seven-minute walk. A full driveway. Our Rambler parked where Dad never parked. Not this time of day. The other two familiar. One gray-blue. The other dull green. Maybe from summer picnics?

I slipped in the side kitchen door. Grandmother Hardy at the stove, her back to me, cartoon-mouse apron I gave Mom one Christmas bowed behind her waist. Pan boiling. From the peels heaped in the kitchen sink, likely potatoes. Her gray eyes always made me need to pee, so I held my breath when I tiptoed behind her into the living room. In a chair there, Dad leaning forward, hands clasped between his knees. The look of a man desperate enough to resort to anything. Even prayer. Aunts Hester and Rachel seated beside each other on the couch. Red-rimmed eyes darting my way. Their already hushed words ceasing mid-sentence. Mom not there. Mom, who had wandered the house all summer, tissue balled in her fist, not there. So bad no one said. Grandmother Hardy came in, long-handled fork in hand, her angry gray eyes telling me if not where telling me why.

I slunk off to my room, my legs not yet long enough for my Buster Browns to touch the floor from my bed. Not taking off my red-checkered coat and hunter's hat. Making up my mind if I should go or stay. But go where? Stay for what? Dad shut the door behind him. Draped his arm around my scared shoulders. Mom was very sick. He did not know when she would come home—maybe not for many months—but come home again she would. He promised she would. Until she did, Grandmother Hardy was moving in to take care of us. I was to listen to her the same as I did to Mom, and if I did, everything would be as it once was. He promised it would. But in the branches of the bare-bone white birches outside my window I heard God's whisper. He's lying. Do not believe him. Nothing will ever be the same for you again. This day…this afternoon… I forever marked it as the day my childhood forever ended, and it did not matter how much I wanted my mother—my mother who it was my fault she had been taken away—to come home again.

Dad kissed me on the forehead. The only time he ever kissed me. Said he needed to get back to the plant. Big order for Boeing. Aunts Hester and Rachel drove home to care for my uncles and cousins, but they also kissed me. Grandmother Hardy did not kiss me, and as she unpacked in our spare bedroom, her angry gray eyes looked across to where I stood watching in the doorway. I knew then. Then I knew.

****

I stepped back from Thoreaux's front porch

window. At least no cat carcasses were strung from the ceiling. Pretty much how I remembered it before I managed to get him shitcanned off to prison. I circled to the rear of the house. Plum, cherry, and peach trees. All nicely pruned. A well-weeded kitchen garden he must have tended on moonlit midnights when he did not have village hooligans skulking about. A rusted lock latched shut the slanted twin storm-cellar doors.

Thoreaux wasn't giving me much choice. For if my estrangement from the world began with my mother being taken away, had his anything to do with the knighthood? An old-style Hollywood stakeout of an old-style Hollywood haunted house seemed called for.

Chapter 8

I sat up all that night in my Hertz rental. Windows rolled down to the chirp of crickets, the fecund whispers of cicadas. Firmament unscrolling. Now and again a screech of whet owl followed by the death-knell squeal of luckless rodent. Thoreaux's silhouetted house looming up out of the dark.

Watched and waited for some sign of life inside but saw only the flutter of faint moon shadow cast by ash and oak, until near dawn when a candle wavered in an upstairs window. Same window behind where a mantel clock concealed the wall safe from which he had taken the funds used to finance our grand adventure.

The candle drew near his bay window where I had seen the spider-webbed letters. Letters still silk-spun with time's passage? Or might he have come this night to find in them what comfort he would? But if he found comfort in their words, why allow them to lie fallow? If not comfort, what words did they hold he could not bear to read, yet must nonetheless keep near at hand if not near at heart?

Had he learned the hard lesson, as I had so many years ago in Judge Biltmore's hushed courtroom: Words have power. Their tales consequences. Consequences tolling on for years. For decades. The wavering candlelight withdrew, appeared in another black-paned room, withdrew again, appeared in a third.

As though he searched for some article misplaced, some object lost, but what article, what object, could so compel him he could not wait until he had the light of day but must search with only that of the miserly night?

Far down the dirt road behind me, where the last of Hanna's hard-scrabbled farmers held out against the damnable creep of modernity, came the betokened cry of cock of which Saint Matthew foretold. With its caw, the candle at once went dark. A scarlet dawn dulled over his cedar-shingled roof. Red sky in morning, sailors...and a small voice, my years-ago small courtroom voice, warned me that I too should take heed, for if Thoreaux had his ghosts—*surely you have yours. Take heed. Take heed.*

****

Having neglected to shop at Crawford's the day before, after I packed it in for the night I swung up Court Street, where even with the grass heavy with dew I had to search for a place to park within a block of the village square. I got my *Cleveland Plain Dealer* at Reash's Newsstand, where I chatted up Keith about our ten-year reunion coming up next summer. A reunion with its too-many questions I didn't want to answer. Questions for which I had no answers, and had no intention whatsoever of coming back for no matter what I might've told Keith. I was headed in the direction of the Country Kitchen when I spotted Clem two blocks down, jogging away from me while pushing one of those three-wheeled strollers jock stores sell to single moms who have no one to watch for them. She wore a pair of barber-pole striped tights. The kind women wear that reveal every calf, thigh, and buttock muscle. Especially every groin-grinding buttock muscle. I stared after her for three sultry blocks until she took mercy to swing her stroller right at Union Street, back in the direction of the *Oracle*. A law. There ought to be a law.

Already a dozen dairy farmers smelling of cow dung, finished with morning milking, crowded the restaurant counter and booths, along with divorced diesel warriors about to head out on the open road saddled up in their eighteen-wheelers, as well as a smattering of early-hour shop owners sporting clip-on bowties and short-sleeved white shirts against the day's coming heat.

Rich steam breaths of frying eggs and smokehouse-cured ham. Just-out-of-the oven Pennsylvania Dutch bread toasting. The sharp clatter of china on china behind the swinging doors of a women-voiced kitchen. Midwest drawls murmuring the village gossip fresh since the day before.

"So, Sid? You hear anything more about this Thoreaux business?"

"Not so much as a whisper. You?"

"Nope."

In the rear of the restaurant sat Lawyer Kauffman, who had represented Thoreaux at his trial where I testified and who later helped Katie and me probate our grandfather's will. Slumped back in his chair with this morning's *Oracle* spread open. Likely their first customer in the door that morning when he came in looking for whatever lonely company might wander in following his hours-long walk before dawn, but at this time of day only he sat at the long table Ray Hurst reserved for the local wise men, where they daily held court to settle the village's many weighty affairs.

"Good morning, Attorney Kauffman."

He lowered his paper, squinting at me over his rimless bifocals. The corners of his mouth twitched as he only somewhat succeeded in stifling an impish grin. Oh, what shenanigans he and my father must have gotten into I can only imagine.

"Well, look at what General Pershing drug in during the dead of night."

"May I take breakfast with you, sir?"

"Why, of course you can, son, of course you can. Proud for the company."

A peroxide-scalded blonde, coffee pot in hand, scurried over to our table as I scooted back my chair.

"I'll be back in a minute to take yours-all orders, doll."

"No rush."

Kauffman's eyes narrowed from across the table.

"Shouldn't be letting go so many liberties with that one, Jeremy."

"Why's that?"

"Told me that twice already this morning."

"Well, no rush on my part." I tipped milk into my coffee. "My working day's over."

"You are looking a might haggard there, son. Bags drooping under your eyes like an old sow's taken fever."

"Thanks."

"In bad need of a shave, too, I might add. So what brings you back?"

"Editor sent me. Thoreaux's knighthood. What's all behind it. Seems to be the talk of the town."

"More like the Tower of Babel at its zenith."

Same old Kauffman. Irascible and vinegary as any

member of the bar you cared to meet. One with a habit some found disconcerting of continuing with them whatever debate he had going on in his head before they interrupted him.

"So how have you been, sir?"

"Beats all how the village is strutting about."

Proud as a peacock amidst a flock of hens in season, he claimed. Speculating on how he must've done something big in the war. Made him tired just listening to their cackling. After all those years they shunned him, even before they packed him off to Lucasville Penitentiary. Letting their kids go about smashing his windows.

"Some singing his praises now would've told you back then if anyone had prison coming to him, Thomas Thoreaux did."

"Coming to him? How do you mean 'coming to him'?"

"Folks now days forget. But once was a time when, except for your grandfather, they didn't think of Thoreaux as any sort of war hero. Not by a long shot. Saw him, if anything, as a slacker. Or worse. A collaborator. In cahoots with the Nazis."

"A collaborator? Why?"

Kauffman removed his glasses, wiping their lenses with a loose drape of his shirt. He said it went back to when he hightailed it out of Hanna in 1938. After he grabbed some national attention for the *Oracle* with his coverage of then young Deputy Constable Durkin shooting down the notorious gangster Clay Turner outside of town in a blaze of gunfire and glory, after Clay held up the Hanna Bank and Trust.

With a Yale education and his head for languages,

Thoreaux found work in Europe as a stringer for the Associated Press until the Nazis invaded France in 1940. Then he vanished. Simply vanished. No one heard from him—not so much as a single letter to his folks—until he came back in 1946.

Head full of what most in the village called his highfalutin ideas. Made a run for Congress in 1948 after Marcus Hanna the elder decided padding his pockets for more than forty years was long enough for decency's sake. No sense getting greedy. Time to let somebody else take his turn fattening up at the public trough. Marcus Junior ran in his stead. An Okinawa-decorated Marine who made certain every voter in Shawnee County knew it. Made certain too they knew he was not about to let Joseph Stalin become a second Adolph Hitler. Which didn't set well with folks thereabouts. They had their fill of telegraphs about sons not coming home and buried on some island atoll they never heard of and couldn't find on the map.

On the other hand, Thoreaux kept talking about good jobs and high wages. Got so the two were running neck and neck. Until two weeks before election day, when Junior drew his big gun. Let Thoreaux have it square between the eyes. Asked him the big question.

"Asked him what was his service record."

"To which he said?"

"Claimed he served. Did his part same as Junior."

"Well, didn't he?"

"You sound like one of Samuel's editorials. Defending him and all. Back and forth it went until Junior asked him if he'd served, then in what branch was it?"

Thoreaux said he couldn't say. Claimed he'd taken

an oath. An oath from which he had not been released. Just like that, the race for the Ohio 18th Congressional was no longer neck-and-neck. Once the votes got tallied, Thoreaux failed to get one vote out of ten. Village saw less and less of him after that. Got laughed at and catcalled to if he dared show his face on the street. Spent his days hid away. Took care of his mother until she passed.

Kauffman emptied his coffee cup, then searched, sour-faced, for Peroxide. Caught her flirting with Reserve Constable Higgins. "Scarcely divorced," he whispered from across the table, her head thrown back in a head-turning horse laugh, one hand on an ample hip and her other on Higgins's shoulder staking her claim.

"There's a story lurking in what you told me, sir."

"And we're all waiting with bated breath for you to let the cat out of the bag."

"Like I said. Sure is a story the village has got itself worked up over."

"Beats all, it does. Just beats all."

Keith Reash had told him that morning that the *Oracle* sold out, day in and day out, before noon with folks wanting the latest whisper of what it was Thoreaux went and done to get a knighthood.

"Clem said her advertising's picked up some."

"Well, at least there's some good to come out of all this tomfoolery."

Had some pluck stowed away in them britches of hers, that girl did, Kauffman said. Even if some in the village said she wore them a might too tight for modesty's sake. Not that he took notice of such matters at his age. Girl had some sass about her, too. Intended on keeping Samuel's presses running come drought or flood. Pestilence or plague.

"I take pity on any soul fool enough to wander in her way."

A flushed Peroxide finally circled over to our table, Kauffman getting me current with other village news as we ate. When she brought us our checks, I stood to go.

"Doesn't make a whole lot of sense, does it?"

"What's that, Jeremy?"

"You'd think after his being shunned, after being the village hermit for going on—what is it, thirty years?—Thoreaux would welcome his chance for vindication."

"Depends on what all it was he done."

"What do you mean?"

"Notwithstanding me being a conscientious objector, I served as a corpsman in Korea. War haunts you. Haunts your dreams. Even when you get to be a white-haired geezer it haunts you."

"Guess you'd as soon forget what it was you saw. The mutilated. The dead."

Kauffman shook his head. That wasn't it. What a man sees in war was bad enough. But it's not what haunts him. What haunts him is what he did. What he failed to do and knows in his heart of hearts he should have done. His betrayals. That's what haunts him. Secrets that follow him, one step behind, when he walks the streets at night when sleep can't find him. Or burns a candle in his window. Night upon sleepless night. Secrets. Haunting secrets. That's why he had taken on his case all those years before.

"You mark my words. Thomas Thoreaux did something, Jeremy. He's got ghosts he wants put to rest and can't. They won't let him. That's your story. If you can find it."

Chapter 9

And breaking news at 2:01 for a Tuesday morning comes out of Portland, Oregon, following the steamy revelations on Sunday of widespread corruption within the International Longshoremen's Union. Allegations including racketeering and murder, not only aided and abetted by their district attorney but local judges as well. Gino Morelli, president of our own Great Lakes Longshoremen's Union, issued a press release stating Doug Rago of the Portland Local had his full and complete support and the workingmen and women of this country knew no better friend than they had in Doug Rago. Morelli called the Portland article a pack of filthy lies, yellow-dog journalism at its worst. Greedy shippers had this reporter Jeremy Michaels and his paper buttoned up in their pocket. Neither Michaels nor his publisher could be reached for comment. Going on to the world of sports, Pete Rose slugged out his thirtieth—

I switched off the radio of my airport rental, parked again down the street from Thoreaux's shadowy ruination. Too bad Henry hadn't listened and let me stay. Likely by now the phone was ringing off my desk. Well, hopefully Sarah, down at switchboard, was picking up my calls. Jotting down numbers. If any got left. Renard would not be leaving his, I knew. Likely never called me from the same payphone twice, but maybe Henry could relax some now. The dirt Renard gave me was panning out in spades. And if Salerno dangled Rago by the short hairs, why not Morelli too? Why not every local toady coast to coast?

Thoreaux's house once more loomed up out of the coffin dark. Dead quiet. I half hoped now Henry would not have me return right away, because after what Lawyer Kauffman told me I was more than a little curious about the details of what all it was Thoreaux did in the war. Wondered why he seemed in no hurry to end his decades-long exile from the human race. Stories can do that. Once you start digging, they grab hold of you and refuse to let loose.

Wondered too if Helen was still in Portland. With a friend, maybe. Maybe with somebody new? Or maybe with her old beau she had ditched for me? If she was, I wondered if she had read the article. If maybe she too had tried to reach me for comment. Well, a guy can hope.

From where I sat parked on Cherry Street, fifty yards back from the intersection with Court, I scanned the rear of Thoreaux's house with the Zeiss binoculars once used by my grandfather for birding, before his eyes went bad. I came across them when I got to snooping through Toby's room. No gardening tonight. Just the dirge of bog crickets. Beams of occasional headlights out on Court Street tomcatting home as they cut through sheets of the June fog ghosting in from Newberry Swamp. Tonight as dead as last night and as dead as the night before. Nothing during the day except for me spotting my old scoutmaster, Noony, as he trudged by, shouldering his bulging U.S. mailbag.

"No, Jeremy. Been years since I've glimpsed so

much as a whisker of him. Or thought I did. Eyes can play funny tricks on a fellow when he passes by them windows of that dark old house of his."

"You sure he's even in there?"

"Oh, yeah. Has to be."

"Why has to be?"

Because every week Noony said he delivered Thoreaux his *Time*. *Economist*. Took the daily *Oracle*. Then there was his Book-of-the-Month Club. Used to deliver Christmas cards. Seemed a lot came from France, and those always seemed to come in a month or so late. But they trickled down to nothing after his mother passed. Couldn't recall when he delivered his last one. Didn't get any bills to speak of, except for his property tax statement the Shawnee County treasurer sent him twice a year.

"Any letters going out?"

"Been years, Jeremy. Maybe five. Maybe more. Can't rightly say."

"I guess it's a safe bet he wants left alone."

"You'll keep a goodly portion of your paycheck next time you're in Vegas risking that wager."

"Anyone in the village who might know something?"

Noony thought most likely my grandfather was the last soul he passed words with. I might try the Kitchen early some morning. One of our village wise men holding court might own up to knowing something.

"Or claim to."

"Did speak to Lawyer Kauffman."

"Oh, he must've given you one ripe earful."

"Oh, yeah."

Noony said he had known Lawyer Kauffman to

stretch the truth some, as did any lawyer worth his salt. Likely got lonely now, with Esther no longer around to take her broom to him. Maybe not quite so reliable in all his particulars as us newspaper fellows would like, but seemed to Noony gossip usually had at least some kernel of truth germinating inside.

"Maybe."

"So you get married up again yet out there? You're in Idaho, right?"

As the quarter moon set in my rearview mirror with me drinking my last cup of cold Thermos coffee, a shadow again came to an upstairs window, followed by the flare of a match strike. I thumbed my binoculars into focus in time to see a profile fade from behind the black-paned window up in his study. His study with their letters webbed with the passage of time.

****

Midafternoon, I got up and, after putting a match to yesterday's pot of coffee, walked out on the porch to get the *Oracle* from Katie's mailbox. I sank into one of her two Adirondack chairs in bad need of scraping and a fresh coat of white paint. Maybe I would do it, before I left, in lieu of the rent she turned down. The neighborhood brats were playing kickball in the empty lot next door. Arguing over whether Billy Satchel really made it to first or had Marla Sue Bartholomew beamed him out on his noggin a half second before his foot touched the rag they used for first base. I opened the paper to read what had transpired in the world since yesterday. Read how since yesterday some of the sand had run a little out of mine. Life can be like that. Beam you on your thickheaded noggin and everything in your life changes in a blink of a blinkered eye.

HANNA WAR HERO!!!

The Oracle *has learned from a source it believes to be credible that our very own Thomas Thoreaux, upon whom Queen Elizabeth will bestow a knighthood on a date yet to be set, served in France during World War II as a member of her elite Special Operations Executive. After rigorous months of training at the Arisaig Complex in Scotland, agents for SOE either parachuted or landed in France aboard Westland Lysander planes capable of landing and taking off on very short, improvised runways. Duties of their agents included organizing resistance cells within one of eighty-some circuits with the goal of sabotage and otherwise disrupting the German war effort, forcing them to reallocate scarce military resources to protect critical road and rail networks in occupied France. The* Oracle *has yet to obtain the actual details of Mr. Thoreaux's service. We have made numerous attempts to speak to him for his comment but have not yet been successful.*

Of course! Thoreaux's boxcar stories. Only they were not stories at all. They were the real McCoy.

****

As I had not checked in with Henry, finding myself out-scooped and once again in journalism purgatory seemed as good a time as any to make amends.

"Been waiting on you to call."

"Heard on the radio our longshoremen story ran on Sunday. Seems to have struck a nerve."

"To say the least. Fair to say we're seeing some decent pushback."

"Yeah?"

Henry said it was not yet eight o'clock Sunday

morning when Rago's mouthpiece lawyer had our fearless publisher cowering on the phone. How he got Stickle's number Henry supposed to be an interesting story in and of itself, since the number was not listed—likely an inside job. No doubt Mouthpiece had Stickle cringing under his kitchen table while he threatened to sue us on charges of libel for every penny Stickle, Henry, and I had and every penny we and our prodigious progeny down to Deuteronomy's third and fourth generation would ever earn.

"Let the bastards sue, Henry. Push comes to shove, I can back up every word."

"May well come to that, kid."

Because Henry said when he got into the office, bright-eyed and bushy-tailed come early Monday morning, our wild boar of a D.A. was waiting to waylay him. Wallowing wall-to-wall, wanting to give me the third degree, rubber hose no doubt tucked under his trench coat. A trench coat he wore everywhere, even in one of our summer heat waves. You see the back of a trench coat ahead of you on the sidewalks of downtown Portland on a blistering day, you can bet your bottom dollar it's our D.A. Sort of a trademark with him. More than a bit put out with us for besmirching his good name. Though how one besmirched a lawyer's good name befuddled Henry. Then he threatened to serve us one and all with grand jury subpoenas. Henry inquired if the First Amendment still remained part of the law school curriculum. Whereupon the D.A. backed off.

"For now."

"Like I said. I can back up every word we ran."

"Back up with a rock-solid source? Not just an earful of barroom gossip."

"Come on, Henry. You taught me better than to go to press without one. Rock solid. Like Gibraltar."

"Uh-huh. Gibraltar's a-k-a wouldn't by chance be one Erec Renard, would it?"

My stomach knotted.

"Maybe. Maybe not. You know I can't reveal a source once I've promised confidentiality."

"I know, I know. Why are you being so touchy?"

"I'm not."

"We've a great connection here, Michaels, a fantastic connection. There's no need to shout into the phone."

"Sorry. It's just…this is a big story for us."

"I know, I know."

The reason Henry said he asked was that, while he was there, the D.A. made noises about an imminent issuing of a warrant for Renard's arrest.

"Arrest warrant? For what?"

"Embezzlement of union funds. Mouthpiece told Stickle he could prove Renard was our source. Had suckered me in to cover his tracks and now demanded an immediate and full retraction."

"How could he kn—"

But of course. My news groupie. The wannabe union man. Looking to get even with the world and took more than a little interest in reading my unredacted trash. Saw his opening to plunder for a fast buck. Likely found Stickle's unlisted phone number in Henry's Rolodex.

"Retraction, hell, Henry. Even if Renard is my source—and I'm not admitting he is—even if he did embezzle union funds, it didn't mean what he told me wasn't one hundred percent scout's-honor truth. Rago's sleazy as they come, and sleaze slithers with other sleaze. It's the sleaze of the world that rats on the sleaze they slither with."

"Sleaze or not, Stickle's looking at giving them their retraction and handing them your head for good measure."

"My— Why?"

"Because besides having a backbone of Jell-O, Stickle's a cheap bastard. Firing you and giving a retraction costs him nada. Plus Mouthpiece made noises on the phone about Rago organizing our pressmen."

"So our fearless publisher is letting himself be blackmailed?"

"Wouldn't be the first time he's caved. Wouldn't be the last. His current floozy is of the high-maintenance pedigree. Plus he loses sleep over making alimony for his three ex-wives. Would do us a world of good if you came up with something more to corroborate other than one sleazy source."

The telephone receiver sweated in my hand. I'd meant to try checking again on those campaign contributions Renard claimed Rago made to our D.A. and three county judges, before I left Portland. But with Helen dumping me, and my wrapping up odds and ends to get out of town, I never made it past being stuck on hold with the Secretary of State.

"Well, do you have something, Jeremy?"

"Nothing nearly as solid as what I've got right now."

Or was it Renard who had gotten me? Set me up in his power struggle with Rago as well as a cover-up for his diversion of funds.

"Henry, you know our D.A. wouldn't be having a

cow unless there was more than a grain of salt in what we ran."

"Yeah, that's what I've been telling Stickle."

"You want me to come back to bolster what we've got?"

"Not yet, kid. We'll let our engine run cold for a while longer. With the D.A. snooping about, no source worth his salt will risk sticking his neck out yet. Especially if the two of us got hauled by the scruff of our necks before the grand jury. No, stay where you are for now. Speaking of which, how's the knighthood saga panning out so far?"

I told him about getting out-scooped, but Henry said he did not see it as the end of the world. Or the story. Not by a long shot. Now we sort of knew why the Queen was handing a knighthood to Thoreaux, but barely knew. We knew none of the down-and-dirty details of what it was he did to deserve it, which was where he would bet his bottom dollar the real story lay, since Buckingham Palace was saying zilch.

"Keep swinging for the fences to get Thoreaux to open up."

Henry said that, with enough gritty details, we could more than make up for not being the first to break the story. Then if our longshoremen story did dead-end on us, assuming it got no worse, it might—might—all get forgotten about after we fleshed out the bare bones of our thirty-year knighthood saga. Our exposé so far was only one story and not yet a whole series. If it did go south, it might all get swept under the rug with a new scoop and New York a breathing possibility for us.

"I'll keep stalling Stickle back here. But you need to flesh out this fable. I've heard a rumor floating about that one of the *Times* editors sold out his soul to network TV. Two recent scoops for us would look really, really good in our portfolios. Also insurance, if need be. But your guy had to have done something. Had to."

What Henry said rang dead-on true. Thoreaux surely had done something. Done something and now lived with the ghosts of what he did. But if Thoreaux had his sins, I had mine. Sins such as putting Henry at risk by leading him to believe our exposé more solid than it really was so I would not have to come back here to face up to my own ghosts. Let him down as I had let down Helen. Beth. Helen and Beth I could do nothing about, not now. For Henry I could. If not with our exposé, then for the story here. I didn't need any more ghosts in my life.

Chapter 10

No, I had no need in my life for more ghosts. I had more than what I thought of as my fair share. One I was reminded of that night when I woke with a start behind the wheel of my Hertz rental, heart hammering my ribcage and me wet right down to my preppy argyle socks.

After Beth died, I thought I would dream of her more, but I seldom did. Only three times in two years. Once we sat in a darkened theater holding hands while we waited for the movie to begin. Not saying anything, just enjoying the evening and each other's company. Another time, stranded in some no-name town in Colorado. One I had never been to but where I walked the snow-swept sidewalks searching for and not finding her. Then tonight. We were going at it again with our old adolescent abandon in my back seat, parked just off Mill Creek Bridge. Went at it until it came to me Beth was dead. Dead and on top of me. At Mill Creek Bridge, where the flames of her mother's Impala consumed her. Our child in the womb. I tried pushing her off, but she came apart in my hands in charred chunks. That was when my screaming woke me. Me wishing I had told Henry to take a flyer. That I had my reasons not to come back.

It took a minute for me collect myself and glance in the rearview mirror. To see the backward writing in the window. I got out. Written in gray dew:

Go away
Leave me alone

Beneath the words, a rock the size of a baseball. Sitting considerately on my car trunk atop yesterday's *Oracle*, I guessed so as not to scratch the paint finish. I'd hit a nerve.

Feeling smug with myself, I got back in and started to reach for the Thermos when I noticed a Chevy Caprice parked in the shadows near Thoreaux's back door. Upstairs, a faint light twisted behind the black-paned window. I grabbed a notepad from out of the glove box and raised my binoculars at the vehicle—like mine, Hertz decal in its rear window. I jotted down the license number anyway. A useless gesture because no way would Durkin trace it for me, but old habits die hard. When in doubt, write it down, as Henry had lectured our class.

I waited. Watched. Near three o'clock, a woman almost skeletal in build, wearing a long-sleeved dress, and of an indefinite age hurried down Thoreaux's back steps. She opened the door to the Caprice and drove away, headlights off. I waited until she turned out of the lane down Court Street before I started my engine, only to stop after going all of ten feet, steering wheel wobbly in my hands. What the...? I got out and walked around the car. This was getting downright old. Just like outside the Port-of-Call. All four tires pancake flat. At least, this time, no baseball bat swinging for my head.

****

Nothing to do at that hour. Dick Simpson seldom rolled up the garage doors of his Quaker State station much before seven. Sometimes not even until well after eight, if Shirley stayed over to fry his breakfast of cornmeal mush and launder their bed sheets. So I climbed back in and was drinking cold Thermos coffee when another figure stepped off Thoreaux's back porch and set out down Cherry Street in my direction. For a second I considered crouching under the dashboard but figured what the hell since Thoreaux now knew he was plagued by a midnight voyeur. Before he got to me, though, he turned left, his corduroy shoulders slumped, eyes cast down.

I got out, sticking to the shadows of the trees lining Church Street. A needless precaution because Thoreaux did not turn around. Had he forgotten I was parked outside? He disappeared into Our Lady of Lourdes through a side door hidden behind a creep of ivy—a secret door that somehow had escaped the notice of the gang of hooligans I tried without much success to run with one summer. We managed, or thought we had, to get into everything we were not supposed to get into, but I guess we were not half as clever as we misled ourselves to believe we were. How could we have missed a secret door? A secret door would have been simply priceless.

After tailing Thoreaux inside, I stood sideways behind a back pillar. He was sitting in the front pew, hands folded, stained glass Jesus hanging on the cross looking down at him. When a door opened in back, a sleepy Father O'Malley, collarless and his sparse hair looking bed-slept, entered from a side room. He stood a minute in the doorway, gray light falling behind him, before he took a seat beside Thoreaux, hand on his shoulder.

"What is it, Thomas? Is it the dream again?"

Thoreaux shook his head.

"What, then? What's so upsetting you seek me out at this hour?"

Thoreaux again shook his head. Father O'Malley waited, but Thoreaux said nothing, his shoulders slumped and head bowed. The stained glass Jesus with eyes cast down upon them began to glow with the unwelcomed dawn.

"Come back to my study. Coffee should be ready."

He rose, his hand grasping the elbow of a badly shaken Thoreaux.

So Henry's reporter hunch had been right! But what was this dream that so haunted Thoreaux? And if it wasn't his dream driving him to seek out the comfort of a priest in the dead of night, what had disconcerted him so much he forgot about me—seemed not to even see me? It could only be his midnight caller. Was she tied to his knighthood? To his dream? To both? If so, who was she? What had she said to drive him out from his decades-long hermitage into the night?

Chapter 11

The note I found late that afternoon taped to the door of his priory said Father O'Malley could be found across town at Newell Field. While I had doubts he would tell me what Thoreaux confided to him any more than I would give up the name of my source to our trench-coat D.A., a reporter grows used to getting a dozen doors slammed in his face before one finally opens, if only a crack.

When I hiked over to Newell Field, Father O'Malley was stuffing baseball bats into an Army surplus canvas bag, his Cleveland Indians cap a little askew.

"Oh, I let myself get talked into coaching girls' softball this summer, after Sam Martin suffered his heart attack. Daughter's our star pitcher, you know. Ten-to-twelve-year-old league. Glad now I did. I have found it something of a blessing. More than a blessing. A comfort. Not having children and never having had younger sisters, I find it wonderful to watch young girls coming upon the cusp of womanhood." He shook his head as he looked out over the field. "Afternoons like this lead me to question the sagacity of me ever taking my orders."

I nodded that I understood, for it was afternoons on fields such as this where I reflected on my own miscarried daughter, who might in a few short years have played here, with Beth and me whooping up in the bleachers when she came to bat or stole home or caught the pop-up fly that snatched victory from the jaws of defeat and got her carried off the field on the shoulders of her teammates.

He listened as I helped him gather up the remainder of the bats and gloves scattered over an infield little more than a wasteland of weeds Bill Newell had cut down with his tractor and mower.

"You know, Jeremy, I haven't seen your face smiling up at me from the pews since you and Thomas got hauled back from Laramie."

"Life made a whole lot less sense after we got brought back. Them packing Thoreaux off to prison with no little help browbeaten out of me."

"I understand. But remember. This is why the Church is here. To help us make sense of life."

"But can it help me make sense of Thoreaux?"

"All I can tell you, Jeremy, is if you wish to know what smolders within Thomas's heart, a good place to start is by looking into your own. Good luck. And God speed."

****

Noony was stepping off Katie's porch when I got back, his smirking grin wide as a raccoon's looking out of a trashcan the morning after a backyard barbecue.

"Got some news for you, Mr. Hot-Shot-Reporter. How's that for turning them tables on you?"

"Yeah? What news you got?"

"Picked up a letter from the town celebrity's mailbox this afternoon. First since I can't remember when. Addressed to the British embassy in Washington, D.C."

"Still have it with you?"

Noony patted his worn leather satchel with 1911 stenciled on its side. "Got 'er right here, safe and sound."

"Come inside. We'll steam it open."

"Not on your life, Michaels."

"Got a six-pack in the fridge," I lied.

"Nice try." Noony shook his head, chuckling as he continued down Katie's driveway. "Nice try, but I'm getting too old to spend my well-deserved retirement in a Federal residential facility. Not for you to worry, though. Thoreaux sent it special delivery. Expect it'll get there tomorrow. So whatever it is, you won't have all that long a wait to find out."

****

Waiting would also leave me pecking at whatever crumbs the newswires left behind. An outcome not likely to get me an invitation to New York. Also-rans trying to break in back there were a dime a dozen. Or less.

Henry more than once had walked me through whatever brick wall I had run into. I had to check in with him anyway.

"Just the man I needed to talk to."

"Why? What's up, Chief?"

"D.A.'s impaneled a special grand jury."

"Trench Coat can't be that desperate. Can he?"

"Can be if our article has him climbing walls about what'll be running next."

"When was the last time a D.A., any D.A., impaneled a special grand jury?"

Henry said not within his memory and not within that of any of our courthouse hacks. Some of whom went back to the days when Lewis and Clark frolicked along the banks of the Willamette with Sacagawea. Henry had posted Collins outside the courtroom to corner what witnesses he could as they came out after testifying in closed court. Definitely had to do with our longshoremen was all Jeff had ferreted out, but with a line of cruisers parked out back looking ready to roll, and maybe twenty of Portland's finest milling about with a half-a-dozen boxes of doughnuts sitting on their cruiser hoods, a slew of indictments definitely on their way down.

"Anything from Renard, Jeremy?"

"Never said Renard was my source."

"Well, have you heard from whoever?"

"No, but I haven't been back in to pick up my phone, either. So far, whoever hasn't trusted me with how to get hold of him."

"Sarah at switchboard's been tracking your calls like you asked. None with a French accent."

"It's early yet. We only spoke late last week. Give him a few more days."

"We've no choice, but let me ask you once more. Are you sure on this guy, Jeremy? I mean absolutely rock-bottom sure. Deep down in your heart of hearts."

This time I kept my voice steady despite my gut dancing a jitterbug on me. "Solid as Gibraltar."

"All right. But I'm trusting you on this."

"Relax. I won't let you down, Henry. Never have."

At least not yet. Not exactly.

"I know you haven't. So we wait. Any progress on our knighthood chronicle?"

I told Henry about the special delivery letter to the British embassy.

"Gotta be his acceptance. Whoever heard of somebody declining a date with the Queen?"

"No American, anyway. You know how we go gaga over any and all matters concerning royalty. Especially British royalty. Lord help us when bonnie Prince Charles finally got around to popping the question to his fair lass. Most Americans seem to have forgotten it wasn't the Ruskies who hanged Nathan Hale."

"Maybe after sending off his acceptance our guy will now be willing to open up."

"Guess it'd be worth my while knocking on his door again."

"Well, remember. Like ice cream in summer, with the newspaper business, two scoops are better than one. The one there in particular, should the one back here melt on us. With Trench Coat now siccing his grand jury dogs on Rago's ILA enemies, I'm getting antsy on my source you've not heard from. Any hope of your hermit now opening up?"

"Reason for my call. Last time I tried, Thoreaux was not so much as opening his door to spit in my face, let alone talk to me."

"Have you considered breaking in?"

"Not seriously." Not until then I hadn't.

"Well, you didn't hear it from me. Just saying. But try not to get arrested when you do. Or shot. We don't need the bad press right now."

****

To avoid arousing his suspicion, I knocked a little less on Thoreaux's door each day for the next three. Fell asleep watching Johnny Carson on Katie's television. Let him think he was running me out of gas and on the verge of packing it in like those hapless news crews he ran off.

On night three, I left my cousin's a few minutes past midnight, wearing black jeans, sneakers, jersey, and the baseball cap—two sizes too small—I found in Toby's room. I decided not to grease my face with shoe polish, on the off chance this might be the one night when Reserve Constable Higgins had not dozed off and not wanting to make excuses for walking nocturnal streets in black face. Though so far I had failed to spot his cruiser. Maybe his night patrols were only the stuff of village lore and legend. Better, though, for me to play it safe.

So using side streets and back alleys, I circled to the far side of town, stepping now and again into the shadows to avoid sporadic headlights. A troubled night. Heat lightning stringing the sky in a chain of crazed cat's cradles off to the west. A night close and clammy. The kind of Ohio night where you woke soaked in your bed sheets. Especially, I only later reflected, if you woke in a house where none of the windows had been opened in thirty years.

The rusted lock securing the storm-cellar door in back, though ancient, refused to snap off no matter how hard I yanked on it. I pulled on the leather gloves I'd also found in Toby's closet, and used a Phillips screwdriver I'd snitched from Katie's kitchen drawer where she kept her collection of possibles.

(*Fair ladies and distinguished gentlemen of the jury, when Reserve Officer Higgins arrested the defendant skulking in the shadows outside the home of Mr. Thoreaux, recently knighted by Her Majesty as Sir Thomas in recognition of his laudatory services, he found State's Exhibit One in said defendant's possession along with other various and sundry assortment of burglary tools.*)

From hasps now orange from corrosion on one of the two paint-peeling doors, I pocketed eight screws and leaned that door up against the back of the house. Then stood listening. Something seemed not quite right, but I decided it was only a case of jitters on my first felony caper. Switching on the flashlight, I crept into the mildewed cellar and made my way for the opposite flight of stairs and past a wall of shelves rough carpentered from two-by-fours holding scores of Mason jars of what looked like recently put-up summer preserves of string beans and applesauce and halved pears.

Four sets of yellow eyes gleamed out of the dark as I passed through his kitchen. The beam of my flashlight ran over a walnut table in the dining room, laden with dust, and a matching hutch holding what looked like Limoges china behind its glass doors. Beside his reading chair, stacks of newspapers and magazines and books. I stooped to pull out one of the magazines near the bottom. A *Time* dated November 25, 1963. On its well-worn and blurry cover, an already phantomy youthful president holding a darkening hand to his throat. Seated beside him his smiling and unaware First Lady who wore that morning in Dallas a soon-to-be infamous blood-and-brain-smeared Chanel suit with matching pink pillbox hat.

A film of decades-old dust overlay every square inch upstairs as well. Ghosts of long-passed footsteps stole down the hardwood floor of the hallway. Rank stench of decomposing small mammals, wood rot, and decay. The doors to his bathroom and all three bedrooms stood open.

The fifth door, at the end of the hall, however, though closed was not locked, and as I entered a slender reed of heat lightning illuminated the room. Illuminated only for a second. Long enough to glimpse a clock set on the shelf of a built-in bookshelf. Glimpse a corduroy-coated figure seated beneath the clock, behind a desk, holding a rifle with a bore bigger than the one I had stared down years before in Laramie, Wyoming, and aimed dead center at a heart that had stopped.

The glow of the lightning faded. The room again coffin black, I did not so much as breathe while I waited for him to say something. Anything. But he remained silent as the tomb.

"So are you going to shoot me?" I said in my small courtroom voice from years ago.

The clock above him ticked.

"Well, are you?"

Perhaps my eyes had been playing tricks on me. Was he even there? But alas.

"Only if I decide not to turn you loose. Let me get this lamp lit. Don't be making any sudden moves. This old Mauser's got a hair trigger on her. Makes just a terrible mess I'd prefer not to have to clean up. A terrible mess. Might decide to leave you to the cats rather than be bothered."

I had no need now to guess where he had gotten hold of a Mauser rifle. Knew he was not spoofing me about the mess it made—he'd seen it first-hand.

A kitchen match flared, illuminating iron-rimmed eyes, runny, behind the flue of a brass hurricane lamp like those once found on bridges of the steel and coal barges that had plied the Great Lakes between Duluth and Cleveland. He creaked back in his chair, Mauser shiny with oil again aimed at my heart. Studying me, and me him.

Easily could you mistake Thoreaux for a Midwest college professor. Maybe a cranky professor of existential philosophy, perhaps, but a college professor nonetheless. Helmet of hair grayed to snow. Brown leather patches on the elbows of his baggy corduroy coat. Ice-pond eyes behind his glasses a watery blue at their edges. Likely from drink, for in the sill of his bay window beside that tall stack of envelopes still spider-webbed with time and yellowed to the color of wild mustard stood a near empty bottle of Four Roses.

"You could call the constable. Have me arrested."

"No, single fellow such as him, tomcatting the town's divorcées, needs his rest. Besides, you'd only come back."

"How do you know I would?"

"Because I'm a newspaperman too. Or was. I remember what it is to want a story bad enough to risk life and limb to lay my hands on it." His finger tapped the rifle stock. "Like to know the name of a man before I send him to meet his maker. Hate seeing anyone buried without a name etched on his marker. As far as I know, we don't have a tomb for the unknown cat burglar. Not yet, though that seems to be the direction this country's headed in. At least if there's any truth in what I've been reading."

"Jeremy."

Those ice-pond eyes narrowed.

"Jeremy what?"

"Michaels. Jeremy Michaels."

His eyes pinched a little tighter behind those iron-rimmed glasses. After a moment, he nodded.

"Been more than a few years since I've been in to visit the eye doctor. Or any other kind of doctor, truth be told. No sense to it. No doubt they're still doling out the same old quackery that'd put a mallard drake to shame." He thumbed the safety on, leaning the Mauser beneath the mantel clock behind him.

I let go my breath.

"Fellow shouldn't get in the habit of shooting down blood kin. Grandson of the last friend he had left in this world."

"I appreciate your sentiment, sir."

The lamp flame flickered in his pond-ice eyes, the edges of his mouth crinkling a sort of smile. "Shouldn't go shooting down my former partner in crime either, I don't expect."

"No, sir."

"Never can tell. He might yet come in handy some day, but what's wrong with you, boy? I'd have opened my door if I was inclined to parley."

"You remember how curmudgeonly some editors get?"

"The lowest race of low sonsofbitches—Samuel excluded, of course—to ever walk God's green earth."

"So here I stand."

"What kind of dirt did he send you to dig up?"

"No dirt. Only find out what services you rendered for the Queen to bestow a knighthood."

A skein of heat lightning webbed the sky outside the black-tinted panes of Thoreaux's bay window.

"Why do you think it took her thirty years to get to it?"

"Queening can be a right tiresome business. Or so I was told once by someone who seemed to know. What between all those fancy balls and teas. Getting her picture snapped for the papers. Likely she leads a hectic life."

"So why take time out to award you a knighthood?"

Thoreaux shook his head. "Go back. Tell your editor it's all a big mix-up. Lizzy Q. has me confused with another fellow."

"That's what you want me to tell my editor?"

"You do still tell the truth like Samuel taught you, don't you?"

"Yes, sir."

"Well, no need for you to go swapping good habits for bad on my account." You can find your way out, I expect. Same way you came in, should you find yourself turned around."

"I can if you want me to."

"Then I'll bid you adieu this evening. No sense in snooping. Nothing to be found."

I looked over his study.

"Nothing much seems changed. Since that one summer. Still have your big rocker."

"You remember?"

"How could I forget? If not for you inviting me in, I would never have come back. For our adventure."

"You were on your way out?"

"Yes, sir. But before I go, thank you for only letting the air out of my tires the other night. Hertz takes a dim view of rental returns with slashed tires."

"What are you talking about?"

"The other night. You let the air out of my tires."

"I did like hell."

"Who would, if it wasn't you?"

"Maybe one of our village rock throwers."

Bushy eyebrows arched in the direction of his study door. I started to go but stopped midway. "Would it be all right if I came back, sir?"

"I'd take it as a kindness if you didn't. But you're probably as thickheaded as I once was."

So was that a yes or a no? Or was it a let-me-think-on-it? Let me think on whether I want to come back into the world?

"You'll hang my cellar door like it was on your way out?"

"Of course," and again I started to go.

"Jeremy?"

"Yes, sir?"

"I'm sorry. About Beth."

I never suspected he knew I was married. Or Beth's name. Or she had died.

"Yes, sir. Thank you."

"I considered coming to her funeral. But it would only have turned it into a circus. That's not what you needed. How you making out?"

"All right. I guess. Try to keep busy."

"So you don't think on it too much."

"Yeah. Pretty much."

"Let an old man hand you a hard-learned lesson. Think on it. A lot."

His eyes darted to the stack of letters spider-webbed by time.

"Think on it. Put it to rest. Find a way. Somehow find a way to put it to rest. If you don't, it will eat away at you. Eat away until the only thing left is a mouthful of an old man's venom spit."

****

After resetting the storm-cellar door, I looked up to his study window, his silhouette outlined behind the black-tinted panes. Looking down. Looking down not at me but at his wind-scoured barn, where I had little reason to doubt a noosed rope I came across one summer could still be found lying coiled beneath a mound of rotting hay.

Put it to rest. Find a way. Somehow find a way to put it to rest. If you don't, it will eat away at you. Eat away until the only thing left is a mouthful of an old man's venom spit.

****

Before taking my leave, I sat on his back step to gather my thoughts. Thoughts taking me back to a summer afternoon when I was eight. Thoreaux must have spotted me from his study window, when I sat on this same step, and for some reason came to his door. In those years the only other person he ever asked in was my grandfather, and even then an invitation by no means a given. Hungry for company that hot afternoon, I guess, but he spent so much time alone, at a loss for words.

So he set me to work in his garden. Hoeing and, during our abnormally dry August, walking up and down sweat-dribbled rows of corn and chick peas with an arm-bursting five-gallon water can in hand. Had me tidy up his cobwebbed barn, where a ten-foot circular saw rusted in its rotted-timber housing. A mule-pulled wagon missing all four of its wheels and a winter sled once used to carry out felled trees sat partially concealed beneath pigeon-splattered tarps.

On its spooned walls hung a collection of mildewed mule collars and J.F. Steiner leather harnesses, their brass fittings now a tarnished verdigris. Remnants from the farm old Jacque bought outside the then village limits that backed up on one of the last stands of original growth forests left in Ohio. Until then a plum orchard and dairy operation that Jacque had converted to a sawmill.

The hangman's rope I found lay beneath a rotting mound of hay. Thirteen hemp coils wrapped above the noose. Stone cold shivers shot up my spine, notwithstanding the summer heat.

When I came in from whatever chores he had set me to, and for which Thoreaux paid me a princely quarter for each day's labor, I found him—if I found him at all—reading in his study. He let me snoop in his bookshelves, where I found a volume on Civil War battles. He said while I was more than welcome to take it down, I could not take it home. I think to keep me there for company. So I sat in the big rocker opposite him. It took me some weeks to finish, and when I did he quizzed me on what I had read. Added his own editorial comments to my accounts of the slaughterhouses fought at Antietam and Bull Run and the Wilderness. At Shiloh, where he told me the loss of life equaled what the British suffered at Waterloo but unlike Waterloo followed by forty-two more battles with a loss of life as large or larger.

Not only did Thoreaux look like a tenured college professor, he knew more about American history than any college professor whose lectures I later suffered through. Yet I cannot call him a patriot. I cannot say Thoreaux loved America, not after it—or at least the village—had turned its back on him after all he had given—but I think what he loved about America was its mythology. Its endless promise, but if he loved its mythological promise, Thoreaux was acutely aware of its numerous failures. Its numerous ambiguities.

"But what about the Civil War, sir?" Holding up his book. "Thousands of Americans died to free the slaves."

"Thousands of Americans also died so other Americans would forever remain slaves. Even after they were freed, it was a freedom in name only. Millions remained slaves. Millions remain second-rate Americans even today."

Having been ostracized himself, Thoreaux shared a strong affinity with the underdog. For those from the other side of the tracks. Its Beths.

He never rushed me to go home. Made up excuses to keep me in his study until near suppertime. Over the many months, he opened up some about himself. Told me some of his family history my grandfather had glossed over. Once or twice even laughed. Maybe he felt he had adopted a grandson, because I sure felt like a second grandpa had adopted me. For that Christmas he gave me a new volume on the naval battles of the Civil War, wrapped in Christmas paper very faded and very brittle, and I still keep it, shelved, back in Portland.

As I was the only person to enter or leave his house, it was only a matter of time before Mom got wind. Likely Noony, our nosey mailman, said something one winter afternoon when he handed her our mail. Now I had lost two buddies. The first after her return from the hospital when she wreaked her revenge on my grandfather for the religious wars waged in her youth when she forbade me to go up to the *Oracle* after school let out and did not relent until we were brought back from Laramie.

So I read a lot. It was the winter I read my father's broken-spine editions of *Tom Sawyer* and *Huckleberry Finn*. The winter I plotted my escape. I held out until the first day of summer vacation to slip out the back door before Dad was up. A flaxen full moon beckoned in the west. Of course we got caught. Sent back. But, oh, what adventures we had that all began on the summer day when he saw me sitting on his back step.

Now here I was back again. Back in Hanna, back to a problematical past. Mine and his. His I was certain could be found in those spider-webbed letters yellowing in an upstairs bay window. Somehow I had to find a way, though I now suspected what they held. "His old partner in crime" he had called me, and while on our spree he came to be my grand weaver of tales. My teller of boxcar stories. Except they were not made-up stories at all but stories from history, true as summer rain. True stories with consequences. Consequences tolling on for years. For decades.

****

When I stood to leave, the storm-cellar door seemed out of line. As I knelt readjusting the hasp, I sensed something behind me and turned to see what it was just as a boot smashed into my face harder than I had ever been struck before. Harder even than the baseball bat back in Portland, and I quite literally saw stars before all went dark, the world timeless, and until the sky began to gray in the east I lay in the dewing grass.

Chapter 12

The swollen right side of my face was black and blue when I studied myself in the mirror late next morning. While tender to the touch, my nose and cheekbones did not seem broken. But not broken by whom?

Thoreaux seemed to be the most obvious candidate only because I could think of no other as I took my first cup of coffee out onto Katie's front porch. Yet, by the time I went in to pour my second cup, that suspicion seemed not likely, considering what he'd said about Beth. But if not Thoreaux, then who? The same jerk who let the air out of my tires? But why? American Legion vigilantes still fighting the last war and upset over his knighthood? Someone who, for reasons unknown, wanted his story to remain untold? A story that, if I was ever to tell it, I somehow had to get my hands on those spider-webbed letters. But how?

As I was fast running out of ideas, even lame ideas, I checked in with Henry.

"Chief, so what's new in your world?"

"Just came in over the wire this morning."

"What did?"

"So what's your angle on why the village hermit turned down a knighthood, for God's sake?"

"He what?"

"Turned down his knighthood."

"No way, Henry. There's no way."

"You didn't know?"

"Not until five seconds ago."

The press release Henry read to me, put out by Buckingham Palace, said that in response to Mr. Thomas Thoreaux's refusal, Her Majesty was with the very deepest regrets withdrawing her offer of knighthood. She did, however, wish to express her gratitude and the greatest of gratitude from her subjects for his services on behalf of the Crown under circumstances she understood to have been most demanding.

"No way, Henry. There's no way."

But after what he told me last night, my gut told me that was exactly what Thoreaux had done.

"Damn. So much for our two scoops."

And our insurance. For a sweaty thirty seconds, I held the telephone receiver to my ear.

"Henry? You there? Henry?"

"I'm here. Puzzling out our angles."

"Angles? We've got no angles to puzzle out. All we've got is one of our scoops melting on the sidewalk."

"Not so fast. This could be an even better story than when it broke. "

"Better? Are you bananas? How could it get any worse?"

"Come on, Michaels. Use your head. I've taught you better. Tell me who turns down a knighthood, to say nothing of a trip to London for a formal dinner with the Queen? Any American, anyway."

"No one I ever heard of."

"Exactly. So why did your guy?"

"I'm clueless, Henry. Completely clueless."

"So is everyone else, and everyone else has got the same question burning on their lips as we do here in the newsroom. Why?"

Why indeed? Again, it all tied back to those spider-webbed letters. Letters Thoreaux could never bring himself to read yet could not put out of sight, let alone burn.

"There's a vulture hovering over this story, Jeremy. A story that might yet seal the deal for getting us to New York and, if need be, keeping our mutual gooses out of the stewing pot back here."

"Speaking of which, anything new with Trench Coat?"

"Quiet. Not so much as a whisper from him in days. No phone calls coming in for you. Too quiet. Something barreling down the pike head on at us, but for the life of me I can't tell you what. Have you been able to talk to our hermit?"

"Did last night."

"Glad you didn't get shot."

No, not shot. Only the bejesus stomped out of me.

"Were you able to drag anything out of him?"

"Nothing but riddles. Riddles inside of more riddles."

"Well, now, with his refusal and the pressure off, you think you can get him to talk to you again?"

****

No, and hell no, he wouldn't talk to me again, but I had to go through the motions. If for no other reason than that when I stood at the end of an unemployment line stretching out the door and down the block while reading some other schmuck's story on the front page of the *New York Times*, I could tell myself at least I gave it the old Bobcat try. After already getting my face kicked in, the worst I figure could happen is I really would get shot for my troubles, but maybe with his eyesight he would miss. Then again, at point-blank range, maybe not.

When I walked out again that evening, the canopy of oak and ash shading Thoreaux's lane reflected the whirling reds and blues of Durkin's roof-rack lights. Two T-shirted boys looking maybe all of thirteen sat in his back seat with their heads bowed, not looking at each other and not likely in prayer, while Durkin stood with a Wellington boot propped on the front bumper of his cruiser as he wrote up his incident report.

"Village went and got itself some excitement tonight, Constable?"

Durkin glanced up, his sour lip curling in a lapdog snarl. A man favored with a long memory, coupled with a miniscule ego, who took not kindly to criticism. Especially criticism finding its way into print. He eyed my face.

"What the hell happened to you, Michaels?"

"Flat tire. Popped on me while I was changing it."

"Gotta be more careful. Curtis Henshaw was changing a tire when it popped on him. Knocked him out cold. Busted his gullet. Done drowned in his own blood."

"How comforting," and nodded into his cruiser. "Is this what passes now days for Hanna's criminal element?"

"Good Lord. Just hope it don't get no worse out of hand tonight than these two hooligans."

"Gets no worse than what out of hand?"

"Backlash settin' in against our town celebrity."

"Backlash?"

"Call it what you want. Was sitting at my desk when the news came in over WKBN. Thought maybe I should run my rounds early. Caught these two chucking rocks at his windows."

"I thought those kinds of shenanigans ended donkey's years ago."

"Ebbs and flows. Flows and ebbs with the times. Folks done got worked all up into a tizzy over Thoreaux's turning down his knighthood. They got to taking it to be part theirs already."

"They ignore the man for the better part of three decades, and now they're worked up into a tizzy?"

"Folks can be peculiar sonsofbitches, can't they? Village done got itself all puffed up they was home to a full-fledged hero. Now that he's hosed them off, they're madder at him than a nest of messed-with hornets."

Durkin pocketed the incident pad in the rear of his service trousers.

"No telling how they're going to take it out on him. I'll have Higgins make a couple of swings by tonight. Give him an excuse to stay awake."

"Likely to be some overwrought divorcées calling the station around midnight."

"We ain't got none in Hanna *that* lonely."

"You been up to the Kitchen?"

"Not of late. Ulcers done got the better of me."

"You talk to Thoreaux at all?"

"Hell, Michaels, I ain't laid eyes on Thomas Thoreaux since I cut him loose after he done served his thirty days for not settling up with the village for the yard work we done for him."

"So you've no idea why he turned down the knighthood?"

"Beats the Sam Hill out of me why."

Durkin said he was surprised they offered it up to him to begin with. What with him having a felony record and all. British consulate down in Washington called to ask about it some months back. Had no cause to badmouth the man. Must have satisfied whatever qualms they were having. Told them the folks back here just overreacted, but Durkin had no idea why he might've turned down a knighthood once it got offered. If anyone might know, his guess would be Clem.

"She's the one who went and broke the story to begin with."

"Be all right if I knocked on his door anyway?"

"It's still a free country. Leastways until them hippie-loving Democrats get let loose again."

I walked up Thoreaux's front steps as Durkin backed down the lane, the village's newest desperadoes sitting in his back seat with heads still bowed, and knocked.

"Mr. Thoreaux. Are you home?" I shouted. "It's me, Jeremy Michaels. Mr. Thoreaux? Are you home? Mr. Thoreaux, sir?"

No gunshots. Only the murmur of traffic out on Court Street. I circled around to his back door and knocked and called and knocked some more and walked over to beneath his study window and called again. Nada. Not so much as a smidgen of a shadow.

As much as I hated to admit it, Durkin was right. I needed to talk to Clem.

****

Early next morning, I took the *Oracle*'s steps two

at a time. If at first outside their twin twelve-foot-tall doors of nouveau stained glass I did not hear Clem's exact words, I did the tone of their rising desperation. At the walnut counter inside stood Edward Jensen, his obstinate pork-pie hat shaking its dissent.

"But Jensen's Hardware's been our best customer since before I took over from Mr. Hardy."

"I know, Clem, I know. But same as you, I've got doors to keep open."

The telephone back in Clem's office started to ring.

"What if we dropped your rate until this all blows over? By twenty percent, say, to make up for any short-term drop in readership. By September, folks will have forgotten. They'll want to read about the county elections coming up in November if not the play-by-play on the World Series."

"For your sake, Clem, I hope you're right."

But Jensen said his gut was nagging him this story would not be blowing over near so quick as she hoped it would. Would be sticking in an awful lot of folks' craw for an awfully long time to come. Near all of them folks his customers. Until Clem went and opened up her big fat can of worms, this was the biggest story to hit Hanna in Jensen's fifty-two years. Then she ran her blamed—excuse his French—story about what all Thoreaux done to get it offered him. Somehow got skittered up, so he turned it down stone cold. Now some of those big-city newspapers and TV reporters had dug up about him going to prison—maybe doing hard time for being a child molester, even—turning Hanna into the laughingstock of the nation.

Clem's phone finally stopped ringing.

"No, this story's not blowing over no time soon.

Until it does—if it ever does—I've got a hardware store to keep open. A family to feed. Tuition for a daughter at Hiram College in the fall. Folks hereabouts so disgusted they're not going to be so much as buying a single issue of the *Oracle*, let alone read it. What really spooks me is there's been some high talk—in my store well within my earshot, mind you—from Shorty Stevens and his whole Chamber of Commerce crowd, about them organizing a boycott of your paper. Not only of you but of anyone caught advertising in it. *Anyone*."

"But Mr. Jensen—"

But Mr. Jensen raised his palm, stepping back from the counter. "I'll bid you a good morning, young lady. I wish you well with sorting all this out. I mean that. I truly do."

He turned, nodding to me where I stood half-in, half-out, and still holding the door open. Then he noticed my face.

"What happened to you, Jeremy?"

"Flat tire. Popped on me while I was changing it."

"You gotta be more careful. Same thing happened to old man Henshaw. Ended up drowning in his own blood."

"So I heard, but Clem's right, Mr. Jensen. By next week, folks will have forgotten all about this and moved on."

"I hope you're right. For everyone's sake, I hope you're right. If they do, I'll be the first one busting down the doors. Red-faced, hat in hand, and begging my apologies."

I allowed the door to sweep shut behind him, the black ice in Clem's eyes melting a little at their corners. "Sorry, Clem."

"Thanks for trying anyway, Jeremy. I appreciate it."

"Sure, but he'll be back. If not next week, the week after, for sure. Just wait and see if he isn't. Hat in hand like he said. Jensen's always been a nervous Nellie. Came in giving my grandfather an earful of grief every time he ran one of his more contentious editorials. It'll give you an excuse to up your rates on him."

"If it's for only a week, I can hold out. Much longer, I may be padlocking my doors. My next three biggest advertisers after Jensen have already pulled the plug on me, but Jensen was by far my biggest. His ads paid a lot of my overhead. Now what? I have to keep this paper, Jeremy. This paper's my lifeblood. I have to keep it. Whatever it takes, that's where I have to go."

The phone back in her office began ringing again.

"You're not picking that up?"

"Why bother?"

Clem said it was just another subscriber hot under the collar, calling to cancel. She had already gotten her posterior roundly chewed on by at least a dozen of them this morning, and it wasn't even nine o'clock. In two weeks' time she might well be picking grapes for that lecherous drunk of an uncle of hers out in Sonoma.

"Folks, as Constable Durkin reminded me last evening, can be cantankerous creatures. Who would have thought they would get themselves worked up over a hermit hardly any have so much as set eyes on?"

"Yeah. Who." She tried to smile. "Well, you're not an advertiser, so you must be here to gut your subscription."

"Not me, sister. I'm just your out-scooped and soon-to-be-unemployed reporter asking if you'd figured out why he turned down a knighthood."

"I was about to ask you."

"Well, even if you don't know, what do you think?"

"That the village has on its hands a crazed misanthrope hermit who hasn't spoken to anyone in thirty years and sees no good reason to get in the habit again."

"I don't know, Clem. He didn't seem so crazy when I spoke to him."

"Nineteen fifty-five hardly counts, Jeremy."

I grinned, not trying terribly hard to imitate her pool-shark persona.

"Some later than that."

"Like later when?"

I explained about last night.

"Gutsy even if stupid, to say nothing of being rude."

"This can be a rude business."

"Yeah, no kidding. So did your old partner in crime let on he was turning down the knighthood?"

"If he had, folks wouldn't have read about it off the A.P. wire."

Clem stood for half a minute looking down at the wood-plank floor, fist tapping her mouth. She cocked an eye up at me.

"Do you think you can break in again?"

"You said that was rude of me."

"And you said this can be a rude business."

The telephone back in Clem's office started to ring again.

"Maybe, but I'd want a diversion of some sort."

"Why a diversion?"

"Because the bore of the gun he had me looking down was big enough for me to plug my thumb in is why. What with all the commotion he's caused of late, he could shoot first and ask questions later."

"You have a strange definition of friend."

"Friendship's not what it used to be, Clem."

"Clearly. So what type of a diversion do you have in mind?"

"Boy, you've got me on that one. How do you divert someone who hardly leaves his house?"

The telephone back in Clem's office at last ceased its ringing, only to begin again.

"Would be quite the front-pager if one of us found out why he left the Queen crying at the altar. What would make it a great story would be if he stood her up for some act of unheralded heroism."

"But if he's some sort of hero, Jeremy, why wouldn't he want it known? Kiss and make up with the village after all these years of shivering out in the cold."

"Therein hangs our tale. That's what's got this story popping on all eight cylinders."

"Well, maybe one of us will get lucky."

"Luck's got nothing to do with scoring on this, Clem. Which brings me to the reason I'm up here this morning."

"I should've known."

"Listen to me. I've got a straightforward proposition for you. Collaboration."

"Forget it, Jeremy. We're competitors, not BFFs."

"Listen to me. This can work."

"No, it can't."

"Listen to me, will you?"

"Forget it. It won't work."

"Will you hear me out for one minute?"

"Okay. You've got sixty seconds, starting fifty seconds ago."

"I propose we work together. Share our sources, share the byline. Publish same day. Promise to publish or perish together."

"Share our sources?"

"Exactly."

"Share our notes?"

"Absolutely."

"No holding back on me?"

"Or you on me."

The telephone back in Clem's office began to ring again.

"So what say, Clem?"

She let go a resigned sigh. "It's like Bob Dylan says. When you've got nothing left, you've got nothing left to lose. But it's understood. No secrets between us."

"I said that already."

"Just want to be certain you mean what you say."

"Why wouldn't I?"

"Because you're a man, for one. A man with a shady history, for another."

Two of us who couldn't bury Beth. Me, I understood why. But after two years, why still Clem?

"So where do we start, Jeremy?"

"Like I said. With a diversion."

"So we get a diversion. So what? What're we going to learn with a diversion if he won't talk to us? Why would he if you—we—break in again?"

"We don't need to talk to him. What we need are his letters."

"What letters?"

"In his study he keeps a stack of letters. Spider-webbed letters."

"So?"

"So who keeps a stack of letters out in the open so he can look at them every day to remind him of what's in them, but he never reads?"

"So what else did you see?"

"A big gun sighted on me dead to rights."

"You told me already. What else?"

I thought. Tried to picture his study in my head.

"An almost empty bottle of whiskey."

Her pool-shark smile crept across Clem's face.

"An almost empty bottle?"

"Yeah."

"So probably not a teetotaler."

"I wouldn't be."

"What label of whiskey?"

Chapter 13

After we came up steps smelling of wood rot and decay from his mildewed cellar, Clem followed me out of his kitchen stinking of cat urine, into the living room where my flashlight beam passed over a face that though snoring seemed not to have found repose even in sleep. Beside his couch stood the near-empty pint bottle of one-forty-proof Four Roses we'd left on his front porch late in the afternoon with a note apologizing for me breaking in.

"What made you think he'd be asleep drunk, Clem?"

"My hunch is Thomas Thoreaux turned down a knighthood because he's a man haunted by ghosts. Ghosts and guilt."

"What made you think that?"

"Life. Come on."

We started up the steps.

"Doesn't this seem a tad too cold-blooded?"

"Don't go backsliding on me now, Michaels. You're the one who started this whole business of breaking in."

"Yeah, but—"

"But nothing. Like I told you. Whatever it takes to hold on to the *Oracle*, wherever it takes me, that's where I'm going."

"So there's no price too high?"

"See it my way. For you, you've always got some other paper."

"If you only knew."

"For me, this is all I've got to hold on to." We had reached the top of the stairs. "Okay, so which room's his study? Let's get to it. I don't want to wager on him sleeping straight through to morning."

We walked to the end of the hall, where I tried the door.

"The sonofa—he locked it!"

"Keep your voice down," she whispered. "He must've thought you'd come back. So must be something pretty important—or pretty damning—he doesn't want to take a chance on somebody seeing. You bring a screwdriver like I told you?"

I reached into my pocket and set to work. Or tried to.

"Oh, for the love of—"

"What now?"

"It's these old-time doorknobs. Screwdriver head's too big and screws too far recessed for me to reach."

"So try another screwdriver."

"I only brought the one."

"Why did you bring only one screwdriver?"

"Because I'm not as smart as you are."

"Save it, Jeremy. Your keen fraternity wit's lost on me." She looked back toward the steps. "Do you want to see if maybe he has his keys on him?"

"Do you want to see what a drunk does when he wakes up with someone's hands going through his pockets?"

"So what do you want to do?"

Downstairs, we shuffled through his kitchen

drawers.

"I can't believe he doesn't keep a screwdriver."

"You want to come back, Jeremy?"

"We were lucky your stunt worked this time."

"Why are you making it out to be *my* stunt? I didn't hear you objecting."

"And no, I doubt if it'd work a second time. I'm surprised it worked this time."

"So why did you try it, then?"

"Because when you've got nothing, you've got nothing to lose."

I switched off the flashlight.

"Now what?"

I canvassed the kitchen, both of Clem's hands fanning her face.

"Why doesn't he keep his windows open in summer?"

"To keep out kids from climbing in on a dare."

"How does he stand it?"

"Maybe he—"

"Maybe he what?"

"Maybe he keeps his upstairs windows open."

"A lot of good that's going to do us."

"There used to be a ladder in the barn."

"So?"

The corner window to his study was not latched but likely had not been raised in years, because I almost fell backwards off the ladder, pushing it open. When the window did open, it creaked with the same death-knell squeal of the luckless rodents I'd heard when I sat outside in my Hertz rental. Clem, in fact, greened some at the gills when she slipped into the musty room thick with the decay one's nose associates with small dead mammals. I lighted the brass hurricane lamp, then sat on the window seat cushion beside her. He kept the letters organized in chronological order starting in 1919, the first written to his mother. Handing half to Clem, we set to work.

"Like you said, Jeremy. Strange he keeps them close at hand—in plain view—yet never reads them." She wiped the palm of her hand on a thigh of her black jeans. "With all these yucky spider webs, it has to have been years."

"Like you said. Guilt. Guilt and ghosts. Can't bear to read them from guilt but wants the ghost of their memories close at hand. Maybe the letters will tell us why."

But the letters did not tell us much of anything. Not at first. Instead, we read trivial family tidings. A third cousin's wedding in Bristol; the death of a maiden aunt in Provence. Numerous births and lingering illnesses. Long separations and reunions. Letters from his mother addressed to him in Montreal and New Haven. A few from Thoreaux to her about school, and later ones about the Eiffel Tower and the Brandenburg Gate. Then more and more warning her of the coming war. Assuring her he would heed her warnings. Not wait until the last minute before getting out. The last written to her dated May 1940. There was only one later letter. From April 2, 1947. In his hand and written in French but absent of postmark or even Thoreaux's signature. A yellowing black-and-white photograph inside the envelope. I handed the letter to Clem.

"Addressed to a Gabrielle Mercier."

"My Aunt Gabby?"

"Is this her photograph?"

Clem shook her head.

"Pretty girl, whoever she is."

She read.

"He's saying he would return in early June. To find out for certain if he sent an innocent girl to her grave." Clem looked over at me. "There's his guilt, I'll bet."

We studied the black-and-white photograph. A girl with laughing eyes and long hair of no determinant color. Maybe strawberry blonde that brushed over her shoulders. A little disheveled, as though she had been lying in the grass. She wore a sweater and calf-length tartan skirt, with a beret cocked at a jaunty angle, and she sat beneath the shade of a tree with her legs pulled to her chest and arms wrapped around them. A picnic basket lay off to one side, an open bottle of wine leaning against it.

"Recognize her?"

Clem shook her head.

"Mom brought few photos with her. The ones she did, I've seen a million times. Maybe some old flame of his?"

"Maybe."

I returned the photograph and letter to their envelope, then tried to arrange the envelopes back into a stack as we found them. Like he was never going to miss thirty years of spider webs suddenly gone. Then again, he said his eyesight wasn't what it was once.

"Could she have been the reason he turned down the knighthood, Jeremy? The innocent woman he sent to her grave?"

"Maybe."

"Why do you think he never mailed it?"

"Clueless, Clem. Completely clueless."

"Why did the letters stop coming?"

"Maybe he stopped writing? Maybe he destroyed them."

"Why destroy those and not these?"

"Again, clueless, Clem. Something incriminating, maybe? Maybe one of them answered his question."

She let go a sigh, shaking her head as she looked over Thoreaux's study.

"So where to now?"

"Clueless, but we're not going to find any answers up here except from the guy downstairs. And he's not talking. At least not tonight he's not."

"Do you think he would some other night?"

"Not a snowball's chance."

"Then this woman's our key, Jeremy."

"I think so too. Come on. Let's go."

"Where to?"

"Back to—"

A man wretched, down the hall. A toilet flushed.

"Is it him, Jeremy?"

"It's not Santa Claus. Maybe he'll go to bed now."

"Maybe he'll get his gun."

A door opened.

"Maybe we should go, Jeremy. Now."

"Maybe you're right."

****

We sat in the dark of my Hertz rental, rind of a new moon rising ghost-gray over Thoreaux's ramshackle abode as Clem opened and closed the glovebox door over and over.

"So did he really go back to France?"

"Maybe, Clem. Thinking about it in nineteen forty-seven. But maybe not. He never even signed his letter, let alone mailed it."

"Why keep it, then? Why not go back after he'd just got his butt kicked when he ran for Congress? Maybe have done him a world of good to get out of Dodge."

"Maybe."

"Maybe—"

The glove-box door dropped with an angry thunk.

"What in hell's this, Michaels?"

"What's what?"

She held my notepad six inches in front of my nose.

"This, Michaels? What's this?"

"Notes."

She pointed.

"This looks like a license number."

"Yeah. It is."

"Whose car?"

"Hertz rental."

"This one?"

"No."

"Whose, then?"

"Woman who came down Thoreaux's back steps couple of nights back."

Clem looked about to feed me my notes for an early breakfast.

"Jeremy. You promised we'd work together on this. Remember? You promised."

"We are working together."

"Not if you're keeping secrets. Don't promises mean anything to you?"

"Who's keeping secrets, and why are you so suspicious of me?"

"Because you're a man with a history, and because you're keeping secrets."

"I'm not keeping secrets if I don't know who she is. That's why I wrote down her license number. Been trying to figure out how I could trace the driver. She was parked over there near that streetlight."

Clem looked to where I pointed, notepad rapping her fingertips.

"Could be she's the woman in the photograph, Clem. Too bad I haven't been in an accident."

"Why too bad?"

"Then I could give Hertz her number and maybe get a name."

Clem shot me a look.

"Just kidding, Clem. You need to lighten up."

"I'll lighten up once we get our story, and I don't need to worry about losing my paper. Did you—?"

"Did I what?"

She pulled out the car rental packet from the glove box and started to rummage its contents.

"What are you doing?"

"Did you pay for the uninsured motorists?"

"I don't know, and what kind of question is that to ask at five o'clock in the morning?"

She read. "Yeah, you did. Why am I not surprised?"

"Why are you worried if I'm insured against a motorist who isn't?"

Clem tossed the rental packet back into the glove box.

"Because, my collaborator in letters, we're taking a road trip this morning."

"A road trip?"

"A short one."

"Where?"

"Cleveland Hopkins. Now take me home so I can change."

"What about me? I could use a shower too."

She sniffed the air.

"No. I can stand you until we get back. Now take me home."

"What about Aimée?"

"Her grandmother will be all too happy to keep her for another few hours. Or days or weeks."

"Okay, but can you ask her to go to my cousin's garage to feed Beatrice?"

"Who's Beatrice?"

"Abandoned cat who adopted my cousin."

"She can't wait?"

"Hate to. Nursing mother and all."

Clem turned away, smiling into the dark.

"You know, Michaels, for a man, sometimes you've got something halfway to a heart almost. Almost. Now roll your buns, buster."

****

Clem came down the back steps of her apartment over the *Oracle* offices, to the alley parking lot. Dressed to kill, if not for the out-and-out slaughter of the male species. She had swapped the black jeans and jersey she wore on our midnight caper for a lowcut scarlet dress with matching heels. I had never seen Clem in a dress, not even back in high school, and I know I stared at her bug-eyed with mouth agape. I mean to tell you, folks, she had nice legs. Nice firm legs peculiar to distance runners, but instead of a purse she carried a hammer in one hand and a small bottle of something in her other.

She set down the bottle of something—I could now see it was a bottle of something red—on the hood of my rental before walking behind the car, the smell of her perfume reaching through the rolled-down window. Halston. Same as Helen wore. She raised the hammer in my rearview mirror and swung, red taillight shattering and me flying out the door screaming.

"What the hell are you doing?"

"Now, don't be getting into a snit, Jeremy." She smiled, admiring her handiwork. "It *was* your idea."

"What do you mean it was my idea?"

"You said it was too bad you hadn't been in an accident. I'm merely accommodating you. Here, hold this."

Clem handed me the hammer, my mouth again agape at the smashed taillight, and returned with the bottle that turned out to be nail polish.

"Now what are you doing?"

"Oh, really, Michaels. Have you ever seen a fender bender where the car at fault didn't leave behind at least some paint?"

She stood. "Okay. Get back in, and I'll follow you up."

****

Clem blasted past me as we were both pulling into the airport and stood waiting in short-term parking as I pulled up outside the yellow door to her decrepit Plymouth Arrow.

"So where to now, boss?"

"Hertz lot, of course."

"Of course. Stupid me."

"No, not stupid. Some days a little dense. But I

make allowances for your being a guy."

"Oh, thank you, thank you, thank you, oh, just and merciful boss."

Clem's reflection smiled in the windshield.

"I'll have you paper-trained yet, Michaels."

When we pulled into the Hertz lot, I headed for customer service out front.

"No, no, no! Not *there*. You really are being dense."

My exasperated hands flew from the steering wheel.

"How am I being dense now?"

"Let me explain this so even you can understand."

"Please."

"Most rentals get rented to guys, right?"

"I suppose. So?"

"So the titans of corporate America might be your typical Type-A psychopaths disguised in suits, but while Philistines, they're not stupid. Not completely. They know sex sells. So they staff their customer service desks with women. Young women. Young attractive women. Sorority and cheerleader types. Women who've perfected to a T batting their painted purple eyes and who keep the top buttons of their blouses undone and lean their ample cleavages into men's noses while they seduce them into buying options they don't need. Like uninsured motorist insurance. Hertz marks it up ninety-something percent, out of which the money nymph behind the front desk gets a decent cut. Multiply that by fifty lust-struck suckers a day, and she can go shopping at Neiman Marcus on her way home. See?"

"Where did you hear all this?"

"I didn't hear all this anywhere. I read it. You should try it sometime."

"Read it where?"

"*Consumer Reports*."

"You read *Consumer Reports*?"

"You might sometime consider expanding your horizons with magazines that don't come with a foldout, Michaels."

"How untitillating. So why aren't we going to customer service?"

"Cheerleader types get hustled a hundred times a day and a thousand times a night, right?"

"I wouldn't know."

"Well, I do. Sweet talk us for a month of Sundays, and you'll still know less than when you stumbled through the door. Now drive us to the garage around back."

"Yes'm, boss."

After I parked before an open bay, we stood behind the rental pretending to discuss the damage until a mechanic sporting a Fu-Manchu mustache and an impressive beer gut lumbered up the steps from the grease pit. Once he spotted us, or should I say spotted Clem's long runner legs, he walked out of the garage bay, cleaning his lecherous oily fingers on an oily rag that looked like it might once have been orange in color, as he sized up Clem. *Billy* was stitched in blue over the pocket of his gray overalls.

"Something I can help you folks with?"

Clem pointed at the shattered turn signal. "We got rear-ended."

Billy stooped to finger the jagged plastic.

"Boy, you sure did. When'd this all go down?"

"Earlier this week."

Billy managed to tear his eyes off Clem's thighs six inches in front of his face and looked up. "Did you by chance pick up their uninsured motorist?"

"Why, yes, we did, Billy."

"Well, smart that you did. This time. Only one time in a thousand you'll need it. One of them rackets Hertz has got running for 'em."

"Really, Billy?"

"Charge you like a gazillion times more than their premiums cost them. *Consumer Reports* ran a big exposé on it all a few months back."

"You don't say."

"Yes, ma'am."

Clem raised her eyebrows, smirking at me as Billy stood. It was all I could do not to kick him in his beer-bloated Fu-Manchu face.

"You folks dropping off?"

"Yes, we are. Plane to catch for San Francisco, I'm afraid. Our family runs a vineyard up in Sonoma."

"Wine?"

"Yes, wine."

"I'm more of a suds man myself, but you can leave the keys here with me. I'll take care of it for you."

"Oh, that's so sweet of you, Billy."

Billy's face reddened to a shade of red deeper than the deepest red-ass red you'd ever not want to lay eyes on.

"There is one other thing."

"Yes, ma'am?"

"We would have called in the hit-and-run, but we were back here for a funeral and, you know, what with one thing after another…"

"I understand. Sh— Stuff happens."

"It sure can, but after she took off, my brother here went after her. I think I was able to jot down the license number, but I'm not certain. She was going so fast."

"Yes, ma'am."

"It was a Hertz rental too."

"No kidding? Well, what are the odds, huh?"

Clem stepped closer, hips almost grinding Billy's, and his nostrils twitched at the rich perfume drifting up from her deep cleavage.

"We really want to make a police report. The woman seemed drunk. What with the way she weaved in and out of traffic, and a playground right across the street."

"I don't recall seeing no damaged car come in."

"Did you work all week, Billy?"

"No. Got me working weekends this month, so I get Wednesdays and Thursdays off."

"Maybe she still has it. Or maybe she repaired it herself if she didn't pick up the uninsured motorists insurance."

"Maybe. Most women have more sense than to fall for that racket."

Clem raised her eyebrows. She smiled. I really, really wanted to kick him in his fat Fu-Manchu red-ass face.

"I'm worried this woman is still out there, Billy. She needs to be off the road. What if it was your little girl in the playground and she ran into the street chasing after a ball?"

"Oh, I'm not married, ma'am."

"Really?"

"No, ma'am."

"Well, I have to say I'm surprised to hear you say so, Billy. A sweetheart like you. I would think you had swarms of girls buzzing all over you."

Clem's thick mascara eyelashes fluttered. Billy blushed all the redder as I searched the inside of the garage bay to see if I could spot a wrench. A large one. A real skull-basher.

"You are?"

"I am. But what I really want is to get this woman off the road. Can't you help me out? Save one of your own kids someday when you have them with some lucky girl. Maybe this woman returned it on Wednesday or maybe Thursday."

"Why not go to the police? You've got her license number."

"Well, like I said, Billy, this woman was driving so fast. I only think we have her number. If we're a little off, I'm sure you can figure out the right number. Maybe her name and address too, to help out the police? If it's not too much trouble. You know how busy they can get."

Billy studied the back door to customer service, his grease-nailed hands working the oily orange rag between his lecherous oily fingers.

"Okay. Sure. Give me a minute."

"Oh, Billy, thank you. You're a dear. A complete dear. Isn't he a dear, brother?"

"Yes. Yes, he is, sister. A complete dear."

Billy disappeared through the back door.

"Clem?"

"What?"

"Don't worry about the *Oracle* folding. You missed your calling." I held out my arms. "Broadway beckons. Hollywood. Television."

Less than five minutes later, Billy strutted across the parking lot, oily slip of Hertz stationery wedged between his lecherous oily fingers.

"Got her number writ down right. But no need to worry none about her hurting no kids. At least not hereabouts."

"Why's that, Billy?"

"French lady." Billy looked at the smashed rear light. "You said you was turning in your rental now?"

"Yes, yes, we are."

I looked over Clem's shoulder as she unfolded the sheaf of Hertz stationery.

Gabrielle Mercier
Ribeauville, France

Likely Colette called her sister about the knighthood. Gabrielle then turned around to pay a visit to Thoreaux.

"We need to speak to my mother," Clem whispered.

"Why?"

"Because Aunt Gabby wouldn't have been here without seeing her and telling her why."

"You mean you didn't see her when she was here?"

"Not since I was a baby."

Billy leaned in the driver's door for the keys.

"Did you say your plane was heading out today?"

"Why, yes, I did, Billy."

Billy let go a love-thwarted breath. "Now ain't that just my luck. You wouldn't happen to be coming back this way anytime soon, would you, now?"

If not a wrench, there had to be a tire iron back in the garage. Had to be.

Chapter 14

Clem stalked room to room through Colette's garden cottage calling.

Maman! Aimée! Maman!

"Where'd they get to, Clem?"

"Likely still at your cousin's."

"Really?"

"Oh, yeah. My daughter's inherited her mother's ardent heart for all matters feline. Just try snatching her away from one kitten, let alone a whole litter. You can forget about it until she falls asleep, and even then she'll wake up howling once she sees they're gone."

"So where to now?"

"Katie's. I've a bone to pick with my mother."

****

Yes, her mother. Another in my grandfather's multi-national extended family. As related by him, Colette Mercier fled to Hanna in 1946, where Colette's aunt by adoption still lived following Jacque's death. The day her train pulled into the Hanna depot she knocked on their door, suitcase in one hand, father-abandoned Clémence bundled in her other arm. Thoreaux answered. Words passed. Heated indictments were leveled and so heatedly denied no Mercier darkened Thoreaux's threshold again until Clem followed me up out of his basement.

They lodged *gratis* in the apartment upstairs from

the *Oracle* until the periodic proceeds began to arrive some months later, cabled to Colette from the sale of her vineyards to Gabrielle, whose property abutted hers and had begun to stagger back from war's wreckage. Colette opened a dress boutique. In the easy-money postwar boom, with the assistance of cut-rate advertising in the *Oracle*, it grew within months into quite the sensation with the ladies of the village. A sort of soirée. Due as much to the learned discourse and a teakettle always kept at a boil in her back storage room as her seamstress's dexterity and the haute couture of her designs that allowed her to raise her daughter in a modicum of comfort.

Clémence got shortened to plain Clem and plain Clem blossomed into the star of Hanna High. Besides making the cheerleader squad and in due course named its captain, she played field hockey in the fall, volleyball in winter, and in spring starred as catcher and homerun queen for the girls' softball team. She charmed Grandfather Hardy to find her summer gofer jobs around the paper. Cleaned its six eight-foot-tall Palladian windows, and, before summer was over, served as his apprentice secretary and bookkeeper. More and more she submitted articles, starting with the sports teams she starred on. But she had her dark side. With no father, she latched onto any boy who showed the slightest interest. So no surprise when a year after graduation Clem married her steady of the last four years, who sold Buicks for a shady Youngstown dealership with rumored ties to the Genovese family. He died five years later with Clem seven months pregnant. Clem had not told me the details. I knew only that Chris managed to get himself killed in a car accident, and that was all my grandfather said. More than likely while steering with his stocking feet and gripping a Stroh's beer in each hand.

Grandfather had sold the *Oracle* to Clem a month before Chris died. She managed somehow to keep the presses rolling after a heart attack felled him. And she made the hour commute two years running over to Hiram College for journalism classes taught by the city editor who drove down two evenings a week from up at the *Cleveland Plain Dealer*. She was not about to allow the *Oracle* to fold. Not on her watch. As Lawyer Kauffman put it at breakfast, woe be unto him who stumbled in her path. Even if that him happened to be her mother.

****

They were not in my cousin's garage, but I spotted them through a rear-door window beneath the broad purple shade of a century-old Dutch maple. A giggling Aimée lay on her back as Katie's crew of kittens rollicked one another off her chest, playing king-of-the-hill, while Bernice napped beneath a picnic table. Colette, thick black hair tied back to keep it off her neck in the muggy June heat, sat on the grass as she teased an ear of my gray kitten with a long stem of grass.

"I see them, Clem."

Colette's wary eyes watched us as we crossed the grass. Sniper eyes, as I overhead my grandfather call them once, when we sat before Thoreaux's fireplace on a snowy February evening. When I asked him what were sniper eyes, he glanced at Thoreaux, who shook his head.

"Go back to your book, Jeremy."

"Well, don't you look so very pretty today, *ma chère*. You should outfit yourself in a dress more often. It much becomes you. Does it not much become her, Mr. Jeremy?"

"Yes, ind—"

"Forget how I dress, Maman. Why didn't you tell me Aunt Gabby was here last week?"

"But I did tell you. I dialed you at your paper. Did my goose forget?"

"You told me you *spoke* to her. You let me think you only spoke on the phone. When I asked what she had to say, you told me it was some personal business. You never told me Gabrielle was here. In person. An aunt who had not seen me since I was a baby. Talking of all people to Thomas Thoreaux. Who you knew I'd been trying to talk to for days."

"Only for a few hours was she here, and how did you know she talked to that…that *connard*? That liar. She swore me to secrecy upon pain of burning in eternal Hell. Did she confide in you?"

"No, Maman. Jeremy saw her."

"Coming down his back steps, Mrs. Mercier."

"I see." Colette stroked my gray kitten that had fallen asleep in the hammock her pleated skirt made between her knees. "Well, since you now know my sister was here, she wished to talk to him because of what she read in *Le Monde*."

"Is this why he turned down the knighthood? Because of something Aunt Gabby said to him?"

Colette's head snapped up.

"Why should what she said to him be of any interest to you?"

"Because since he did, I've lost almost all of my

advertisers. Every day more and more of my subscribers. My paper is going under and taking me bankrupt with it. Are those good enough reasons?"

"The less I know of that *connard* the better. Those English brought him back, and that is all I have to say."

"Are you going to help me save my paper or not?"

But with what I thought too much fervency, Colette claimed she had nothing more to tell. She'd found her sister waiting on her boutique steps the morning she spoke to Thoreaux. Demanded to know what she knew of the knighthood. All the while, or so Colette claimed, refusing to tell her what it was she and Thoreaux talked about or why she even made her journey. A journey Colette could not fathom.

While true her sister remained a woman of property, an owner of one of the finest vineyards in all of France and a high-ranking member of the National Assembly, by no means was she a woman well off. Her voracious vineyards consumed every sou they brought in and more, much more, just to keep up, burdened as she was by usurious loans. Her sister was not one to throw away meager resources on matters of frivolity.

"Now especially, with your uncle Dominique much ill."

We were getting nowhere fast with Colette. I had dead-ended out of leads, even bad leads. Quickly dead-ending out of time. If I wanted to tell this story before somebody else grabbed it, if I wanted Henry to keep his job and us—or me—to get to New York, I had to talk to this Gabrielle. From what Newbie told me in Thoreaux's driveway, ABC News already had their man in London digging into it. Who knew how many others were doing the same. Only a matter of time before one of them unearthed my mother lode. It was too good a story. One, as Henry had said, with Pulitzer written all over it.

"Will she talk to me, Mrs. Mercier? If I went to see her? Go to France, I mean."

Now it was Clem's head that snapped at me.

"You would, I fear, be disappointed, Mr. Jeremy."

"Why?"

"My sister cares not for Americans. Not even a little."

But even if Gabrielle cared not for Americans, why would her sister discourage me from speaking to her with the survival of her daughter's newspaper in the balance? It made no sense. Just as Gabrielle's journey here, without more, made no sense. Or so Colette said. Just as it seemed to make no sense Gabrielle would refuse to tell her sister why she came. If in fact she had not told her sister. How likely was it she had not, after the two of them survived the Occupation as sisters in arms? What was it with them and their secrets? They kept them as much under lock and key as Thoreaux did his.

A lazy Sunday breeze sent a leaf tumbling through Katie's grass, setting the crew of kittens off in chase, except for one Aimée carried over to Colette.

"So, Mrs. Mercier, you must be something of a cat fancier too."

"Some, though not as once I was. As with so much in my life, the Occupation changed with me everything."

"Even with cats?"

"Most especially with *chats*."

The barbarity, she claimed, I could not imagine.

Life so desperate. Take food. While the *Boche* ate well, quite well, they kept the French to a mere eight hundred calories a day. Wild game proved difficult without firearms. If caught, a hunter risked a quick bullet to the temple as cure for his hunger.

"*Chat*, however, if properly prepared, can prove most hardy fare."

"Cats, Maman! You ate cats?"

"But of course we ate *chat*. Why not? They grew fat on our barn rats. True they could be difficult to catch as one by one their friends disappeared, but worth the effort. They tasted a lot like chicken. Oh, yes, it is true. You gut them—"

"You gutted cats!"

"What? You think we swallowed them whole, my goose? We are not sharks. Of course we gutted *chats*. How else to eat them? You make a stew with wine and a little garlic the way you gut and cook a chicken. Gabrielle who taught me how."

Colette sat for a minute considering as she stroked the kitten Aimée had brought over to her.

"No. I must discourage you from speaking to my sister. She is resolved not to speak of this business. She a woman of much resolve. So did the *Boche* learn to their grief. No, never should you underestimate her resolve. Never."

Chapter 15

From the driveway I waved goodbye to the ladies, Katie's phone greeting me on my way in her side kitchen door.

"There you are. Been trying to get hold of you all morning."

"Out working a new angle on our knighthood saga. What's up, Henry?"

What was up, Henry said, was Trench Coat had once more busied himself with squandering taxpayer dollars. Gone all in on a legal shopping spree by conniving his select committee of vigilantes—spun to the gullible media as a grand jury—to indict Erec Renard. Not for embezzlement like the D.A. carried on about in Henry's office only last week. But for the murder of Kid Twist. A murder Renard led me to believe was Doug Rago's handiwork. If it was, Renard's indictment was one risky roll of Siuslaw casino dice for Rago. With an indictment, he had handed Renard all the more incentive to go all in on taking him down.

But maybe Trench Coast was not as stupid as he pretended. Rago had served his nefarious purpose. So maybe it was time to put him out of his misery like any rabid dog. Using Renard to do the dirty let him keep his hands clean for his next move up the political ladder. Governor or senator. Then again, it would also not surprise me either if Renard for reasons of his own *was* behind the murder of Kid Twist. He had kicked around enough, not only in Portland but back in Brooklyn, where as Father Connor had told me, the docks were as rough and tumble as they come. But where was Renard?

"Sarah get any calls for me since the indictment?"

"Yeah, your bank. You're overdrawn. Again. They're threatening to close out your account."

"Can't be. I still have checks left. Anything else?"

"No one sounding French. Any guesses where your guy's hiding?"

"Maybe Tijuana, but he'll surface."

Soon. Wherever he'd gotten to. Much too severe a case of the hots for Rago's job to disappear for long.

"D.A. still demanding a retraction from us?"

"Yeah. Got to frothing at the mouth over it near the end of his press conference."

"Stickle still of a mind to cave?"

"Definitely."

Not six seconds after the last press conference question got evaded, Henry said Stickle had him on the horn for a good hour grinding his ear to hamburger. So far Henry had kept him towing the line. Told him our D.A. was blowing smoke inhaled from a substance of dubious legality after I caught Rago with his arm elbow-deep in the cookie jar. It would take a little more time to play out, but at day's end a Pulitzer, with the advertising dollars a Pulitzer would bring in—that would take the sting out of Stickle's alimony—was more than a passing possibility.

"But it's touch and go with him. His backbone could mush to Jell-O on us in a wink of a rat's eye."

"You want me to come back?"

"No. Stay where you are, kid. No sense getting whacked over a story."

"Whacked? By Rago?"

"By Rago. By your source, whoever he is. Our D.A. Those judges named or think they're about to be. By disgruntled detectives on the take down at Pearl District. Pick a number. No, stay where you are for now. Keep working the knighthood story. Hard."

"How bad's it looking for us, Henry?"

No way to say for certain, Henry said, but if our inept D.A. could somehow, by fair means or foul, pull off making his charges against Renard stick, there was a real chance of us getting simmered in the juices of our own potboiler. Trench Coat would spin it to make it look like we were so gullible we let Renard sucker us in to divert attention away from his double-dealing shenanigans. If he did, our reputations would plume right up the old smokestack.

"You sure I shouldn't come back, Henry?"

"No, stay put and keep digging. As deep as you need to dig. It may be all that's going to save our bacon. And at the end of the day, that's all a newspaperman's got. His reputation."

His reputation, sure, but it's not all some of us had. Like Thoreaux, some of us had a past. A past not past. Predacious. Forever behind us. Had us forever looking over our shoulder. Getting closer. We only need wait for the night for it to catch up.

****

Twelve iridescent numerals circling Katie's Big Ben clock gleamed a cat-eye yellow. I lay a minute as I listened to the night to be certain she no longer lingered. Certain she had ceased her relentless catechism of culpable conscience.

Why won't you walk away? His heart's broken, Jeremy. Why won't you walk away?

But it was because his heart was broken I would not, could not, walk away.

I pushed back the sheet damp from disconcerting dream, dressed, and set out. A starless night. A night heavy of air thick with past. A fisted-heart past not about to let go. Not until I gave in to the damnable demands it levied on a coward's conscience.

Desultory headlights glistened over dewy grass. Now and again the plaintive howl of a mongrel dog. Down from the *Oracle* at the far end of Union Street festered one of the village's older neighborhoods. Twin rows of two-story houses with roofs of gray slate green with lichen, and only one looking as if a paint brush had touched its winter-scoured walls in recent memory. As was the *Oracle*, put up in that same smug prosperity befouling the final days of the Roaring Twenties by shopkeepers and machine-shop owners and proprietors of garages employed to keep running Model Ts that broke down if their inept drivers so much as glanced at a pothole. Houses built in haste and lack of craftsmanship by slipshod carpenters as the end of the age, preached from pulpits fist-pounded on Pentecostal Sundays, charged toward them. Clueless of the twin world cataclysms lurking around the corner of history to engulf them and put an end to a way of small-town life much too sweet to have endured for more than the decade it did.

Here, among the vestiges of a broken-promised past, Beth grew up. In the last house before the street dead-ended at the now boarded up and window-shuttered C & W Brickworks. Her shaggy lawn long uncut. Driveway a field of asphalt overgrown with dandelions. Even more ramshackle than its neighbors, with an askew Johnson Realty sign rusting out front with no way to tell for how long it had been up for sale. Even in the hazy night through windows coated with years of dust I saw someone—Nameless relatives? Shylock realtors? Agents for the State of Ohio seeking recompense for the cost of Mrs. Brennan's bare-bones asylum hospital?—had stripped the house that now sat barren of furniture likely auctioned off in one of those ubiquitous small-town yard sales held every other Saturday morning on front lawns in the summer. Empty since Judge Biltmore had committed Mrs. Brennan to Massillon. Not only wild-eyed crazy but had driven crazy every other denizen of the village with her endless end-of-the-world harangues. Even Beth. Especially Beth.

But it's me, not her mother, who bears the blame. Maybe for me, in finding Thoreaux's past, the fist of my own would at last let me go.

****

Reserve Constable Higgins, with his roof rack lights strobing the night, rolled up behind me where I stood on the frost-buckled sidewalk.

"Oh. It's you. Durkin told me you was back in town."

"Yeah, it's me." My hand raised to my brow. "Would you mind?"

"Sorry." He switched off the Border Patrol flashlight blinding me.

"So what're you doing skulking about in the dead

145

of night?"

Higgins received the respectful response I thought his perceptive question deserved.

"Standing."

"Got us a report called in of a suspicious person. That'd be you. Prowler maybe, or peeping tom even."

"No. Only me. Couldn't sleep."

"So you took to carousing the streets?"

"About the size of it, Higgs."

"Village already has itself one crazy. It's not shopping for two."

"Well, this crazy's headed back to his cousin's. Goodnight, Higgs."

"Night, Michaels." Then he sort of smiled. As if in the night he saw we shared a bond common to men who had rolled the dice at the crap table of love and lost their shirts. "Goodnight and good luck."

"Good luck?"

"With getting some sleep. Sometimes grabbing those zees can be one mean bitch to pull off when what you've done has you by a handful of the short hairs. A complete bitch. Ask our village celebrity. How long's it been since he caught himself a good night's sleep? Whatever it was he did. Got to be a doozy."

A doozy no doubt it was. No doubt too I was not going to find what it was walking the streets at night. At least not those in Hanna.

****

Near noon, when I pushed open the *Oracle's* twin twelve-foot-tall doors of nouveau stained glass, Clem stood at the counter between two stacks of unsold newspapers.

"You think you can nudge Jess Walters to come in

146

to mind the shop for a few days? A week at most. Maybe twist Colette's arm to take care of Aimée?"

"Jess can be nudged, I suppose. My phone's pretty much stopped ringing, so there won't be all that much for him to mind. Wouldn't have to twist Colette's arm very hard. But why?"

"We've wrung about as much out of this story from here as we're going to."

She eyed the two stacks of newspapers.

"A week, you think?"

****

The iridescent numbers glowed a few minutes past two when Katie's phone woke me.

"H-hello."

No one answered, but someone was there.

"Hello. Who is this?"

I listened, not breathing, until the empty void of nothingness followed the disconnecting click at the other end of the line.

Chapter 16

Clem and I landed at de Gaulle only to discover Hertz had snafued our reservation, big time. Some sort of global medical convention caused them to overbook their rentals. Like what doctors do to patients to keep their waiting rooms filled, sundry paramours adequately provisioned, and them swinging away on the country club greens by four o'clock.

"Please try us again tomorrow, monsieur," said the ferret-faced clerk, who could not be troubled to look up from his reservation book, drumming his manicured fingers while he waited on hold. "Better luck tomorrow you should have."

"I don't need better luck tomorrow." I shoved my reservation under his hairy nostrils. "Look! I reserved a car for today."

"Sorry, monsieur. We have no automobiles left in our lot. None." He pointed over his shoulder at the curtained window behind him. "See for yourself should you not believe me."

"Look, you—"

On which affable note Clem dragged me away by the elbow.

"Let it go. Let it go, Jeremy. Better we start out fresh anyway."

Better, she said, for me to learn to navigate French roads on an early Sunday morning with fewer Paris drivers taking aim at me. Her *maman* had warned her they were merciless, more than willing to run down hapless pedestrians in a New York minute. Even made something of a blood sport of it.

"But—"

"Let it go, Jeremy. It's not worth the aggravation. Let it go."

****

So let it go I did. Slowly. We rode the RER B into the city as Clem studied her little red guidebook. She found for us a quaint pension- –she insisted on calling it cute—off the Rue Christine, where we got two rooms, showered, and set out to explore. It was the first time for me outside the States, and the first time Clem had traveled more than a hundred miles from Hanna since Colette brought her there from Ribeauville.

The two of us strolled along the sidewalks while we window-shopped the boutiques and small stores, me greatly admiring a vintage Viscanti Medici fountain pen.

"See something you like, Jeremy?"

"Maybe someday. Not now."

Medieval chanting murmured down into the street. We climbed a flight of marble steps to peek inside a candle-lighted cathedral. Not wanting to disturb the dozen or so shabbily dressed parishioners celebrating Mass, or to give up our exploring, Clem and I listened for only a minute to the twenty-voiced choir. We read outside of nearly empty bistros the posted menus I only sort of understood from what little I remembered from one disastrous year of French in high school. One I'd managed to pass only because Mrs. Brocklehurst took pity on me. Or more likely cringed at the thought of having me in her class again. The sidewalks, too, were almost barren of people, which seemed odd for an early Saturday evening. Clem pointed to the darkening northwest sky.

"Probably know enough not to get caught out in a downpour."

"What about us?"

"We're tourists. What do we know?"

So we walked on. She had changed into a white summer frock short enough that from the wandering eyes of the few men out and about I judged it was not only me of the opinion it did justice to her runner's legs. I kept feeling the urge to take her hand as we walked, so kept both of mine firmly clasped behind me. Clem kept both of hers far out of temptation's way with holding the little red book while acting as our tour guide. Now and again she looked into its pages for confirmation and translated the French far beyond my forgotten capabilities.

"Hey, Clem."

"What?"

"You know, with those gargoyles squatting up there, that could pass for Notre Dame."

Clem flipped a page of her guidebook.

"The grand lady herself."

"No fooling?"

Then as we started to cross the street to purchase a postcard to send home to Colette, the skies opened up in the downpour forecast by Clem. The two of us were drenched by the time we sprinted to the other side, Clem's white cotton frock clinging to her slender figure. We stood huddled in the shallow arched doorway of a closed bakery, its windows refracting the bursts of staccato lightning and the shops across the street but a blur. The temperature had to have dropped ten degrees inside of ten seconds, and Clem stood shivering, with her arms wrapped around her shoulders.

"You cold?"

She shook her head, goosebumps prickling up and down her arms.

"Liar."

"I'm fine."

"When this lets up, we'll go back to change."

"Don't be silly. This is a dream come true."

"Getting soaked in a bucket drencher, to say nothing of hypothermia, is your dream come true?"

"Where's your romance, Michaels?"

"Romance?"

"Yes, romance. R-O-M—"

"That's all right. I think I remember."

"Good. There may be hope for you yet."

"Me? What about for you?"

"All my life I've wanted to get caught in a rainstorm on the streets of Paris on a summer evening."

"But aren't you hungry?"

"R-O-M-A—"

"Okay, okay. I get the picture."

"We can go back to that bistro we passed, with those heavy wooden chairs, and sit outside. They'll be ecstatic for any business they can get on a slow evening."

So we watched the rain for a few minutes more as it slowed to a drizzle. Clem stood in front of me under the arched doorway, me breathing in deep the jasmine scent of her wet ringlet hair. She was right. This was indeed a dream come true. A moment in time. A moment like so many others in my life I had let slip by. If it rained until morning with us standing there, I would be one happy guy. But did I really want her in my life come morning? And the morning after? Did she want me? Was there even anything left in me to give? Was there anything anyone would want? Had Helen been right?

"Come on," Clem said. "It's almost stopped," and after purchasing Colette's postcard at an open-stall newsstand, we set off to cross the street back the way we came.

Clem was looking up at the sky dreamy-eyed as she stepped off the curb, letting the mist wash over her face, not looking out for oncoming traffic. She failed to notice a little black Peugeot, its tires at most an inch from the curb, as though its driver indeed was on the hunt to fill his bag limit for pedestrians. Black beret pulled down to bushy eyebrows behind the whisking windshield wipers and barely poking above the steering wheel. Headed for her dead on.

"Isn't this the—"

Clem! and I yanked her by the shoulders back up onto the sidewalk and into my arms, the Peugeot swerving at the last second.

"Are you okay?"

"I...I think so," but her face had paled as white as her dress. "Are you?"

"Yes, I'm fine," and looked down the street to where the Peugeot had barreled around the first corner it came to.

"The bastard didn't even slow down."

"I guess *Maman* wasn't kidding about Paris drivers."

She pushed herself out of my arms—with reluctance, I thought. Or maybe hoped. "Come on. Let's go find that bistro so I can have a drink. A large one."

****

We both did. While finishing our second large ones as a dozen little black Peugeots whizzed past the Bistro and cross-haired pedestrians scurried across crosswalks, Clem and I decided to take the train to Ribeauville next morning rather than deal with crazy Paris drivers. We returned to our pension, exhausted with jet lag and shaken by her close call. She to her room, me to mine. So much for any R-O-M—at least on that night. Probably for the best. An envelope addressed to me lay on the floor when I unlocked my door. It seemed early to receive our bill.

If you value your miserable lives, turn back. Tonight! Not tomorrow. Tonight! Do not forget. I watch you. Always.

The desk clerk claimed, yawning and rubbing sleep from his eyes, he had seen no one go upstairs other than guests and staff since he came on duty. I showed the note to Clem, who wore a bathrobe slit open halfway down her chest and toweled rain from her hair as she opened the door.

"Who would write such a note, Jeremy? Someone else out to get Thoreaux's story, maybe?"

Or maybe one of my blackguard cast of characters back in Portland, but I saw little need to give Clem anything more to worry about that night.

"Maybe. Steve or Stanley from ABC said they already had someone over here working the story. Then again, maybe it's something more sinister."

"More sinister how?"

"Maybe this isn't from some news competitor. Maybe Thoreaux got blackmailed to turn down the knighthood. Maybe this note is from someone who doesn't want his story published at all."

"Who?"

"I don't know. Just looking at all the angles."

"So what do you want to do now?"

"Find out what made him turn down the knighthood to begin with. To find out that, we need to start by talking to your Aunt Gabrielle."

I crumpled the note and dunk-shot it across the room into her wastebasket.

"Don't do that."

Clem snatched it back out, smoothing the note flat and reached to the bureau for her purse.

"Why not?"

"In case we get another note."

For a long time I stood in the dark at the window looking out at the lights of Paris before I went to bed. Sometime during the night my telephone rang; again someone silent was at the other end.

****

A peasant girl maybe six months with child answered the door to Gabrielle's stone villa with a slight curtsy, a slight tipping of her kerchiefed head of vulpine red hair that swept down to her waist. Something familiar about her. Something troubling I could not quite put my reporter's finger on, but something.

"*Suis moi.*"

She walked us through the darkened house to a shaded patio that looked out upon row on row of vineyards that began at the grove of olive trees abutting the patio and ran on until they disappeared over a distant rise, a breeze blowing off them that carried down a hint of ripe pear secreted from their leaves. The peasant girl waved us to three wrought iron chairs circled around a table, then vanished, wordless, into the gloom of the house. Clem nodded after her.

"You see that black Peugeot parked beside the garage?"

"It and a hundred more from the train. They're like what Volkswagens used to be in Ohio a few years ago, when every other kid in college drove one."

Sunday cathedral bells tolled two miles below in the village of Ribeauville, from where Clem and I had walked after a late and too-large lunch. We sat. Watched as dozens of yellow-breasted Ortolans flittered in and out of patio lilacs until they rose with a sudden *swoosh*, startled into seeking out whatever sanctuary the vineyards offered. Startled as I was by an iron-haired woman in mourning dress darkening a villa doorway that had only a wink-of-an-eye before been framed in sunlight.

Clem pushed back her chair to cross the flagstone patio to where she kissed a reluctant cheek.

"Jeremy, this is my Aunt Gabrielle."

But instead of offering me her hand when I stepped forward, she gave a curt nod to our chairs, blue-razor eyes taking their measure. Eyes so icy sharp they rattled Clem, and Clem not one easily rattled.

"Y-you are w-well, Tante?"

"I am," she answered, her words whispery, spoken in a voice as if ghosted out of a haunted past.

"And Uncle Dominique?"

"Your uncle has not left his bed in months. Your intrusion is most mistimed."

"S-sorry. Should we—"

"No, no, no. Now that you are here, let us get on with whatever it is you want."

"Well thank you for seeing us. Considering your circumstances. Your vineyards, too. You're a busy member of the National Assembly. The pride of our family. *Maman* tells me you perform much good there."

"I try, my dear." A vein-gnarled hand dismissed the air as if it chased away a pesky fly. "I try. So you operate a newspaper in America."

"I do, yes."

"How unfortunate."

She said she did not care for newspapers. Especially American newspapers. Always snooping for dirt. Getting it wrong when by accident they stumbled on something. Or worse. Invented it out of thin air when the truth failed to titillate.

"Some do, to be sure, but most of us struggle to get it right. Which is why we are here."

"Yes. Colette rang me but gave me little by way of details. Always the flighty one. So what is it you wish to know? As you say, I am much busy here."

Clem glanced at me. Not the friendly family reunion she expected.

"We won't take up much of your time, Madam Mercier."

"It would be a relief if you did not."

"Really, only two questions."

"Only two?"

For only two questions we incurred the cost of such a journey? Had our easy American money made us spendthrifts that we wasted resources on plane tickets for only two questions? Clémence could have rung her. Written her, even. She would of course have penned a reply. Then we need not have bothered. She would not have been bothered.

"We had to come anyway."

"Oh? Why is that?"

"Thomas Thoreaux was offered a knighthood."

"So I read." She sighed. "The English can at times be a most befuddling people."

Politicians the world over, I was beginning to see, were all cut from the same cloth. She was no different from my trench-coated D.A. back in Portland. Corner them, and they cast about for a diversion. Any diversion.

"Why was he, do you suppose?"

"For services rendered, of course. Why else do you think, young man?"

Then throw in a dash of rudeness to see how much mileage they can get with a little bullying.

"Yes, of course, but what services exactly?"

The fingertips of her right hand tapped those of the left, her lace sleeve slipping up her arm as she reassessed the chessboard after a poor opening gambit and revealing a runny stain that inked the gnarled veins bluing her wrist.

"I am sorry. You traveled a far distance for so very little. Oh, Thomas was an occasional visitor here in those last months before the *Boche* came, but that is all."

She said his junk of a Citroen passed often back and forth over the frontier. But after the Occupation, she never saw him. Just as well. Never would she have tolerated him to take refuge there. Not in her villa, not in the barn. Not even in a hayrick far out in the fields. For her to allow him could have proved the grandest of follies. Too much risk. For him and especially for her. She last saw him on the day *Boche* tanks rolled through Flanders. They sat at this very table. Musing over their morning coffee. When word came over the wireless, her cousin leaped to his feet and dashed out the door behind us. "Bound for the front," he bellowed over his shoulder. Followed by scores of her neighbors. Many she was never to see again.

"So you were here during those years, Madam Mercier?"

"Yes, of course. Where else? Maintaining the quality of our vin—"

When she caught me watching her thumb rub back and forth over the smudge inking her wrist, those razor-blue eyes pierced into mine, her hand giving the laced sleeve a quick concealing jerk.

"Now, please present me with your second question so I may see about my vineyards. Attend to my sick husband."

"Certainly. Why was it you flew to America?"

Gabrielle sighed an unpersuasive breath of sympathy.

"I much worry for him."

"Worry?"

"Do you dare doubt me, young man?"

"Of course not. But why worry?"

"With good reason, why else?

Thomas, she said, returned only once after that day *Boche* tanks rolled through Flanders. The spring of 1947. To offer his testimony in the trials of their *collaborateurs*. After he had lost so many cells to the Gestapo. One lowlife lawyer sought to turn the tables on him. Accused Thomas of being the true *collaborateur*. Of masking his own treachery by making counterfeit claims against his client.

"Accused Thomas of carrying the Reichsmark coin."

A specially minted coin the Nazis struck in gold and the *collaborateurs* sewed into their pockets to present should they ever be questioned, so they might save themselves by proving to their interrogators they were the traitors they claimed to be.

"Do you believe Thomas collaborated, Madam Mercier?"

The fingertips of her gnarled right hand again tapped those of the left as do the calculating fingers of a master chess player plotting her next move.

"We can only speculate. But would it not explain why he refused this honor of knighthood? Did not want it to come to light it was his treachery that resulted in the Dachau deaths of dozens of *Maquis*...the thirty-eight shot in the village." She nodded to Clem.

"Your own father perhaps among them."

"My father, *Tante*? How can that be? *Maman* never said..."

But Gabrielle waved away Clem's objections with her dismissive hand.

"My sister lives in the fog of a fantasy world of her own making."

One where she could only hope her niece had not taken refuge. Thomas in any case so distraught that on the same evening as the lawyer leveled his damning charges it proved providential she found him. On the top ladder rung in their wine cellar. Rope in hand. It took her until dawn to talk him down. Begged him to give himself—to give life—one more chance. "So perhaps there is some truth to the accusation."

As much as I hated to admit it, Gabrielle was right. Shame of his treachery would explain much. The claims made against him during his disastrous campaign for Congress. His years-long hermitage. The recurring dream. Pre-dawn visits to Father O'Malley. Hangman's rope hidden beneath a hay mound in his barn. His baffling refusal to accept a knighthood that could bring him reconciliation with the village. Yes, treachery would explain much. If true.

"This the reason for my journey to see Thomas."

Did she succeed? Gabrielle could not say. Thomas was a man who believed himself in much need of forgiveness. For the taint of treachery upon him? For the betrayal of his courier, her death never suitably explained?

"Who of us can say?"

To say nothing of the unsent letter we found in his study. His asking if he had indeed sent an innocent girl to her grave. Was she this courier?

"If true, the story of one more woman betrayed." The chess-player fingertips of one guileful hand again tapped those of the other. Gabrielle turned to Clem. "A story as old as woman, is it not?"

Clem nodded. The account of the courier's betrayal, though thirty years distant from her own, a betrayal Gabrielle knew from Colette but one I was unaware kindled Clem's coal-black eyes in what I would only recognize too late as the avenging fire of surrogate requital, just as Gabrielle surely intended.

Her cousin, when she saw him in America, a man still poised beneath the barn beam of a past life. Those who sought to tell his story must watch their own step with the gravest of care. For upon their shoulders they carry a great burden. A great obligation for their questions.

"The anguished answers those questions may solicit. Be prepared to live with them."

She checked the time on a heart-shaped watch she wore on the breast of her mourning dress and rose, our interview ended. As we stood to go, twigs snapped out in the olive grove.

"Dogs," Gabrielle said, looking neither into the grove nor at us. "My neighbor has a most infuriating habit of letting his damnable hounds run wild. I will need again to instruct my groundskeeper to set his traps."

****

The early evening breeze that hinted of pear skittered ocher-dust dervishes along the quarter-mile lane that ran from Gabrielle's villa up to the road, vines head high on either side of us. A half-dozen burly men—in black berets and peasant smocks absent of collars and color-dyed a wild riot of reds, blues, and greens—slogged a hundred feet ahead, shouldering their hoes and long-handled pruning shears, boisterous in their end-of-day laughter and horseplay though in the vineyards since breaking dawn on a Sunday. Our innkeeper had counseled us, as he carried our bags upstairs, that this was the season when all invested with their success must labor among the grapes seven days a week if this year's vintage were to have any chance of being remembered in Paris salons.

"Next to soil, weather is all-important, but as in all matters of life, we must give God every chance to perform His miracles," he'd counseled.

We turned into the well-rutted road taking us back to Ribeauville. For a pensive mile we continued in silence, Clem, I was sure, devastated by Gabrielle's revelations. Now we needed to figure out how to salvage what story we had.

"Penny for your thoughts, Clem?"

A kid's face at Christmas lighted up.

"We've got it, Jeremy! I know we do. We've got the ending that's going to save the *Oracle*."

"We what? After what your aunt told us?"

"Yeah, not what I had in mind, but she for sure gave us solid copy to make hay with."

"Make hay with? Are you kidding? What she told us will kill Thoreaux."

"After he betrayed his courier. So what?"

"So what?"

"Aunt Gabby gave us the greatest gift a reporter can hope to find stuffed in their stocking."

"Which is what?"

"The gift of *scandal*. Pure, salacious scandal." Clem stopped in the middle of the road, running her future headline between raised thumb and forefinger. " 'Queen Narrowly Escapes Awarding Knighthood to Traitor Spy.' And think! It was *me*, *my* article, that forced Thoreaux to turn down the knighthood that saved her royal arse."

"You can't be serious, Clem?"

"Couldn't be more."

Nothing, Clem claimed, sold papers like scandal, and this one was a double doozy. That the Queen came so close to knighting a traitor. You had to ask yourself what bumpkins this lady employed to fact-check for her.

"Maybe her bumpkins did check, and maybe she wasn't duped. Maybe Gabrielle got it wrong. On purpose. Didn't you see how hostile she was? Maybe Gabrielle wasn't straight with us."

"No way, Michaels. I can smell the stink of male duplicity a mile off."

We were, Clem was certain, going to make those newswires sing. All we need do now was dig up more copy while we were there. Then we could stretch his entire sordid story out over a whole week when we got back. Maybe more. Circulation—to say nothing of her advertising—would moon shoot past Mars.

"Best of all, we can make the bastard pay. *Maman* was right. He is a *connard*."

"Whoa, whoa, whoa, and more whoa, Nellie. Weren't you listening to what Gabrielle said?"

"Hanging on every word. Were you?"

"Yeah, especially the part where she had to talk him down."

"Well, isn't that a traitor's just deserts?"

"Wait a minute. We don't know—"

But she brushed away my objections with her aunt's dismissive hand. We were reporters, Clem insisted, and this a story. A story that, besides bringing much long-delayed justice to the world, would save her newspaper. Allow her to make a life for her daughter.

"But what Gabrielle told us isn't a story, Clem. It was smeared speculation. Unproved. Propounded by a desperate lawyer saying anything to save his more desperate client. Maybe it could be a story, but we better be dead certain on our facts before we play God. We need to follow this road back to the beginning to see where it began."

"I can see where it began and where it takes us."

She saw all too clearly it was nothing but a dead end if I thought it was going to end somewhere over the rainbow. Facts were facts. Thoreaux was not the unsung hero I had talked myself into believing. Not someone turning down knighthood out of false modesty or a reluctance to remember what he wanted to forget. He was a traitor. Complicit to murder. One who buried his shame a long time ago and didn't want it dug up.

"A buried past we can bring to light. That we as reporters have a duty to bring to light."

"But you're jumping to conclusions based on a single allegation. An allegation we have yet to verify. There have to be others here who remember him. Even if Gabrielle believes it, she also admitted she never saw him during the war. We need to at least verify."

"Verify? Verify what, Jeremy? Verify he was a traitor? What is there to verify? Didn't you hear what Gabrielle said? Dozens exterminated in the ovens of Dachau like so many cockroaches because Thoreaux sold them out. Those thirty-eight in the village. Stood with their backs against a stone wall. That's our story, Jeremy. The one we're running with."

"But we shouldn't jump to conclusions based on one conversation, even if she is your aunt. You can't tell—"

"But I *can* tell. Believe you me, I can tell. This is one rot I can smell."

"What rot?"

"The rot of a man who wants you to believe he's

other than who he is. If nothing else, I've learned that lesson in life."

"Lesson, Clem?"

But she had stopped in the road, beaming, seeming not to have heard.

"God bless my Aunt Gabrielle is all I can say. Bless her for giving this girl a new lease on life."

She laid a hand absent of wedding ring on my shoulder and shifted her weight. I must have blushed, for an impish smile slipped across her lips I had not seen since before Beth crashed into a concrete bridge abutment.

"What are you doing?"

"Unstrapping my sandals."

"Why?"

"So I can take them off."

"Oh. Stupid me."

"Sometimes, Michaels, sometimes I gotta say you can be dense as lead. But today I don't care."

She took off her other sandal, her long ringlet curls swinging into my face, me again breathing in her jasmine scent.

"There. Much better."

"So why are you taking them off?"

"Because I've not walked barefoot down a dirt road since Colette took me berry picking."

"You are feeling giddy."

She handed me her sandals.

"What?"

"Silly. Be a gentleman and carry them for me."

"Yes, ma'am."

"By gum, Michaels, I may have you nearly paper trained."

She set off down the road, claret-colored sunset before us, her slender figure showing through the white muslin of the same summer frock she wore the evening before, when we'd been caught in a Paris downpour. I took my sweet time catching up.

"It seems to be working out. It really, really does after all. Finally."

After all, Clem asked, what did she know about the nuts and bolts of the newspaper business when my grandfather sold out to her? She was certain she couldn't keep it afloat after Chris died. How could a mere girl with nada know-how and no college run a newspaper *and* raise her first child all alone?

"You did, though. Double feathers in your bonnet for doing so."

She again stopped in the road, hand shading her brow. "Is that the river down there?"

"Seems like. Can't tell for certain, with the sun in my eyes."

"Come on." She reached for my hand. "Let's see."

When we had almost reached the river, Clem pointed. "Oh, look! Kittens."

"Where?"

"Along the bank. See them? Following their mother. Their little tails sticking up. Aren't they cute?"

"If you say so."

"Oh, stop being such a fuddy-duddy grumpy, Jeremy Michaels."

When we made it to a meadow along the riverbank, she plopped in the grass, her long fawn legs spreading out from beneath her frock. "Come sit."

We watched the kittens trek single file through the cattails, hopping like little rabbits over one another.

"Your Aimée would go crazy."

"Yeah, no kidding. She'd be chasing after them." Clem sighed. "Something for us to look forward to when I get back."

"Us?"

"Yes. Me and Aimée."

Oh. That us.

"Maybe we'll adopt the litter in your cousin's garage. Another something to look forward to. Along with the story. Keeping the *Oracle*." Ghost-gray fingers of evening fog reached from the river. "I'm grateful I had it then. The *Oracle*. When Chris died. It's what kept me going."

"I know. Something, anything, to hide away in."

"It's not only he died. It's how. I was there."

"There?"

"When our car got pulled out. From the stripper cut. After they crashed through the guardrail. Rolled down the embankment. Where they ended up."

"They?"

"Corey somehow managed to get his tow truck down. Search-and-rescue hooked up his chains. I was standing beside him when he pulled them out."

"You keep saying them. They."

"Chris. Charlotte."

"Charlotte? Not Charlotte the—?"

"Yeah. Her. Of all the women for a husband to be caught with, with his pants down. Her."

"I'm sorry, Clem. I hadn't heard."

She had watched as water drained out when Corey towed up their old LeSabre. Hair plastered over their scalps. Chris wearing the white shirt he'd asked her to iron that morning. Said he wanted to look super sharp.

Could feel a hot sales day coming on. The tacky red, white, and blue tie with stars and stripes he wore around the lot. Fourth of July weekend and all. She was leaning against Chris's shoulder. No seatbelt. Clem had walked around to the driver's side. Looked in the window. Chris's fly down.

Her cheeks began to quiver.

"I'm sorry, Clem. Really, really sorry. How do you live with a betrayal by someone you thought you knew? By someone you trusted."

"You don't, and you never get over being played the dupe. You promise yourself never again. Never again. But the anger never burns away. Not ever."

"Surprised I hadn't heard."

"Corey saw too. He opened the driver's door and tucked Chris in before Durkin got there. Zippered him up. Said not to worry. He'd never tell. He must not have. At least I have one man in my life I know will never betray me. Too bad he's faithfully married. I hope she knows how lucky she is."

"There's others, Clem."

"But ever since, he's carried an ad with me. Week in, week out. Doubled down after Thoreaux crashed and burned."

"Corey's a good man. Always was."

She sighed a long, despairing breath. All giddiness gone.

"I'm so tired of it all, Jeremy." Her temple fell to my shoulder. "So very, very tired. I'm ready to let this story go. Let the *Oracle* go. Just let them go. It's not worth the remembering."

I waited for her to raise her head, but instead she placed a hand on mine, her shoulders shuddering. It's a woman crying that will dupe me out. Every time.

We sat. The river flowed. Almost dark when she leaned over, kissing my cheek. "Thank you. I've been holding that inside me for what seems forever."

I turned my face to hers. Looked into those bottomless coal-pit eyes. Shoulder so soft under my hand. Did I want—did I really want—someone in my life again? Could I find the courage this time to risk giving myself? Did she really want me in hers after the betrayal she had gone through? Could she let go her anger? Could she trust again?

But maybe if this time I could give of myself, I was the one who could help her let go. Because I too felt as if I had been holding it all in for such a long time.

Chapter 17

The quarter moon was setting on the other side of the river as we walked hand-in-hand across the stone-arched bridge into Ribeauville, Clem still barefoot and wearing this goofy smile. A goofy smile I'm sure matched mine. As we circled the fountain in the center of the square, the cathedral tower tolled midnight. The end of one day and the start of a new one, perhaps tolling the end of one story and beginning of another, the cobblestone square empty except for us. Us and a black Peugeot parked in the alley facing the window of our room. One of a hundred or so I had seen since the night before.

****

The patio off Clem's room, where we breakfasted the next morning on croissants and slices of fruit, overlooked a well-tended garden. A fifteen-foot obelisk of stark gray granite stood at its center, affixed with some sort of plaque and capped by a bronze crucifix. Toiling beneath it, wearing a raggedy thug cap, was a gray-haired gardener who snipped at the blood-red chrysanthemums with his long-handled pruning shears.

"Oh, what beautiful flowers, Jeremy. Can we check them out? Just for a minute, maybe. Can we?"

I raised my eyes over a cup of eye-opening Turkish coffee. Her face positively glowed that morning, and she wore the same goofy grin as when we'd crossed the bridge at midnight. I nodded. Anything to keep that big smile on her long unhappy face a little longer.

"You were up and about early this morning. Where'd you go?"

Clem reached over to the bed for her purse. "Here."

I unwrapped an oblong box. Inside was a vintage Viscanti Medici fountain pen like we had seen in a Paris storefront.

"Clem, you shouldn't have. It's too expensive."

"Oh, don't be such a fuddy-duddy grumpy, Jeremy Michaels. Of course I should have."

"Where?"

"On my morning walk. Saw it in a stationer's store. He has a whole shelf of nothing but antique pens. Do you like?"

I weighed the pen in my hand.

"I do. The balance. Thank you, Clem."

A petite cat, heather-colored but with white fur underneath when you stroked her coat against the grain, chose that moment to slide off Clem's lap and leap to the spot on the bed where she had snuggled between us all night after we found her last night mewing outside the door downstairs. Now she settled back to sleep.

"I think I'm going to call her Doriane. What do you think about Doriane for a name, Jeremy?"

"I don't know if I would."

"Why not?"

"Grandma Hardy claimed you were courting nothing but a boatload of bad trouble if you dared name a cat you didn't intend to keep."

"Oh, fiddle-dee-dee on her superstitious hocus-pocus."

A pox on any man foolish enough to ever stand in

171

her way.

Clem scooted around in her chair, her hand held out. "Doriane!"

But Doriane slept on, or pretended to. Not so much as giving you the courtesy General Pershing would by thumping her tail.

"I christen thee Doriane."

"Suit yourself."

"When haven't I?"

So true.

****

We passed into the garden by lifting the rusted latch to a cast iron gate on the other side of a narrow alley outside the back door of our inn. At the obelisk we stopped to read the weathered plaque.

"What's it say, Clem?"

"It's a memorial. To the thirty-eight."

Clem ran her finger down a long column of names.

"So many."

"Yeah, thirty-eight is a lot."

"No. I mean so many Merciers. Like maybe half. There's Henri. Simone. Mathilde. And then Aristide. Jeanne. Lorin. Dashielle."

"Thirty-eight's a lot for such a small village. But why so many Merciers?"

Clem read down the list again, shaking her head, me adding it to our growing list of questions. We continued along a brick path that wound through the lush flowerbeds until we reached a park bench shaded beneath a willow tree where the gray-haired gardener we saw tending the flowers from Clem's balcony sat fanning a face shiny with sweat with his thug cap. Beside him, a wicker basket of clippings.

"*Bon matin.*"

"Good morning, sir."

"Ah. *Américains*? On holiday?"

"A working holiday. Are you the gardener for the inn?"

"It's gardener, yes, but not for the inn."

He explained that the village elders had appointed him as caretaker. Their garden while small held their village's large and most dear memories. They wanted someone they knew would give it the devotion deserved by his comrades.

His finger made a circling motion around one ear.

Also the war left him a little *outré*. Tending their garden they thought a more fitting reward than screaming in the inmate choir at Simeon Asylum.

"You fought in the Resistance, then?"

"Yes and why not?"

"No reason why not. We're honored to meet you."

Clem's lips brushed my ear. "Maybe he knew Thoreaux."

"How did you come to join the Resistance?"

"After our surrender of shame by the coward Pétain, I came home from the Army. I had marched off with my head held high, only to worm my way home on my belly. Those of us who returned did what we could with the help of those English dropped from the sky."

"Perhaps you remember a man named Thoreaux. Thomas Thoreaux. He was one of those English."

The old man's time-clouded eyes stared into a thick bed of chrysanthemums. He shook his head.

"My memory grows feeble. Such can be the curse of old age. To grow no wiser and nevertheless to forget much. I recall no such name, but it's as well. Those

English who dropped from the sky never trusted us with their true names and were wise not to. Had I known, in time the bastards would have had it out of me."

"He was an American," Clem said. "We understand he was in charge of a circuit here."

"Oh." The old man's creviced face brightened. "You mean Anton. I was his dynamiter of trains. Like this"—and he made an inverted "V" with his hands—"I made the trains go like this. That is how we knew him. As Anton. Daniel too. His telegrapher. A good man as well."

"What happened to Daniel?"

"Betrayed." The old man pointed his pruning shears. "You can yet see on the wall before you the pock marks their bullets made."

Here, he said, was where the thirty-eight breathed their last. Hallowed ground for the old men of the village, possessed as they were by their ghosts. Old women too. The innkeeper claimed his patrons told him often of rising from their beds in the dead of night—for no reason they could name—and looking out into the moonlight where they glimpsed before the memorial a mourner dressed in black on her knees.

"They rub their eyes, look again, and as smoke up a chimney she is gone."

"She?"

"A woman, they say. A gray-haired woman. Always a gray-haired woman."

"Do you believe in such sightings?"

"Perhaps. Perhaps it is true. They died so young, the thirty-eight. Half-lived lives. So perhaps it is true. It would make sense. If any sense is to be made."

"Make sense?"

"We are haunted here by much guilt."

"Why guilt? Why not honor?"

"*Collaborateurs.*"

Clem elbowed me.

"What about Anton's courier? Do you remember her?"

The old man's gray eyes smiled.

"Ah, yes. Remember her well, I do. For it is true what they say about old men. We always remember the pretty girls from our youth. Now, what was her name? A girl most striking. Fearless, and obvious to all she and Anton much in love."

"In love?"

"Oh my, yes, but a bad thing to fall in love in time of war. Always is heartbreak a risk of love, but no time more so than in time of war."

His time-clouded eyes again searched the bed of blood-red chrysanthemums.

"Adrienne. Adrienne may have been her name. Or maybe something like Adrienne. I remember she came from the next village over."

"She was not English?"

"No, *Français*, and so brave, that one."

"She died here too? Her name perhaps engraved on your stone?"

"No. No, but she would. For of us all, the Fates spun the worst of fortunes."

He said when he came home after his liberation, after he ceased his year-long wandering in the mountains, they told him of her capture by the Gestapo only days after his own. She did not come home. Died in Dachau. Betrayed. How betrayed and how she died? The particulars he never heard, but none there died with pleasantness. The best death one could hope for was to starve. Electrocute one's self on the wires. Shot in the back while making a doomed escape.

"For the best death is one we choose ourselves. Not one the Fates choose for us."

"Could Anton have had a hand in her betrayal?"

"Not would I have thought, but we lost so many. Often the Gestapo only need wait on the ground for new English to drop from the sky. Rot there was. Somewhere."

The old man considered for a moment before he continued, "Do you know who you must talk to? Father Paul. The elders appointed him caretaker of our village archives. What is not written down on paper"—a finger deformed by arthritis tapped the old man's temple—"he carries here. Everyone tells him everything. Especially us old ones gasping on our deathbeds."

"Where do we find Father Paul?"

Cathedral bells tolled across the village square.

"There. There you will find him."

****

We crossed the cobblestone square and entered the gothic cathedral with its cavernous ceiling, our footsteps following behind us as they echoed off the forty-foot walls of gray stone.

"What say, Clem? Should I give out a holler? See who's home?"

Clem, her face darkening to the same chrysanthemum red as in the garden, took exception to my inspiration for juvenile humor.

"You small-town hick. Don't you dare holler anything. You hear me? Not word one." She threaded her arm through mine, yanking me off balance back toward the doors. "Let's see if someone's outside."

Behind the cathedral we found a nun bent between two rows of tomatoes spading into the earth that from its very distinct odor I recalled from my days of toil in Thoreaux's garden as chicken crud.

"*Excusez-moi.*"

The sister straightened, drops of sweat dotting her white wimple. She listened to Clem with her respectful head bowed, thorn-scratched and broken-nailed hands laid one over the other, resting on the spade shaft.

"*Merci.*"

Clem returned to where she'd left me waiting in the grass at the edge of the garden.

"Father Paul's with an ailing parishioner but should be back in an hour."

"So how do we kill an hour?"

Clem grinned that impish smile, giving me a wink, and again threaded her arm through mine as she pulled me out to the street.

"An hour should be just enough time for me to have my way with you, Michaels."

From behind the front desk of Un Hôtel Ribeauville, the eggheaded innkeeper—who wore the massive mustaches of a master sergeant and dressed in a uniform of khaki with a high tunic collar and epaulets—called out as we entered the front door, fanning the air with an envelope.

"Monsieur. Monsieur Michaels. A letter. A letter has found its way to you."

"I'll meet you in my room." Clem let go my arm and started for the stairs. "Unless you want a spanking good hiding, don't keep me waiting."

I crossed to the front desk and took from the

innkeeper an envelope with no stamp and addressed only to *l'Américain.*

"Who left this?"

"I know not, monsieur."

"Well, who was minding your front desk?"

"At my post I have been all morning. Only once with my back to the door when the telephone rang. When I turn around, there it lay."

"You saw no one, you say?"

"No one. But—" The proprietor lowered his head, a fist raised to his lips, his eyes darting to the front hotel window. "There."

"There what?"

"There, as I turned and saw the envelope, I saw also the back of someone. Hurrying past the window."

"Do you know who this someone was?"

"I saw only his back."

"Can you describe him?"

"Less than a second did I see him."

"Try."

"Average. Average height. Perhaps a little shorter. Trim. No, more than trim. Thin. A skeleton. Dressed in black. Hair, maybe gray."

"Dressed in black."

"Yes, monsieur."

"His hair gray."

"Maybe."

"The gardener told us of a midnight mourner your guests claim sometimes to see praying at the memorial. Dressed in black and hair of gray."

The innkeeper raised a finger to his lips.

"Superstition. That is all. Idle talk."

"Still, very odd."

"Yes, monsieur. It is most mysterious."

"So why are you handing this to me?"

"You are my only American guests."

"Odd my correspondent knew that."

"The mystery grows deeper, but do you know what else is odd?"

"No. What?"

"When I answered the telephone?"

"Yes?"

"There was no one at the other end."

"Your midnight mourner, perhaps?"

"Superstition. That is all."

I opened the envelope.

Rentrez chez soi.

My face must have betrayed that I remembered at least some rudiments of my high school French.

"Nothing disturbing, I hope, monsieur?"

I turned the letter around to show the innkeeper. "It seems our presence is not entirely welcomed."

The proprietor's face reddened.

"I am so sorry, monsieur. Rest assured I will get to the bottom of this outrage. Rest…"

"Michaels!"

I flew up the steps, the innkeeper two steps behind, Clem in the doorway to her room, hand over her mouth. There lay little Dorianc. Green cat eyes open. Lips parted. Gray entrails spilling out on the bedspread.

Chapter 18

Our mortified innkeeper carried Clem's bags down the corridor to a new room at the far end of the inn, voicing apology after apology and swearing to get to the bottom of the outrage carried out within his inn.

"Never have I heard of such an indignation in our village. Not since we drove out the bastard *Boche*. Never, and on a helpless *chat*? Who would suppose such a crime?"

Upon returning to my room, I discovered my passport missing from my duffle and reported the theft to our more than flustered innkeeper.

"For someone who wants us gone, he certainly is making it difficult for us to leave."

"Again, I am horrified, Monsieur Michaels. Most horrified."

"I'm glad we had our money on us. Should I report my loss to the police?"

"Allow me. You have been through enough today. Truly enough."

"Why would someone want my passport?"

"From time to time the police circulate bulletins. American passports, they claim, bring the highest prices on the international black market. Drug dealers and arms merchants and other such vermin. Vermin they must be, to slaughter an innocent *chat*."

Later he brought up a complimentary bottle of

cognac, but it did little to calm our frayed nerves.

"Where's this story taking us, Jeremy?"

"Deep into someone's past. Has to be some story. Some story someone wants kept buried six feet under."

"We can't quit. We can't."

No, we couldn't, and I could not let Henry down, should my longshoremen's exposé go seriously south. I needed to call him tomorrow to see what was up.

"No. I've never quit a story in my life. Neither have you."

"And no matter who it hurts."

"We're not going to start walking away with this one. It's too important. To us both."

We ate dinner in Clem's room. Inside, not out on the balcony. Turned in drained before eight o'clock, the summer sun not yet set. Clem crying. Her arm again threading mine and lying very close on the side of the bed away from the door, back of the desk chair jammed up under its knob.

****

The next morning, still shaken, we once more crossed the cobblestone square. Inside the ancient alder doors we came upon a priest without coat but wearing his cleric's collar and kneeling, yellow tape measure stretched between his hands across a stone floor, with a pencil stub wedged behind the cauliflower ear of a boxer. Blue eyes full of boyhood blithe darted up to greet us.

"*Bonjour.*"

"Good morning."

"Good morning." His tape measure retracted with a swift whirl as he stood with a clumsiness common to the middle-aged who one day surprise themselves to find they are forty pounds overweight, half struggling to his feet before he had to push himself up the rest of the way with hands pressed to his knees. "Our old cathedral attracts many tourists and therefore is good for the livelihoods of our parishioners. The shops, their wineries, and of course the inn. The church, she too, alas, like her aging caretaker, falters with infirmities each year. More repairs than funds for proper renovation, but we do what we can. I regret we offer no tours until after lunch. Can you return then?"

"Would you be Father Paul?"

"Oh, of course. You are the Americans our Sister Beatrice spoke of. Truly am I sorry for the travesty occurring in your room. Truly."

"You've heard?"

"Oh, we are such a small village. Small and therefore take more interest in one another's affairs than some would find decent. Not a fly gets swatted here without word of its demise buzzing every ear. I pray you do not take this outrage as indicative of the hospitality our village offers."

"No. We do not. We have found this to be a lovely village. Truly lovely. The people very kind. Very helpful. The flower gardener...next to the inn."

"Old Julian."

"Yes, Julian. Julian was most helpful. He said you are the keeper of the village archives."

"Indeed I am."

"Perhaps you can help us." I explained. "His name is Thomas Thoreaux, but you might know him as Anton."

"Anton? Yes, of course I know of Anton. On many a rainy night by the fireplace my father told me tales of

Anton's exploits. Of the trains and bridges. A valiant man. How is he?"

"You may have read of Queen Elizabeth offering him a knighthood."

The priest said he had not. He no longer read newspapers, the news they brought too disturbing, but bravo for Anton. He deserved to be honored for his bravery.

"Yes, but he turned it down."

The furrows creasing Father Paul's forehead deepened.

"His refusal is what brought us here. To find out why."

"This seems most odd. Why refuse such a deserved honor?"

"He won't say. We're both newspaper reporters, Father. My name is Jeremy Michaels, and this is Clémence Mercier. We both have family from here."

"Yes, the Mercier name is an old and honorable one in our village."

"Thomas, Anton, came back after the war. Took part in the investigations of your collaborators. Offered evidence. We thought we might find something in your archives to explain his refusal."

"Perhaps. Come. Let us look and perhaps together solve this mystery."

****

We followed the priest into a study smoky from a dozen honey and beeswax candles. Books musty with age lined all four walls from floor to ceiling, with our only light coming from those dozen candles and a clerestory of stained glass depicting Saint Matthew's Passion that ran above the top shelf twenty feet up.

Father Paul held out both hands. "So where to start?"

"He returned in the summer of nineteen forty-seven."

Father Paul squinted along the long rows of shelves before he crossed to a ladder set on twin brass trolley rails. He pushed the ladder along one wall of books almost to the end, then climbed the steps midway up where, with the elbow of a black shirtsleeve, he dusted book spine after book spine until he pulled a volume from the shelf and joined us at a twenty-foot table.

"Crafted from Bastogne walnut by the same Venetian artisan who carved the front doors of our cathedral some five centuries ago."

From his shirt pocket, he fished out his frameless bifocals and, with the same care as were this a text of scripture hand copied by medieval monks at this very table, opened the leather-bound book. As he read, doors out in the corridor opened with a soft click, then swished closed. Learned voices passing outside pondered sacred mysteries in the barest of Latin whispers. After some minutes, a finger tapped the scrawled page. "Mercier?"

"Yes, Father."

"No, child. At the inquest. On September sixteenth nineteen forty-seven. Gabrielle Mercier gave testimony that while held at Dachau she…"

I bolted upright in my chair, turning to Clem seated beside me.

"Gabrielle never told us… In fact she said… Did your mother ever…?"

"No. Never."

Father Paul smiled.

"Such is not so very strange here. Few wish to speak of what they saw in those years. What others did to them. What they did or had done unto others. From out of a deep shame or perhaps from a fear of revenge."

"But to have…" I glanced again at Clem. "What did she testify to, Father?"

His index finger continued down the page.

"Here it is. While at Dachau, held in an adjacent cell a woman known to her. From the next village over. A courier in their circuit."

"Their circuit? Are you sure it says *their* circuit?"

"Clearly it does."

"Does it give the courier's name as Adrienne?"

Father Paul read.

"No, Gabrielle gave no name. She said this woman somehow managed to escape—a small miracle in itself—only to be recaptured twenty kilometers away. On the road leading away from a convent. Outside Petershausen."

"What else?"

Father Paul read on, turning the page. Cathedral bells tolled the hour.

"Executed by the SS. Because she was *Maquis*."

"Anything more?"

Father Paul's finger traced the table's winding wood grain as he skimmed down the page. Turned another. After a while, he looked up, shaking his head.

"No. Nothing. Only executed because she was *Maquis*. Members of the inquest seemed concerned more with whether it was Anton—your Thoreaux—who betrayed her into German hands."

"What did they decide?"

"Evidence inconclusive."

"So…possible?" Clem said.

"Yes." Father Paul closed the book. "Possible."

"Likely, even."

"I think not. Not when by the fire my own father told me of Anton's heroism."

I sat back in my chair. "Seems like for every answer we dig up, we find two more skeletons alongside it."

"Perhaps you see now why, because of your questions, your digging up the past, what happened in your room did happen."

The French, the priest told us, nurse a national mythology. That of a nation of the brave fighters of the *Maquis*. Stymieing the Nazis at every turn while they awaited the return of their allies, who had abandoned France to face her ravagers alone while they licked their wounds in the safety afforded across the Channel. It was, alas, mythology founded on the basest mendacity. For nations, like men, wear blinders when it comes to finding the mote that sties their own eye. The many who openly collaborated found themselves standing in the dock before legal tribunals. For others, for the worst of the worst, their collaboration strongly suspected could not be proved up in a court of law. Retribution found other means. They were found hanging in barns by their thumbs with mouths gagged—a favorite sentence. Labeled as suicide by an intimidated coroner. Even now, thirty years later, our questions could arouse disquiet among those still at large. Those made to suffer were burdened with long memories. Harbored scores long in need of settlement. However long it took. The village's last barn hanging was less than a year before.

Father Paul wiped his glass lenses with a loose

shirt cuff. "You must be careful where your questions take you. Be discreet with whom you ask your questions. So you will not be caught in the silk of their intrigue."

A dancing-leg spider lowered itself at the far end of the table from its web.

"Where do Clem and I go from here, Father?"

"Petershausen, perhaps. Maybe there the courier sought refuge. Perhaps someone there yet who remembers. Once a sister procures her orders, common is it for her never to leave. There to be buried."

He pushed back his chair and walked behind his desk. He would write us a letter of introduction. It might help. Nuns he had found to be reticent. The nature of their training.

"The least I can do to make up for the inhospitality you suffered here."

He took an envelope from a drawer when he finished, before showing us to the cathedral doors, where he told us to let him know what we had found. We set off across the square to pack for Petershausen, Clem rushing ahead of me.

"This story just keeps getting better and better for us, Jeremy."

"And worse and worse for Thoreaux."

"Well, it's high time this score got settled. It *was* Thoreaux who betrayed the courier to the Nazis. I know it was. The tribunal thought so too but just couldn't prove it, but he as much as admitted it in his letter we found. Petershausen will be the last turn of the screw. Then this bastard is finally going to pay."

"But at what price?"

"Doesn't matter. Let the chips fall where they may,

Jeremy. Let them fall where they may because not only is the bastard going to pay up, this story is going to save the *Oracle*. I'm sure of it now."

"But those falling chips are making less and less sense. Why did Gabrielle lie to us? It might change our story."

"It's not going to change anything unless it changes the worse for Thoreaux and the better for me."

When we entered the inn, a wart-nosed crone I had seen feather-dusting its numerous nooks and crannies stood talking to some sort of official in a dark blue uniform and garrison cap. Maybe about my stolen passport. Maybe she had seen someone, but when she saw us, it was me she jerked her bony finger at, and the officer hurried across the lobby.

"Monsieur Michaels?"

"I am."

He seized me by the elbow.

"You will please come with me now."

"Why? What is it?"

"The *juge d'instruction* has issued a warrant for your arrest."

"Arrest? Arrest for what?"

"For the murder of Julian Barnet."

Chapter 19

Clem caught up to us out of breath.

"Where are you taking him?"

The officer did not bother to answer but yanked me by the elbow across the village square. Sidewalk gawkers stopped and stared, whispered to one another, hands cupped over their mouths, while shopkeepers shaking their gray heads, with brooms in hand, gathered to gape in doorways.

"I asked you where are you taking him? Tell me!"

"To our village prison. Tomorrow morning this one appears before the *juge d'instruction*. Now I must ask you please to stand back. To stop following us, mademoiselle."

"I will not. I'm going with you."

"You will, mademoiselle! If you persist in this unlawful behavior, I will be forced to arrest you as well. Then you will learn our prison is not so very pleasant, as this fine fellow is about to find out."

"Arrest me? Arrest me for what?"

"For interfering with the sworn duties of an officer of the *Police Nationale*."

Clem's face raged a Roussanne red. Looked as if she was two steps from kicking this clown in the back of his popinjay head.

"Stay back, Clem. Talk to Gabrielle about finding me a lawyer. It's not going to do us any good if they

189

toss us both in the slammer."

The officer jerked me back around.

"Quiet, you. Learn your place, if you know what is good for you. Here we do not coddle our criminals. Not like in America."

"Oh, really? How do you know how we coddle criminals in America?"

"Because on television I watch your *Columbo*." He jerked my arm again. "Now walk faster. Stop dallying. Dallying does you no good."

He dragged me on for several blocks until we entered a side street where a half dozen doors down we passed into a squat limestone building with a sign above the front door reading *Ribeauville Police Nationale*. After they got me printed and snapped my not-so-smiling mug shot, their unshaven jailer, who had an enviable scar jagging across his cheek to a smidgen below his right eye, led me down a flight of stone steps into a cold dank basement that smelled a little of chlorine and a lot of stale urine. We passed between twin rows of cells to the end, where he unlocked the iron-barred door and waved me in.

"*Entrez!*"

My cell had to have been in use since before the guillotine-giddy days of the French Revolution. Stone walls the color of ash, with a single barred window, two feet square, ten feet above the stone floor. A rust-stained sink absent of soap or towel beside a disgusting-looking toilet with a single sheet of paper the thoughtful prior occupant left hanging off the spool. A low-wattage bulb behind the jailer threw off just enough light for me to follow long trails of rodent droppings across the floor to where they vanished beneath an iron cot.

The key rasped in its lock; heavy-footed steps mule-clopped down the corridor. No TV. No radio. Nothing to read, not even in French. Not even sagacious epiphanies scribbled on the walls. I sat on the cot, studying the crisscrossing trails of rodent droppings, and after a while I stretched out on the wool blanket reeking of men. Many men. No other prisoner in any cell when we walked down the cellblock. One of my doper sources back in Portland had told me over a cup of take-out coffee about how a favorite gambit of prison guards was to isolate you for your first thirty days to encourage your thinking twice before making trouble. I guessed my captors had something similar in mind to make me more willing to talk. If that was the game they played, it worked. I was more than ready to confess to any and all crimes no matter how many or how heinous.

Some hours later, my jailer brought me a bowl—absent of spoon—of what had to be horsemeat stew, and a quarter loaf of brown bread without butter, and a tepid half-cup of coffee. Thirty minutes later he came back to collect my dirty dishes.

"Your portions don't leave much for the rats to nibble on, do they?"

Les orteils. He grinned. "They always find your toes. Very industrious, our rats."

Footsteps again mule-clopped down the corridor. Then nothing. Shadows and pedestrians at street level passed my iron-barred window where the soft light of a summer evening grayed to black, but the electric bulb out in the corridor would burn all night. Water dripped somewhere. Cell doors creaked open and closed.

Voices, most likely imagined, most likely those of prior tenants, whispered words of despair. Rodents scurried and sniffed in the dark, and what sleep I got I did with my shoes on. That night, like the nights to come, was long in passing, and my paranoia ran rampant.

Where was Clem? How long could it take to find a lawyer? Even some shyster lawyer? Or with me out of the way, was she running her story without bothering with my byline? Was now the time she exacted her revenge for Chris? For Beth?

****

Beth. That night I dreamed of her. Two dreams. One I could have held dear if not for the second that left me badly shaken and sick to my stomach. The first found us again in bed in our apartment above the *Oracle*, me with an intent ear laid to her swollenness, she holding me, her mousy hair covering me like a blessing. From it, I somehow slipped into the second dream with no distinct doorway between the two. Found myself again standing at the covered bridge that spanned Mill Creek, a dozen steps from where we had conceived our child. Smoldering hulk of scrunched steel surrounded by deputies. Their red-and-blue lights spinning, the front of the stolen Impala smashed back to its melted windshield where a shriveled and blackened figure sat, what was left of her head askew and nearly severed at the neck, our second child she carried, either knowingly or not, at least suffocated if not broiled within her womb.

Had to be going ninety easily, Jeremy. At least ninety. Why couldn't you have kept her hands off them keys?

Me waking in the night to consider one more along

the way who I had let down. Whatever retribution waited for me was well deserved.

****

My iron-barred window had begun to gray overhead when I again woke, shivering and stiff with cold. I pushed back the thin wool blanket carrying its scent of uncounted men and started to circle my cell. Tried without success to slap some warmth into my arms and shoulders while I tried to think. Think on where I was, how I had gotten myself there. Tried not to think of what Clem might be doing or not doing.

A few hours later, me only a little the warmer for my efforts, the jailer reeking of garlic brought in another bowl of horsemeat stew and brown bread still without butter and a cup of coffee that this time was at least hot. Life was starting to look up. He grinned his lizard smile at my feet.

"All made it through the night?"

"All made it."

"This is good. Toes can prove most useful here."

"Or anywhere, I would think."

"Yes, but especially here. In prison toes can prove especially useful."

"Why, especially?"

"For when you find yourself deep in troubles where your fists prove lacking and forced to resort to your feet. Toes are good for one's balance." He arched up on his. "Leverage."

"Jailers here do not keep order?"

"And risk injury ourselves?"

He shook his head. Jailers there not so very stupid. No, when problems arose, they preferred to allow us to sort them out among ourselves. They only placed their

193

bets. As on the cock birds that savage one another in back alleys.

"Not wagering as much on you as on the birds because prisoners, we find, are possessed of less heart."

"A little cold-blooded, aren't you?"

"Perhaps, but we need some little entertainment to make the time pass, no? Now eat up. In here you never know when your next meal might find you. This is no restaurant."

Clearly. Thirty minutes later he returned.

"So when do I go before the judge?"

My jailer shrugged.

"Do not be in such a rush to meet your fate."

The judge, my jailer informed me, liked to sleep late. Some mornings most late, depending upon his luck with cards the night before. His luck with the ladies. Once up, he did not like his breakfast to be a hurried affair. Liked to digest the fine points in *Le Monde*. Ruminate over his coffee on the state of the world. What he could do to right it.

Great. A jihadist for a judge, looking for infidels.

"You will see him when he finds himself ready to face the world." My jailer smiled. "Better he not be rushed while he ruminates. With a little luck, you may even find him in a good mood."

"Is he often in a bad one?"

"Almost always. Gout, I hear it whispered. Also he does not like Americans so very much."

"What does he have against Americans?"

During the war, my jailer told me, our bombers had leveled his village to rubble. Buried his mother under their house. A glad-handing colonel claimed it one of the misfortunes of war. That was how we referred to our innocent victims before we relabeled them as collateral damage. Then they were the misfortunes of war. Americans paid his grieving family ten thousand francs, but his mother just as dead, mistake or not. Just as dead and the ten thousand francs soon dissipated by his brokenhearted papa in the wineshops.

"No, he hates you Americans even more so than does he the bastard *Boche*. Which in this country is considerable. I almost feel sorry for you today. Almost."

****

Hours later, my jailer returned in the company of the popinjay flunky who took me into custody the morning before and now stood outside my cell clanging his baton across the bars as would a xylophone-playing baboon and waking me from a morning nap.

"Stand up! You go before our judge now."

"Where're we going?"

"Next door. Come." He grinned. "You dare not keep this one waiting."

I stood. Looked around my cell speckled with rodent droppings, and suspected my absence would not be for long.

They led me up the stone steps, a firm hand on each elbow, and through the police station to a side door. It opened at the front of a whitewashed courtroom fissured with helter-skelter cracks, and on the opposite wall were three six-foot-high barred windows. Officer Popinjay prodded me in the spine with his baton toward an empty table near the front, where he pointed to a straight-back chair.

"Sit, you!"

I considered barking at him like a dog but thought

better of it.

At an adjacent table, a portly gentleman of middle age, wearing a white shirt in much need of an iron, and a rumpled suit, its coat splattered with what were likely gravy stains over the lapels, sat shifting through his papers.

"Who's he?"

"Your *procureur général.*"

"What does he do?"

"Sends vermin such as you to prison for rest of your worthless lives. Like the district attorney in *Columbo.*"

"May I speak to him?"

"You certainly may not! Don't be an American idiot. Do you know nothing of decorum?" He slapped his palm with the baton. "Now sit and be quiet."

He returned to stand before the door by which we had entered, his tiny hands fig-leafing the tinier crotch of his tight trousers. Behind me a courtroom gallery packed with glaring spectators. Along the back wall maybe a dozen police stood at ramrod attention. Behind my table in the row of seats before the bar sat this guy who looked about my age, wearing glasses with black octagonal frames and, notwithstanding the summer heat, a serious charcoal-gray vested suit, penciling notes. A reporter for the local paper, I guessed.

After some minutes, the rear courtroom doors creaked open, followed by a stirring among the spectators. Clem had approached one of the guards nearest the door, her finger raised at me, spectators now glaring at her too, whispers of *Américain, Américain* circling the packed gallery. The guard gave Clem a curt nod to a back courtroom bench, she shaking her head at me as the row of reluctant spectators rose to make way for her. *Nothing yet*, she mouthed.

Gabrielle I should have guessed would be less than helpful in seeing me get sprung. One of those I suspected who had secrets they wished to keep nailed closed and buried six feet under along with any and all inquisitors. Then again, if Clem wanted to run our byline as only hers in the direction she wanted to go with it… Or maybe I was only rattled from a first night in the slammer with my new furry friends.

So we waited. Twin ceiling fans churned the already warm air as blue-bellied flies, sensing where the soon-to-be dead meat could be found, skulked about my table. Fifteen minutes passed before a shrunken figure, also wearing a charcoal-gray suit and wiping his sallow face with a handkerchief, entered by the same side door as had I and Officer Popinjay. He sat behind a plain table similar to mine at the front of the courtroom, his with a two-foot stack of brown manila files at each corner. He seemed not to notice the crowded courtroom as he reached for the top file on the stack to his right, glanced at its tab before tossing it back and reaching for the top file on the other stack, and read before scowling up at me.

"So, an American."

I stood. "Yes, your honor."

Officer Popinjay rushed toward my table, the judge glowering at me with his bushy arched eyebrows.

"Unless he wishes his legs shackled to the table, the prisoner at all times will abstain from standing except when entering or leaving this courtroom."

I dropped back into my chair. Officer Popinjay now hovered so close behind me I smelled the stale breath of his morning coffee while his right hand grasped the handle of his baton hanging at the ready from his left hip.

"Yes, your honor."

"The prisoner will also abstain from referring to me as 'your honor.' "

I was, he said, in neither a Texas cowboy court nor did I find myself even in a slightly more civilized English court of law. If for some reason I must address him at all, I was to do so as *Monsieur le président.*

"Yes, *Monsieur le président.*"

"Silent, you!"

So silent I was. His now chili-pepper-red face turned to the other table.

"Monsieur Henri."

Monsieur Henri stood. *"Oui, Monsieur le président."*

Monsieur le président explained that since their prisoner had the grave misfortune of being an American, doubtless endowed with little appreciation for the elegance of the French language, they would conduct the hearing in English for my sorry benefit.

"Yes, *Monsieur le président.*"

"The American prisoner is charged with the serious and reprehensible crime of the murder of our beloved village gardener, Julian Barnet, valiant hero of the *Maquis.*"

"Yes, *Monsieur le président.* This is correct."

"The police report states a farmer found Monsieur Barnet yesterday morning hanging from a rafter in his barn thirteen kilometers outside our village."

"Yes, *Monsieur le président.* This is also true."

"It was no suicide. You are confident you can so

prove?"

"Yes, *Monsieur le président*. I am confident. Not with hands bound by wire behind his back."

"So what is your evidence with which you propose to convict the American?"

"This." Monsieur Henri's dainty fingertips withdrew from his open briefcase something inside a plastic as he would a dead mouse by its tail. "The American prisoner's American passport."

"Where was it found?"

"Nearby. Dropped in the dirt. Only a few meters from the deceased's feet. Perhaps lost in the death struggle."

"Any more evidence of note?"

The morning before they found Monsieur Barnet, Monsieur Henri noted that a maid at the inn had spotted him in their Remembrance Garden speaking to the American. Doubtless being lured to his death. The likely motive robbery, as the deceased's pockets were empty.

The courtroom murmured. The judge again glowered at me.

"Very well. The American prisoner is bound over for trial at our autumn session."

Sometime, he said, in October, on a date to be set should I fail to confess. Until I did, I was to receive no favors. He nodded at Officer Popinjay, standing behind me.

"Instruct his jailer. Now take him away and send in my next case. I have a date for lunch."

I started to stand, then thought better of it.

"Am I not permitted to speak?"

Now not only the judge but the prosecutor

glowered at me.

"Absolutely not!"

Unless addressed, I was to remain silent or the next time I had the misfortune to appear before him not only would I be shackled to the table but he would order my mouth gagged as well.

"Now call my next case."

I stood. Clem was nowhere to be seen. Spectators were all nods and smiles. All except the one in the serious charcoal-gray vested suit seated behind me, who continued to write in his notepad. No doubt that evening I would be making great copy.

****

My endless days somehow did pass; my nights, with the insipid light of a pale moon in its endless cycles circling the gray stone floor, more endless still. When he walked me back to my cell after the hearing, I asked Garlic Breath about visitors, but he reminded me the judge had ordered I was to receive no favors, and anyway the custom in this precinct was that prisoners accused of high murder received no visitors under any circumstances, so as not to taint their eventual examination, which, he promised, I would find if not entertaining at least educational.

"I'll bet."

Next day when I asked about a change of clothes or getting hold of some reading material, he said none had been brought. Had Clem even tried? I asked if I could get word to someone, but he said it was not permitted. No favors. None. The day after, when in desperation I asked about seeing a lawyer, my jailer laughed so hard tears filled his eyes, and it took him a moment to catch his breath.

"W-where do you think you are? No, you will meet with your lawyer the day before trial, like everyone else. This is not America, you know."

Clearly.

So I made endless circles of my cell. A thousand, two thousand circuits. Slept a lot, and tried not to drive myself crazy with questions, and managed to drive myself crazy anyway. I did prevail upon my jailer to bring me a roll of toilet paper, well, more like a quarter roll, which he told me would need to last a month, or maybe even two. After using a few precious sandpaper sheets to sweep my cell floor clear of rodent droppings, I did pushups and sit-ups until my arm and stomach muscles ached. Two times a day, my jailer brought me a bowl of horsemeat stew they must have prepared once a week, at most, as it grew more rancid with each serving, still with no spoon, and a quarter loaf of brown bread without butter.

Then, to keep myself from going crazy, I tried to work through whether Thoreaux was a hero or traitor. Tried to work through how the gutted cat tied in with a dead Julian.

****

A long nine days after my arrest, I woke from a late morning nap to see looming outside my cell the suspected reporter who had sat behind me during what passed for a hearing and wore today the same serious charcoal-gray vested suit. This guy had to have ice water running through his veins, because I was sweating just lying there. Again notepad and pencil in hand, which seemed odd. No way would my judge permit an interview. Bent over beside him, Garlic Breath rattled his key in the lock of the door to my cell before he pushed it open and stepped aside.

"Thank you, François. That will be all."

"Yes, *Inspecteur*. I will be on duty at the foot of the stairs should this wretch make trouble for you. Call out, and I will be to your aid with your next breath and his last."

"Thank you for your concern, but I expect no trouble."

"With Americans one can never be certain. Cowboys and gangsters, the lot of them."

My cell door creaked closed, the inspector chuckling as I elbowed myself up.

"So which are you? Cowboy or gangster?"

"Little of this, little of that."

"How are you enjoying your stay with us?"

"Lovely. Just lovely."

"I know, I know. Please accept my apologies."

He crossed to the wall opposite my cot.

"I am Inspector Inman and have been assigned the duty of investigating the murder of Monsieur Barnet."

"It wasn't me."

"A sweet old man, our Julian. Well loved. Antipathy against you runs quite high in the village."

"I noticed."

"So safer for you in here while I carry out my duties."

"I'm willing to risk it the other way."

"In their performance, I spoke to your friend, Clémence Mercier. A charming girl. Really most charming."

"I think so."

Or thought so. I did not care what Garlic Breath said. How hard could it be to get word to me? Or a lawyer? Not nine days difficult, surely. What was she doing out there? Sightseeing? Wine tasting? Polishing her solo byline?

"She asked me to tell you she has had no success in finding a lawyer."

Not only did antipathy against me run high, the inspector explained, but would run high against any who dared to represent me. The loss of clients for whatever would remain of their abbreviated careers was not worth whatever fee I would pay.

"Do you think this true?"

"Possible, I suppose. Though my experience is lawyers thrive on publicity, and your trial would bring much. She also told me you are a reporter back in America."

"On that accusation I plead guilty."

"So I had someone from home office go to our national library. They subscribe to newspapers from all over the world. Even to yours."

"It's a good paper. We've a first class editor."

"I had photocopies made of some of your articles. The recent one on corruption within your union of longshoremen particularly impressed me."

"Thanks. A lot of hours went into that article."

"Particularly impressed because corruption among our longshoremen is rampant as well. My own father worked the docks in Marseilles. Before his arrest."

"Arrest? Arrest for what?"

"Like you, for murder. A murder he did not commit."

"Also like me."

"He nevertheless served twenty years in prison. His conviction the reason I became a policeman."

"To find the real killer?"

"No. I know now the real killer was likely silenced within hours if not minutes, to keep the names of his paymasters secret."

Did that same need also explain the murder of Kid Twist back in Portland?

"Or the real killer fled the country and therefore was impossible to find. No. I became a policeman to prevent such injustices in the future."

"I can explain my passport."

"I know about your passport."

"Oh?"

He said he had spoken to the innkeeper, who explained his delay in reporting it stolen. His mother, who had been ill for some time, took a sudden turn for the worse. She lived several kilometers outside the village, and he and Father Paul spent all the night and next several days there. He knew too about the gutted *chat*, and Father Paul was kind enough to pay him a visit as well.

"A good man."

"He says the same of you. I've come here today to ask a favor of you." He held out his pad and pencil. "Can you write a little something for me? You can refuse, if you prefer not to. It will not be held against you."

"Why?"

"I wish yet not to say."

"Will it get me out?"

"It may well."

"Or it may keep me here."

The inspector smiled.

"A life absent of risks is not so much of a life."

"Tell me about the risks of life."

Well, what the hell. I took the offered pad and pencil.

"What should I write?"

"Oh, anything you like. Preferably in French."

"My French is an embarrassment."

"In that case, English will serve as well."

I wrote what I could remember of *Mary Had a Little Lamb* and handed the pad and pencil back to the inspector.

He chortled as he read.

"It gladdens me you have not lost your sense of humor while here as guest."

"Nor have I lost any toes."

"Such is good. My father once told me of the utility of toes in prison."

He removed a small envelope from inside his coat, withdrawing from it a smudged sheaf of paper. He looked from it to his pad and back again.

"As I suspected."

"As you suspected what?"

"You and he not the same."

"He who?"

Inspector Inman held up the contents of the envelope in one hand and his notepad in the other.

"The handwriting. Not even close."

"So?"

"So." He raised his right hand. "This is the letter we found on Monsieur Barnet when we cut him down. Written in French. Do you want me to translate?"

"Please."

" 'Dear Maurice. It has been a long time, my old friend. Almost thirty years. But I write because I now know the name of he who betrayed our thirty-eight. Who betrayed you. Our blackguard remains alive and near at hand. His black heart still beats, but not for much longer. Meet me tonight at our old rendezvous, and we will plot our revenge so at last justice will be done. Viva la France! ' Signed Gilbert."

"Who is Maurice?"

"Julian's *nom de guerre*."

"Who is Gilbert?"

"He for whom we search."

"Also a *nom de guerre*?"

"Likely."

"What's his real name?"

"We know not. Yet. But we search. Diligently."

A sparrow landed between the bars of my iron-barred window, me watching it, it and the inspector watching me. "What troubles you?"

"Would it have been common to have more than one *nom de guerre*?"

"I cannot say. One had, I suppose, as many as necessary to keep one's self alive. Why do you ask?"

"No reason, Inspector. Just puzzling out the angles, as are you."

"Your innkeeper showed me also the note left for you at the front desk by the fiend who gutted the poor *chat*. Clearly written by someone not our Gilbert. Even perhaps by a woman, from the penmanship."

"You're right. Now I think back on it, it could have been. I wasn't paying attention at the time."

"No. This note found on Monsieur Barnet was written by a man. Your young lady showed me the note slipped under your pension door in Paris. Both written by the same man."

"And I get to wait in here until you find him."

The inspector smiled. He did not think that would be necessary. I was not the man he sought. Of this he was now convinced. The son of the innkeeper was on duty on the night of Julian's murder. No one came or left. There are no back stairs, and too far for me to drop from our balcony. I would have broken my legs on the cobblestones. Or worse. The son did, however, report seeing Monsieur Barnet pass through the hotel lobby near eleven o'clock, only whistling the son off when asked what he was about at such an hour. The owner of the barn where Julian was found told them his bedridden father was indeed a member of the *Maquis*, his barn used by them during the war as a rendezvous.

Inspector Inman stepped to the cell door. "*François!*" He looked back at me.

"I will speak to the judge."

"I hope you catch him in a good mood."

"Yes, I know, I know. A testy one, my uncle."

"Your uncle?"

"Yes. My mother's brother."

While his father languished away his years in prison, his uncle took him in under his wing. He enjoyed his wine too much and therefore suffered from gout, but he liked his nephew. They should have me out in time for me to enjoy a most pleasant dinner with my most charming friend.

"Yes, most charming indeed."

Dinner we would have. Pleasant, after nine days, I had my doubts, and now I also had new doubts about Thoreaux in addition to what Father Paul had told us. Might he have been Gilbert as well as Anton? The answer might lay buried in Petershausen.

Chapter 20

"What about me, Clem? Couldn't you have made some sort of an effort to get word to me what you were up to? It was, after all, my neck. My neck and my decision to make, you know. Not yours, and certainly not his."

"Fine. You're right. You're absolutely right. I was wrong."

Alone in her room that night, I made the attempt, well started for all of five seconds, of enjoying a promised pleasant dinner with Clem. Our innkeeper warned us not to risk going out. Repeated what Inspector Inman said about much ill will afoot in the village. Much malignant and ugly whispering. Villagers seething at the rank stupidity of their judge to authorize release of an all but proved murderer, claiming he suffered from gout in the head as well as his extremities. As a precaution that night, our innkeeper had stationed both his sons behind the front desk, two Holland & Holland shotguns they used for pheasants stashed underneath.

Clem claimed he was right to take precautions. She could feel in the air the palpable ill will of the village toward us as soon as Officer Popinjay dragged me off to the station. When she started knocking on their doors, she found most lawyers already gone on month-long vacations, and none left behind would so much as touch my defense. She was about to board a train for Paris, but Inspector Inman cautioned her they would come horribly overpriced if they would come at all, and anyway, it might not be necessary. He asked her to give him a few days more, but Clem should under no circumstances try to see me, so she would not taint his chances for getting me out.

"Taint? Taint how?"

"He wouldn't tell me. Only your judge could be a testy one."

"Yeah, no kidding, but tell me this. How much time did the two of you spend together, anyway?"

"I don't know. Better part of an afternoon. Why?"

"Because you certainly seemed to have cast your spell over him."

"Jeremy, you're being absurd."

"Absurd, am I? Tell me then how you two spent the last nine days together."

"We didn't spend the last nine days together."

Clem claimed they had only spent part of one afternoon. In his office. With the door wide open so all the dirty little minds could satisfy themselves.

But she seemed too insistent there was nothing more she could have done to spring me.

"You should've gone to Paris anyway."

"I thought I could trust him, but have it your way. I was wrong."

"And while you were busy being wrong, what did you do with all your free time while I sat in their sorry excuse for a hoosegow?"

"I was out looking for a lawyer. *For you*. Sitting in waiting rooms until they found two minutes to give me the time of day."

"Well, from the results, that should have taken you all of half of a short morning. If that. What else did you do?"

"Read a lot."

"What else?"

"Did Father Paul's cathedral tour one afternoon."

"What else?"

She did not answer.

"What else, Clem?"

"Oh, visited a few wineries."

"So while I rotted in jail, you went sightseeing. Did some shopping too, I imagine."

Clem whipped the napkin from her lap, half her meal unfinished.

"Excuse me, but before a plate lands in your face, I'm going out for a breath of air."

****

Okay, I was being a bit of a bastard. Or maybe a bit more than a bit. So no great shock, once Clem got back hours later, rather than me she preferred to face the wall when we went to bed. Next morning while she showered I went down the hall to my room to check in with Henry.

"Where the hell've you been, Michaels? It's been damn near two weeks!"

I explained.

"Good Christ! You okay, kid?"

"Yeah. I'm okay. The inspector running the show here seems to be on my side. For now. But you're familiar with the fickleness of cops. Speaking of which, anything new with our longshoremen?"

Our ever-corruptible D.A. had held another press conference that morning. He confirmed Renard had indeed once found employment on the Brooklyn docks, but not off-loading ships like he told me, but as a mob enforcer where he separated shippers from sizeable chunks of their bank accounts. A year or so back, the mob sent him to Portland, where not only did he shake down our shippers for the Local but went into business for himself on the side. Banking the proceeds God only knows where, because the D.A. had not been able to trace them even with assistance from the F.B.I. Likely banked under an alias using a Social Security number he bought on the black market across town in the Pearl District. Or maybe down in Tijuana where he may be taking a siesta. For now. Turns out when Renard went into business for himself, it wasn't for Crackerjacks. He went in big time. Squeezing these chumps so hard the general manager for Orient Shipping started crybabying the blues to Rago's eyes and ears down on the docks. Late Kid Twist, by name.

"D.A. blowing smoke, you think?"

"Hard to say."

"Trying to keep Renard quiet and out of town?"

Henry wouldn't put it past him, but I'd better get what I could get over here, just in case he wasn't and this blew up in our faces before I got back.

****

I carried my packed duffle down the hall to Clem's room. As she stood at the bed folding clothes into her suitcase, the two of us making strained attempts to restore some semblance of civility, I stood at the twin doors of paned glass looking down into the wet cobblestone square through a gray drizzle that had begun to fall sometime after midnight.

"Will we be back after Petershausen, Jeremy?"

"A chance, I guess."

"Well, I'll pack everything so we don't have to come back if we don't need to. Even with our innkeeper as nice as he's been, I feel violated here."

"Yeah, no kidding violated. Look. I'm sorry about last night. I—"

"Forget it. You've been under a brickload of stress."

I tried again.

"Yeah, but that's no ex—"

"Forget it, Jeremy. Just forget it."

But the tone of her voice said she was not about to forget it. Told me I had one hefty bill coming due for last night's dinner.

"Whether we come back depends on what the nuns tell us, I guess. We may have more questions for Father Paul. Maybe even Gabrielle."

"You were right, you know. For every answer we unearth, we're digging up two more questions buried beneath it."

"Or three or four."

Questions like: were Thoreaux, Anton, and Gilbert one and the same? Was the woman in the cell next to Gabrielle's the same as this Adrienne—Thoreaux's lover—Julian had spoken of? And why did Gabrielle lie to us, saying she busied herself with her vineyards during the war?

"Why didn't she tell us she survived the Hell of Dachau?"

"Good question, Clem. What do you think?"

"Maybe she's one of those Father Paul told us about hiding secrets. Maybe Thoreaux's using them to blackmail her. To keep her silent about his selling out."

"Maybe. He was, after all, born in Hamburg. His father—his real father—served in the German army during World War I. So did he get recruited while stringing for the A.P from Berlin before the war?"

A vindictive fist struck Clem's palm.

"I know he's the one who betrayed the thirty-eight, Jeremy. I know it. He has to be."

"Why has to be?"

"Because if he didn't, they would be the thirty-nine. What are the odds?"

Clem snapped her suitcase shut, her reflection from where she sat on the bed facing my own in the paned glass.

"I know he's the one who betrayed them."

As much as I hated to admit it, he could well have. What were the odds of his being the last man standing? Then again…

"I don't know, Clem," I said turning to her. "My heart tells me no, but I really don't know."

"Well, I do know because my heart's screaming yes."

"Screaming yes because it would save the *Oracle*?"

"No."

Well, maybe, I told Clem. But what if Thoreaux just failed? What if he dove into a runaway river and got swept up in it? He was, after all, only an amateur. Did we really want to heap more shame on him? From what Gabrielle said, he had stared suicide down once. Maybe more than once. Maybe it was only his own luckless bungling he wanted to hide.

"Do we really want to send him up that ladder of guilt again by running a story we got wrong, and for our own gain?"

"We're not getting it wrong, and I told you before, Jeremy—however far I have to go to save the *Oracle* is how far I'm going, and I don't care who pays the price."

"But our jobs are more than about running a scandalous story to save our hides."

Or should be, I told Clem. We should be telling the truth. Dragging it out of the night by the scruff of its neck kicking and screaming to hold it up to the light of day so we can all learn and maybe not forever repeat our follies. Reporters may be our last hope. But our stories should not be harming the innocent for our own gain.

"You can unsaddle that white horse you're saddled up in anytime, Jeremy."

Thoreaux was not an innocent, Clem insisted. He was a participant. A part of history. And participants who were a part of history forfeited their right to hide out in ramshackle houses.

"Who says?"

"I do."

"Don't you think maybe you're being just a little coldblooded?"

"Don't you think you're being a little softhearted?"

It was, I said, not about being softhearted if he wasn't the one who betrayed the thirty-eight. Thoreaux was too well remembered there. Julian remembered him well too, and he had served with Thoreaux.

"He had to have done some good, don't you think?"

"No. Whatever good Thoreaux did, he did to cover up his duplicity. I think he duped them just like he duped you."

So there we were. I turned and again looked out her window through a gray drizzle into an opaque morning.

"Boxcar stories."

"What?"

"Box—"

But at that moment a flash of lightning burst directly over the square, the explosion of thunder rattling the panes in Clem's patio door. Something—someone—across the square in the cathedral archway? Or was it only shadow? Only me jumpy at gutted cats and a hanged old man and nine days locked up in a jail cell with toe-nibbling rats for company and a jailer whose enthusiasm would have proved an embarrassment even to the Nazis?

"What were you saying, Jeremy?"

"Lost my train of thought." I crossed to the bed and took hold of her suitcase. "First let's find out what our story is before we decide whether to run with it."

"We have our story, and I am running with it. Better with your byline once you're satisfied, but without you if I have to."

Us bickering now over what we had or did not have made no sense, but I couldn't deny Clem could be right. Maybe what we found in Petershausen would tell me for sure.

Downstairs, our innkeeper stood at the front desk.

"Your train leaves in twenty minutes, Monsieur."

Clem had been right about me at times being a little dense. It didn't occur to me until that moment that if there was indeed someone spying on us from across the street, he might be the key to the gutted cat and to dead Julian, and the gutted cat and dead Julian the keys to unlocking Thoreaux's secret. I pointed to the stand of umbrellas behind the front desk.

"May I borrow one of those?"

"Of course, Monsieur. They are there for our guests' convenience, but my driver will soon be up front."

"Jeremy, where do you think you're going?"

"Something I want to check out over at the cathedral before we leave."

"What?"

"Something. Wait here. I'll be right back."

"You better be right back."

I crossed the cobblestone square, but the cathedral archway stood empty. I stepped back out into the rain just as a raincoated figure darted out of another doorway on the same side of the street and turned at the corner three blocks farther down. I hurried as best I could, umbrella held up against the wind and drizzle, to the next corner and turned down the street and stopped. A dozen passageways and alleys on each side. But no figure in black.

Chapter 21

"*Ach, ja,* remember well, I do. How can I remember not such a ghastly day?"

Sister Agnes's pleading eyes looked up at us from her bed in a room that smelled of diapers at a nursing home where her Mother Superior had directed Clem and me with reluctance and then only after reading Father Paul's letter.

"Do not trouble her, I beg you. While God gave this one the heart of an angel, no longer is it strong."

An understatement. Her parched skin bunched in rolls on arms thin as dried sticks and looking just as brittle, but when two unexpected visitors appeared in the doorway to her room, her eyes of robin's-egg blue sparkled within the deep sockets of their leathery nests. A Bible well thumbed lay on her bedside table, only partially concealing what looked to be some sort of German movie magazine, also well worn, with two pectoral-endowed young men half naked on its cover. I laid my hand near hers.

"Go on. Please tell us, Sister. It's important, or we would not trouble you. Can you tell us what you remember?"

Those pleading eyes turned from mine to the thick quilt covering her legs with its enigma patterns of interlocking hexagons.

"I remember watching from a chapel window when

217

the SS captured her on the road that led away from our convent. Their dogs falling upon her. Tearing at her. Taking her down as they would a wild doe."

A horrible day, Sister Agnes remembered. Many horrible days she saw in those years, but this day far and away the worst. She was confronted with evil—blunt, naked evil—and helpless to do anything more than pray. Pray and bear witness. Never could she forget. Never could she forget such a face.

"The Virgin's face, but so horrible a day."

She looked up from her quilt.

"Though I see now so few visitors, I wish you had not come."

"We will go soon, but this is important. Do you by chance remember this girl's name?"

"No." She shook her head of white hair fine as spider silk. "She never told us. A young girl clad in the black-and-white rags of the camp. Holding close to her breast a daughter."

"A daughter?" Clem about jolted out of one of the chairs we had pulled to the sister's bedside. "She held a daughter?"

"Yes. Not a day old, poor thing. Born in the dead of winter. Only by the grace of Providence alive."

I pressed on.

"Where was this baby born, Sister? Surely not at Dachau?"

"No, no, no. Never there. Only a kilometer away from the old convent."

"Where?"

"Like our Savior, born in a stable in the dead of winter."

Wrapped, she said, not in swaddling clothes but a

horse blanket stained with manure. That is why she had to escape. If she gave birth in the camp, the SS would have taken the child. Tossed her in the air for target practice.

"How fortunate your convent was nearby when her time came."

"Fortune had nothing to do with her coming. She had her journey well planned, this one did. Another prisoner summered at a farm near the convent when a little girl. The child may well have been born there. Now please go. You promised me you would. You don't know how these memories so upset me. I have answered your questions. Now please go."

"We will, soon, but you did not allow them to stay with you? Hunted as they were?"

They did not, Sister Agnes said, and the girl knew she could not. Knew for the nuns to harbor an escapee would be their own death sentence. A summary bullet to the head though they be nuns. For while Jews were the most reviled, all who lived their faith lived lives of gravest peril. Nuns there were spared only because they were German and kept their silence and because so many German officers claimed to have been baptized by the Church. Though how any could make such an outrageous claim was beyond her feeble grasp. Not after the crimes committed. Sisters from Poland had told her how before they entered their convent soldiers stood outside drinking brandy while drawing lots to determine who of them would go in first. Salivated in anticipation at being the first to desecrate a virgin.

The girl did not stay with them long. A few hours. They fed her. Took a little of December's chill out of her bones. Found her proper shoes because she had bundled her feet in grain sacks. Then she left. She who insisted. Her daughter she believed stood a better chance without her. Sister Agnes said she was right, but it truly shattered her heart as nothing before or since to watch the mother trudge up their lane drifted with snow. She now knew they should have made her wait until dark because it was plain from her striped rags she was an escapee, for which the SS would pay a most handsome bounty, but the girl said convents and churches would be the first places they would search, for nothing in their black hearts stood sacred, and the girl wanted to put as much distance between her and the child as she could.

"I can't." Clem shook her head. "I can't imagine."

"You are a mother?"

"A three-year-old. A daughter too."

"Always can I tell." The sister forced a smile. "Young mothers have an air of worry about them for the well-being of others. But can you please go now."

Clem nodded, started to get up, but I put my hand on her knee.

"We will. We will, but tell us what happened to her baby."

"Will you then truly go?"

"Yes. Truly."

Sister Agnes said that they hid the baby. Lived in mortal terror the SS would return. Feared as they broke down the convent door the little one would start to squall. For surely they knew the girl was with child when she escaped. Had likely already drawn their lots as to who of them would use it for skeet, and now she was without child. Set upon in the snow on a road with footprints leading away from our convent.

"Did they ever return?"

"Maybe a month later."

"Why so long?"

"Who can say?"

For we should never forget—whatever monsters the SS were, they were bureaucrats first. Like bureaucrats the world over, they lived by a curious logic all their own, such as it is, which is no logic at all, and they from a people who gave Kant to the world.

"Did they find her when they came?"

"No."

The Sister's eyes beamed for the first time since we told her why we had come. Already their little one far away. Taken by a *parteiisch*. A partisan who showed up on their doorstep.

"Not a French partisan?"

"And why not?"

"Would it not be unusual for a French partisan to show up on the doorstep of a convent in Germany?"

"It must be. It only happened to us once, and never were we to see or hear from him again."

"What did this partisan say?"

Through a sort of underground, Sister Agnes said word had reached them. Knew the child to be in the gravest of danger and needed to be bundled off to safety.

"Did he give a name, this partisan?"

"He called himself Gilbert."

"Gilbert?"

"Such is what he said."

I glanced at Clem.

"Are you sure he gave his name as Gilbert?"

"I am very sure."

"His nom de guerre, perhaps?"

Sister Agnes said such would not surprise her. For when he told them, he did so without much conviction. Either in his words or his eyes. He stayed with them until it grew dark. Then he and the child slipped away, the little one bundled up inside his coat. He said he could not take her to the mother's house because the Germans would surely have it under watch. Instead he would carry her up to the Monastery of Saint-Martin-du-Canigou, run by the Community of the Beatitudes, high in the Pyrenees. Very remote. Very far removed from anywhere the Germans had shown much of an interest. The way up treacherous, especially in winter. He claimed to have carried there a score of allied aviators as well as many young Jewesses about to be freighted off in boxcars. From there the two of them could make their way into Spain and in time she would be across the frontier to Portugal and then on to South America.

"Did this partisan tell you anything more?"

"Very little."

Nothing of consequence, Sister Agnes said. Only the mother had been betrayed by someone he called her circuit leader. Why betrayed, the *parteiisch* did not say.

"Did the partisan say what became of the mother?"

Sister Agnes turned away. She nodded. The SS raped her. Took turns sitting on her head. The German doctor who used the prisoners in his experiments gave the girl an injection of phenol. A drug addict himself, he misjudged the dosage. Determined her weaker than she was. When she woke screaming as the *sonderkommandos* slid her into the oven, they started to bring her out, but the SS leveled their machineguns.

Ordered them to continue with their work. Laughed even as she burned. Screaming for mercy. She was a *terroristin*, a terrorist and a pig, they said, and so she should die like a pig roasting on the spit.

Clem's eyes shifted to mine, a hand cupped over her mouth.

"Now, please leave. Please."

"Sister Agnes. Is there anything more you can tell us about this girl? About her child? Anything at all you can remember."

"No. There is not. Now please leave. I beg of you. Please leave."

Tears welled in her eyes, and I placed my hand on hers.

"You have been most helpful, Sister. We thank you for sharing your memories, troubled as they are."

We crossed the room to leave, but at the doorway, Clem turned back to her.

"Sister, one more question. Please. Then we will go. I promise. Did this girl by chance tell you her daughter's name?"

"*Ach, ja.* She did." The old nun wiping at her eyes with the bed quilt tried again to smile. "An unusual name but also very beautiful. English rather than French, but nonetheless a beautiful name for a beautiful little girl. A saint's name. Thomasina. Her mother named her Thomasina."

Chapter 22

We arrived at the station early enough to grab seats on the side of the train that would face Dachau. When we came in from Ribeauville, it had been near dark, and through the dense gray of fog the brick apparitions rising out of the dusk, blurring past the windows, looked like what they were. A city of the dead. A twentieth-century Valley of Bones out of Ezekiel.

The night before, over dinner, we talked about taking a tour. Not out of macabre voyeurism but to understand that which we could not understand. The wife of the hotel's proprietor, however, told us when we inquired at the front desk that because the next day was some or another Catholic feast day, Dachau offered no tours.

Clem refused to stay the extra day. Biting at the bit to get home to run our story and so save the *Oracle*, before someone else dug it up or maybe the British, miffed at Thoreaux's snubbing their Queen, let the cat out of the bag.

I was torn. Sister Agnes had shaken even more my already shaky confidence in Thoreaux, but I held out hope on the slim chance we didn't have the whole story. I wanted to keep digging. At least that is what I told myself, but perhaps once again I was walking the world wearing Father Paul's blinders. Perhaps Thoreaux had been a collaborator. It looked bad and yet did not run true to the boxcar stories he told me. Then again, maybe they were stories he had to tell himself.

"What is wrong with you, Jeremy? We have his story, and we should run with it. Just run with it. Let his chips fall where they may."

"I'm not so certain. At least not all of it. Something seems amiss."

"Amiss like what?"

"This isn't the Thoreaux I know. This story we're getting is not adding up."

"What about it isn't adding up?"

"Something I can't put my finger on, but something."

"Give me one of your somethings. Just one."

"Well, the partisan who took Thomasina away went by Gilbert."

"So?"

"So a Gilbert is a suspect in the death of Julian. It's the signature on the letter they found on him, that lured him to his death."

"Again, so what, Jeremy? There must be a gazillion Gilberts running around."

But there weren't a gazillion former partisans running around with the *nom de guerre* Gilbert. This was too much a coincidence. If she ran the story as is and got it wrong, Hanna would tar and feather her. She'd be out of business with no hope of holding on.

"No. You're wrong. Dead wrong. They'll be thanking me for exposing Thoreaux. For telling them they were right all along to scorn him all these years for being the fraud he is. He'll be the one they tar and feather."

I was not the only one wearing blinders. We see

what we want to see, but that night she again turned away from me.

****

Next morning it turned out there was no need for us to have gotten there early. After we bumped our way down the aisle of an only half-full coach, with bags strapped over our shoulders and a couple of babies smelling of spoiled milk crying, Clem insisted I sit by the window. Perhaps hoping if I saw the magnitude of death wrought here I would accept we had the right ending for our story.

Our train at last lurched out of the station, a troubled sky making up in the west. We passed Dachau a few minutes later. Or started to pass, as it stretched on and on. I had expected something more of the compactness of the camp I once saw Friday nights on *Hogan's Heroes*, but so vast was it that from a distance Dachau could have been a Volkswagen assembly factory or a Baer chemical plant. Or one of Sinclair Lewis's sprawling slaughterhouses in Chicago. Later I read the Germans had converted it from a munitions factory. Clem rested her chin on my shoulder as the razor-wire fence, orange with rust, rushed by.

"So this is where she died."

"Yeah. I guess so."

"One more mother betrayed. One more woman used. This time, though, the bastard's not getting away scot-free. This time he will pay."

"Maybe we're being too harsh. Too quick in our rush to judgment."

"How, Jeremy? Tell me how."

"Maybe the partisan had reasons of his own to mislead Sister Agnes. If he was in fact Julian's killer, I

226

have to question his character."

"Why are you being so pigheaded? Thoreaux betrayed the mother of his child. Likely for a woman he had stashed away on the side. It's a story as old as Genesis."

And as new as a LeSabre towed out of the dark depths of a deep stripper cut. With her jaw set, those black eyes burning coals, her reflected face in the window scared me. The fiery ferocity of the self-righteous has always scared me. Especially those out to avenge some supposed wrong. An insane self-righteousness with a logic all its own that once set in motion hurtles to insane outcomes. Like those passing by our window.

"Clem," I said softly. "Thoreaux's not Chris."

"Did you not hear what Sister Agnes said?"

They had raped her—they gang-raped her. They took turns sitting on her head before some dope-fiend swine of a doctor shot her full of phenol, but the incompetent bastard got the dosage wrong, and when they slid her into the oven its furnace heat must've made her come to. Couldn't I feel the flames? The heat? Couldn't I hear her screams? Sister Agnes could.

"Now, night after night, I will hear them too. How could he have done what he did to the mother of his child?"

"Clem, we don't know for sure what he did. We don't yet have the whole story."

"We don't need the whole goddamn story. We have enough to run with what we've got to make him pay."

"We can't run with what we've got if we don't know what we don't have."

"What is it we don't have, Jeremy? What?"

"I don't know what we don't have, but we at least need to talk to Gabrielle again."

"Why?"

"Because we know now she withheld facts from us. We know now she was a prisoner here. Maybe she withheld more we don't know about."

"What was it she withheld, Jeremy? What?"

"That's my point. We don't know what she withheld. We don't know what we don't know. We need to talk to her again. We're going back to Ribeauville anyway to change trains. What's an hour of our time?"

"Fine. I'll give you an hour of my time and not a minute—not so much as a single second—more. Then we're running with the story, and if we're not running it together, I'm running it alone."

"Fine."

"Fine." She stood. "I need some air."

The door at the back of our car slammed shut so hard when she went out its glass rattled, and every accusatory eye fixed on me when I turned around.

I looked out my window, the razor-wire fence blurring past. The night before, after Clem went up to our room, the wife of our hotel proprietor and I had talked some more. She grew up in Dachau. As a little girl she remembered the cattle cars carrying their human cargo always came at night. They had already confiscated the prisoners' leather shoes in order to recycle them into boots for their troops, and those prisoners herded off the trains wore wooden ones. Recycled from prisoners past and would be recycled again. Passing by her house on their way to the camp, that is what she most remembered. The clopping of hundreds—some nights thousands—of pairs of wooden shoes beneath her window on the cobblestone street in the dead of night.

Chapter 23

"Jeremy, why do you insist on proving to the world the male of our species is made up of pigheads? We've got the story, for Christ's sake."

Thomas Thoreaux had sold out the mother of his child, Clem insisted. That was why he turned down the knighthood. Why he didn't want the world to know. That was it. That was the whole ugly ending to our story. There was not going to be some other, no matter how much I kept digging. Get over it. This was the story, and it was the story that was going to save the *Oracle*.

"But it's not adding up, Clem."

"Sweet Christ!"

Clem's anger echoed up into the vaulted ceiling of the Ribeauville train depot. Late that morning, we had walked there, down from Gabrielle's villa where the expectant peasant girl again ushered us through the gloom of the house and out onto the patio. Something was still familiar about her. Something disconcerting. Disconcerting as Thoreaux's story Clem was so dead-on certain she had got right.

A swarm of Ortolans fluttered in and out of lilac bushes that bordered a path paved with squares of rough-chiseled stone leading from the patio, as fog-distorted voices within a morning mist rose from the vineyards. We followed the girl through doors swung open to receive the day's bounty into a forty-foot barn built of stone, then down a long flight of steps into a dank cavern lined along all four walls with white-oak casks that reached to the ceiling. Clipboard in hand, Gabrielle stood at its center. With her iron-gray hair pinned back, she looked every inch the severe estate mistress as she gave orders to three workmen shirted in collarless smocks who, with their tool belts of worn leather hung with a hodgepodge of hammers and diverse tools for working wood and metal, might have been her barrel coopers. When Gabrielle saw us, her razor-blue eyes narrowed to the thin sharpness of a well-honed knife.

She gave final orders to her workers before she shooed them up the steps, then stood rapping the bulging clipboard against her leg.

"That will be all, Thérèse. See to lunch, please."

"For three?"

"I think not."

"Yes, Madame."

"*Tante…*"

But with a quick finger to her lips and a cutting razor squint, Gabrielle shushed her. We waited for the peasant girl to labor up stone steps cut out of limestone bedrock, her kerchiefed vulpine hair sweeping her waist, and not until the iron-slatted cellar door creaked behind her did Gabrielle address us.

"I must say I am most surprised you two have not tired of your adventures here and returned to America."

"We take the noon train to Paris, *Tante*."

"Speedy journey, then."

"But we have one more question before we do."

An annoyed sigh escaped Gabrielle's lips.

231

"Very well. Ask your tiresome question, if you must, but be quick about it. I have a vineyard to run."

"Father Paul read to us from the war crimes archives. You were a prisoner in Dachau during the war. Not tending your vineyards here."

"How is it any business of yours where I was?"

"From there we traveled to the convent outside of Petershausen where Thoreaux's courier sought refuge after she escaped the camp."

"What are you getting at?"

"He sold her out to the Gestapo, didn't he? It was Thoreaux who sold her out."

The clipboard ceased to rap her leg. What could have been a smile seemed about to crease Gabrielle's lips until she caught herself.

"Thomas believed her the double agent betraying the cells within his circuit."

"Giving the Germans a courier."

"In the end, yes."

"For money?"

"Perhaps."

"A courier who knew all the secrets of all the cells within his circuit."

"If true, she sold them long before. His tattered circuit lay in rags. No more damage could she inflict. If true."

"If true? Was she in fact a double agent?"

"I cannot s-say."

"And they executed her."

"That I can say. Yes."

Clem turned to me, smirking her self-righteous smile of satisfaction.

"There's your confirmation, Jeremy. Now we can

go home."

But what was it with Gabrielle's hint of a smile when Clem placed the blame for the courier's death on Thoreaux?

"Why, Madam Mercier, would the Gestapo execute their own double agent?"

"They are a most barbarous people, their Gestapo the worst of their worst. Perhaps she knew too much. Posed too much risk. Perhaps they suspected her of lying. Who can say why they did what they did?"

"Was it Thoreaux who betrayed you to the Gestapo?"

"No, I suspect not."

"By who, then?"

"I-I cannot say."

"Cannot or will not?"

"As you wish."

"Why did you not tell us all this when we first came here?"

"Tell me, Monsieur Michaels, how does one betray another of one's family who has suffered enough?"

"No." Clem shook her head. "Here you are mistaken, Tante. A man who betrays the mother of his child can never suffer enough. Never. A special roasting pit in Hell burns for such men. We're going, Jeremy."

"One more question."

"*Oui?*"

"What was the name of his courier?"

Gabrielle's face clouded for a second. But only a second.

"Adèle. Her name was Adèle."

"Can we go, Jeremy? Are you satisfied now?"

When we reached the top step, I looked back down into the cellar. Gabrielle, face no longer clouded but smiling as she wrote on her clipboard, right sleeve slipping a little up her arm as she wrote, revealing the runny smear. Her concentration camp tattoo that, unlike memory, had begun to fade. Another something not adding up. In a modern history course I took in college, taught by an old Jewish professor from Krakow who somehow survived four years in the camps, I learned the Germans tattooed only their inmates at Auschwitz.

I caught up with Clem outside the house, a black Peugeot—not there when we arrived—parked beside the garage.

****

Inquisitive heads of overhearing passengers hurrying to purchase their tickets turned to where we sat on a long wooden bench set against the stucco wall. A gray-mustached man who had been trying to read his morning paper a few feet from us gave up and moved to the end of our bench, where he unfolded his copy of *Le Monde*, making a miffed show of snapping open its pages.

"Do you think if we spoke to Colette she might tell us something we might've missed?"

"Colette? She's not going to tell us anything we don't already know."

"Why wouldn't she? She told you about Thoreau's SOE service."

"No, she didn't. I asked her what she knew as soon as the A.P. story broke over the wire."

"And?"

"And she refused to discuss squat-diddly with me. Just ranted on about what a *connard* Thoreaux was.

234

Now I can see why."

"So who was your source?"

Clem's coal-black eyes that had been scorching mine dropped away. She began rummaging through her purse.

"Clem?"

"Oh, Jeremy," she said, not looking up, "what's it matter who my source was?"

"If it doesn't matter, tell me who it was."

Clem, finding her compact, inspected the corners of her mouth.

"Remember our deal, at your insistence, when we started? No hiding sources from one another."

The compact snapped closed with a sharp click. She stared ahead.

"So who was your source?"

"Oh, if you must know. My father."

"Your father? But your father's one of the thirty-eight."

"Another of Gabrielle's…misstatements."

"Why would she misstate your father being stood up against a wall?"

"In my family, Jeremy, we bury secrets beneath vast mountain ranges of misstatements."

"Can't you see now why I say there's too much not adding up? Too many secrets not getting told?"

"Maybe not *everything* is adding up and getting told, Jeremy, but enough is for us to run with what we've got. Enough to see to it Thomas Thoreaux, the *connard*, the Judas murderer, gets what he deserves."

"I'm not so certain."

"Well I *am* certain. Dead certain."

"So when did you talk to your father?"

"What's it matter when?"

"Come on, Clem. When?"

"Oh. The day before you came back."

"He called you?"

"No."

"Where then?"

"He stopped in."

"And told you Thoreaux served with the SOE?"

"So he said."

"How did he know?"

"Said he knew Thoreaux from before the war."

Passengers returning from the ticket counter walked by us, Clem's eyes following them rather than looking at me.

"So when did you last hear from your father before?"

"Never so much as a birthday card."

"So some guy shows up at the local paper a few days after A.P. breaks Thoreaux's story, claiming to be your father."

"Not claims. He *is* my father."

"How can you know he's your father when you never saw him before?"

"Colette keeps a photograph tucked in her Bible."

"So why did she leave him?"

"She won't say."

"Why won't she?"

"My guess is they never married. Like Julian told us, war's not the best time to fall in love."

Peacetime was turning out no picnic either. The more we talked, the more that was not adding up. Then a light flickered. Flickered as it had on the drizzly streets of Portland the night before Thoreaux's story broke. Flickered, shadows receding, then snuffed out. Such is the diaphanousness of memory. A hunch left to smolder. But it couldn't be.

"What's your father's name?"

"What's it matter what his name is?"

"Clem."

"Oh, Renard, if you must know. Erec Renard."

In Clem's face I saw the shock of my own.

"What is it, Jeremy?"

"I know Erec Renard."

"Know him? Know him from when?"

I explained the when. The where.

"Did he tell you anything else, Clem?"

"He said the *Oracle* hadn't changed by so much as a dust mote since he'd stopped in twenty years ago, looking for Thoreaux. But by then Thoreaux was in prison."

"Funny that when he came to Hanna that first time he didn't bother to look up you and Colette. Another something not adding up."

"What my father did or didn't do twenty years ago has nothing whatsoever to do with our story, Jeremy."

"So you're telling me that within days of Buckingham Palace announcing a knighthood for our village hermit, your father, who you never saw before or even heard from and who your mother refuses to discuss, shows up in Hanna and it has nothing to do with our story?"

"Not one iota."

"It does, Clem. It has to. We're just not puzzling the pieces together, and until we do, it's too soon to run our story. We'll get our heads handed us on a pewter platter and maybe destroy an innocent man in the bargain."

"We have puzzled the pieces together, and he's not innocent, and he doesn't deserve to have his life back. He deserves to pay."

So there we were. In a train depot going nowhere. I rose, handing Clem her ticket when I returned. She looked at my empty hand, looked at me, her eyes holding my answer before she asked the question.

"Where's yours?"

"You'll have to go home alone."

"So you're abandoning me too."

My hand fell on her knee.

"Clem, Thoreaux is not Chris. Neither am I."

But she shoved my hand away, hard, her coal-black eyes ablaze. "Don't you dare touch me, mister!"

Except for the echo of her voice lost in the vaulted ceiling, the station was still as a held breath.

"Clem, we don't know the whole story."

"We know enough to make him pay!"

"Something's missing. Something."

"No, it's not. Please, Jeremy. Come home. Don't abandon me too. Please."

"I can't, Clem. I won't. Not without the story. All of it. I can't—I won't—destroy a man without all of the truth. Without all of it, I'll have nothing to go home to. I'll have betrayed myself."

"You'll have me. Am I not more important than your being certain you've got your entire goddamn story?"

In answer, I did not answer, which was answer enough. We sat not speaking until her train pulled in. Clem stood, bags in hand, eyes burning.

"So you getting the *Oxford Unabridged Edition* of

your story is more important to you than I am?"

"No. Of course not."

"Don't lie to me, Michaels. Don't you dare, and for a change stop lying to yourself. It is. You know it is."

"I'm not lying to anyone."

"You know what your problem is? Your problem is your story. No, make that stories. As in you use your stories to hide inside of. As in you use your stories as an excuse to feel for everyone else in the world except those who need you the mo—"

She turned away for a moment, eyes wet at their edges when she turned to me again. My stories were who I was, she said, but I buried myself in them as an excuse not to feel. She could understand my being numb to the world.

"But it's been more than two years since the baby and Beth died."

"Beth?"

"Yes, Beth. Remember her? I don't know how many times she came downstairs to talk after she lost the baby."

"Why?"

"Why? Why do you think! Because she needed someone to talk to. You couldn't, or wouldn't, leaving her only a loony-tunes mother."

"What did she talk about?"

"You! Who else? You were her life, Jeremy."

"What about me?"

"Exactly what I just told you."

"And what did you say?"

Clem said she told Beth she just damn well better get used to it. A man would never be there for her when the chips were down. When she needed him the most,

239

he'd dump her for the game going on at the next table. Count on it.

"You told her that? Her in and out of jail? Drinking herself into an early grave?"

"Someone had to tell the poor kid the facts of life. You sure weren't doing her any good. If she knew, maybe she'd move on."

"Move on. From me. How often did you two talk?"

"Every day. Some days two or three times."

Another hunch.

"When was the last time Beth came downstairs?"

"When? What's it matter when? What matters is she came down, a lot, and she came down because of you."

"It was the day she killed herself, wasn't it? Two days out of rehab. The day she crashed head on into Mill Creek Bridge."

Clem's eyes seared into mine.

"Don't you dare try crawling out of your guilt cocoon on my back. Why do you think she drove head-on into goddamn Mill Creek Bridge? No, it was you, not me, who dropped the keys into Beth's hand. Admit it, you coward, and admit you're using this story to purge your guilt over Beth's death. You think by somehow saving Thomas Thoreaux it will make up for how you treated Beth. Well, it won't."

I said nothing. Nothing because…maybe I was.

"I'm right, aren't I? Aren't I? Down the road. That first night. Along the river. I thought you'd changed. I thought we'd started something, but you're like the rest of them. Like you always were."

"Clem, I—"

"Forget it, Michaels. I don't want you so much as

on the same plane as I am, let alone in the seat next to me. I can make it home without you, thank you very much. I'm used to it. I'd begun to hope those days were behind me for good. How could I have been so stupid? Again. So go on. Go on and get the rest of your goddamn story."

"Clem, I—"

"Oh, shut up, you stinking coward."

"*Tous à bord,*" the station master called from the door, passengers standing, moving out onto the platform. "*Tous à bord.*"

"When you get back with that last measly morsel of your goddamn story that isn't going to change one iota of anything that matters, I don't want to hear about it. I don't want to hear from you. Not a letter. Not a phone call. Not so much as a postcard. Nothing. I can read about whatever it is when they get around to handing out the Pulitzers. And I hope you'll be very happy," she said, twirling in a sharp pirouette to hurry across the station out onto the platform.

So it ended. There I was left. Like Clem, alone. Again. The one stop neither of us wanted to get off at but one reached from our own decisions. Our own self-deceptions. Me alone because of not being able to reconcile myself to a story only half-told, because a story only half-told was a whole lie. Perhaps worse than a lie because not only does its teller mislead his listener, he misleads himself. A story that in its half-telling raised its own troubled questions: Who was Gilbert? Had Gabrielle been held at Dachau where the SS did not tattoo their prisoners? If not, why claim she had? What became of Thomasina? Should I find her, what would she want with a father who sent her mother to the ovens? But if she does not, how does Thoreaux find his forgiveness? How do I find mine?

Those troubled questions raised their own, because if I found their answers, if I at last found my story, how would I tell it to the world? Shaming the man who, before I pushed him down his path to prison, was only one of two who showed me friendship in a friendless world? Be the one to push him off his ladder? One more betrayal, one more failure by me.

Yet if I failed to tell his story, had I not betrayed those duties drilled into me years before by my grandfather and later by Henry and by Thoreaux himself in those hours he apprenticed me to the truth in his study? The duty to seek it out. To tell the truth no matter how ugly. Pay whatever bill came due. For how else are we ever to learn from our collective follies? How else are we not to repeat over and over again the desperate lessons of Dachau?

Perhaps all that was needed to stop a new Dachau was one person willing to risk telling the hard truth. Perhaps that person was me. Me who, as Clem claimed, saw his place in the world as astride a white horse. But if I failed, if I were no longer a reporter, no longer a teller of hard truths, who was I?

Her train at last whistled out of the station. Rasp of steel wheels on steel rails. Steel rails millions rode to nightmare deaths. One nightmare death in particular. A death giving rise to so many questions I had to answer before I could let go of Thoreaux's story. Lay it to rest for us both. Had to—more than had to, for in those murky shadows of the why of his story lurked the why of my own.

To answer the one was to answer the other. A story

now more than a story about who was Thoreaux but about who I was. About who I was to be. For I knew deep down that in finding forgiveness for Thomas, there too somehow would I find my own. Knew that in saving Thomas, I would save myself.

I rose and again stood in line at the ticket counter. Questions, so many questions. With so many questions, what better sanctum to search for answers than within the walls of a snowy mountain monastery high above the clouds of the world's obscurity?

I did not know what answers I would find there. Knew only the answer I'd hoped I found here with Clem was smoke in the wind. After I bought my ticket, on my way out of the depot I reached into my pocket. Let my fingers roll the gold pen she gave me our first morning there. A morning aglow with hope. A hope now run dry as faded ink. I continued out to the platform, metallic knell of a trashcan ringing from the tossed pen behind me. Ahead, a speck on the horizon far down the tracks. Coming closer.

Chapter 24

I switched trains at Gites and from there up to Vernet les Bains, high in the Pyrenees, where I took a room. Even this late in June, when I came downstairs the next morning my breath smoked into the rafters. At the breakfast table, I asked the waiter as I rubbed my hands, blue from cold, if it was always this frigid in summer.

"Not yet summer here. Here we yet remain in the moon of May. Summer still some weeks to come. Also we had a much hard winter. Sheep froze where they huddled. Came early and stayed too long. Short summers always come later after much hard winters."

"Good to know, but tell me after such a hard winter how does a stranger go about getting up to your monastery?"

Two fingers of one hand walked across the palm of his other.

"Really?"

"Only the last ten kilometers, monsieur. At least they tell me ten kilometers. I have never ventured there myself. Few of our villagers do. Except those who believe their souls misplaced and in need of finding. What would be the point?"

"Why no roads?"

"Oh, our terrain is *perfide*. You understand? Very treacherous. Besides, our brothers desire very much to be left alone with their God and their prayers."

"What do the brothers do for provisions?"

They grew it, my waiter told me. Herded it. Spun and weaved it. They were very industrious, their brothers. Then too they had a man, of sorts. Should they lack for anything they could not grow, herd, spin, or weave, they sent him down into the village.

"How does he get his purchases back up, with no roads?"

As seems true for waiters the world over, mine was a standup comedian in training, on the lookout for an audience upon which to hone his skills. He performed for me his imitation of Charles Laughton playing Quasimodo, one side of his face screwed up and hunched-over with his arms swinging and lifting his legs in place as though weighed down with lead.

"But will the brothers welcome a visitor who has not misplaced his soul?"

The waiter tapped a reflective finger on his cheek. He supposed they would. He knew no reason why they would turn away such a request, but never had he heard of anyone not bereft undertaking such a journey.

"Why would one, if in full possession of his senses?"

Despite his misgivings as to me not being in full possession of my senses, the waiter sent the hotel boy out to track down the chicken farmer who had come halfway down the mountain before dawn to sell his capons to the hotel's chef, then found for me a pair of wool trousers and a heavy shepherd's sweater.

"Our weather can turn quite inclement."

"Many thanks. I'll have them cleaned before I get them back to you."

"Not to bother. I do not know why I have not thrown them out long before. Many years has it been since I herded for my father."

"Your father no longer herds?"

"No. No longer."

Wolves got into his flock one night, and he took it upon himself to reproach them. Never should one reproach a wolf, my waiter warned me. Especially a wolf in the company of friends. Because they suppose themselves full of much dignity, wolves lacked all sense of humor.

"I'm sorry for your loss."

My waiter shrugged. "Many years ago has it been."

A bell rang downstairs.

"I need to return to my tables."

"Many thanks again anyway."

"But of course. At your service, monsieur."

****

Snug as a bug in a rug, surrounded by a dozen empty wood cages, I rode in the back of the farmer's redolent cart, dried brown droppings pasting a bed of chicken feathers to its splintered floor. We followed the gravel-paved main highway for several miles before cutting off onto a washboard dirt road used by mountain woodsmen to bring their felled trees down—by snow sled in winter—for sawing at the local mill. Up and up into the mountains he drove us in his two-wheeled cart for some hours before pulling in his team of white-faced mules.

"This is where you get off, my friend. If you have yet to come to your senses."

I hopped down and walked with more than a little stiffness around to where he sat up front.

"Is there some reason why I should come to my senses?"

But he only shrugged as I reached into a back pocket for my wallet and handed up a ten-franc note. He pointed to a path. A not-well-worn path easily missed.

"*Douze* kilometers from here."

"I heard only ten."

"*Douze.*"

"They told me in the village ten."

"Told you by one who never set foot up there. By that fool of a waiter. Like father like son. It is *douze*, I tell you."

"Have you ever set foot up there?"

"Me? What? You take me for a fool too? What man not crazy in the head would undertake such an arduous journey?"

"And on foot."

"And uphill. Steeply. Are you in much condition?"

"No, not really, anymore."

"Rest often, then, is my advice." Should I become ill, he said only the wolves would find me, and they cared not what they ate, those wolves. Wolves would eat even my bones. My boots. He eyed my waist. "Even your belt. Rest often. That is my advice."

"Many thanks for your advice."

"Another thing. Do not come between wolf pups at play and their mother."

"What if I do?"

Worn leather reins slapped the lathered rumps of the chicken farmer's mules. "You might remember your prayers in those last seconds God in his grace allots you."

****

If I wanted to know what became of Thomasina, I had no choice but to chance becoming a wolf's breakfast burrito. I followed the chicken farmer's advice, resting every fifteen minutes, more often when I grew winded. Kicked myself for giving up jogging because of a little Oregon drizzle. Then I had no choice but to take my time crossing a bridge woven from hemp rope, grasping for dear life its guide ropes as a fierce gorge wind blew me from side to side far above a stream I heard rather than saw through the thick vegetation below but sounded like it had to be hundreds of feet beneath my stammering knees. Two and a half wheezing hours after setting out, I reached the stone walls of a monastery somehow built on the edge of a sheer rock precipice. As the waiter had said, it had a garden and pastures dotted with couple-colored cows and some goats and a few sheep. A reassuring hum chanted from inside their tile-roof chapel. The eyes of the first brown-cassocked monk coming down the dirt path widened when he saw me, and he listened with his head bowed.

"Brother Luke may be able to tell you. He is charged this year with the keeping of records for the monastery. Our librarian, so to speak. Follow me."

****

We found Brother Luke in the kitchen, stenographer's notepad in hand, taking inventory.

"Our monastery has no electricity, of course."

"Of course."

Only a stream-cooled milkhouse that preserved for a few days or maybe a week, at most, he said. So even though they were self-sufficient, they did not wish to waste those bounties the Lord had blessed upon them.

"No. Of course not."

"Come with me. We keep the records of our visitors in the library."

First, though, Brother Luke removed from a library cabinet an oblong leather-bound volume, something similar to a deed book you might find in any county courthouse.

"This is our current log."

He explained that each year a new brother was selected to maintain it. This was his year to be so honored. In their logs they kept meticulous records of what transpired there each day. The weather. The fairing and failing of their crops and herds. Illnesses afflicting a brother. Names of those few visitors each year received by them. Brother Luke held out to me his stenographer's pad.

"You will spell your name and give us your address?"

I did as asked, and after Brother Luke copied it into the monastery's log, he waved his hand across the shelf of books lining one wall. Now I would join their library that went back to their founding in the year of our Lord one thousand-nine.

"I'm honored."

"Now what was the date your partisan fled here with his little one?"

After I provided him with the date Sister Agnes gave me, he crossed the stone floor to the wall-length bookshelf where he ran his finger along the spines of a row of books similar to the one on the table before me, bound in tanned leather from the monastery's own herd.

"Here."

He opened the book on the slanted shelf of a stand-up desk—the library had no chairs—and leafed through its pages, me looking over his shoulder. He ran his finger down a column, then turned to the next page. Then another. He flipped the pages back, looking at the pages before the first page he had read, shaking his head. He raised his eyes in puzzlement to mine.

"I am sorry, but I see no entry. No visitors at all near that day, even providing for difficult travel in time of war. Is it possible the sister gave you the wrong date?"

"Possible. Sister Agnes is very old. Not in good health. Then again, she found that day very traumatic. Is it possible their arrival did not get noted?"

Furrows creasing Brother Luke's brow deepened.

"While possible, not likely."

They received so few visitors, their arrival always noted, but a partisan with a refugee infant tucked under his coat? Coming to them in the dead of winter would be noteworthy indeed. Such visitors would be entitled to at least a whole page of their own, if not two.

"Did you receive many refugees during the war?"

"I was not then serving here as a brother, but I have heard some came to us."

"Is there anyone who was here?"

"Only Brother Theodore remains with us."

"May I speak to him?"

Perhaps, but he must caution me—when Brother Theodore fasted, he could be quite cantankerous. Brother Luke smiled.

"I think you Americans would call him something of a pill."

****

He led me along a narrow goat path that switchbacked up the dizzying steep escarpment to where Brother Theodore lived apart. A hundred feet below a one-window cottage cut from rock, Brother Luke turned, his hand raised. "Wait here. Allow me to go on ahead." He smiled. "I go to prepare a place for you."

So I waited. Looked down upon where Vernet les Bains played hide-and-seek as sly blue-black clouds winked open and closed. Stood shivering even with my heavy shepherd's sweater. Brother Luke did not return for a good fifteen minutes but was beaming when he did.

"Luck is with you, my son. Now that he grows resigned to his hunger, Brother Theodore's mood is much enhanced."

"I worried. You were gone so long."

"He can be quite the testy one if interrupted before he comes to his final amen. Better to allow him to finish. You may go on up the rest of the way now."

When I pushed aside the wool-blanket door, I found an unwashed and emaciated figure with a head of hair coarse as stubbled spring wheat in winter sitting on the dirt floor before a table knee high, the ascetic room smelling of overripe onions. Shadows cast by three flickering candles washed over the text open before him, but he smiled when he looked up, half his yellow teeth gone. He held out his hand.

"Please, pilgrim."

I sat opposite him, folding my legs before me tailor-style.

"So tell me the purpose for your making so arduous a journey?"

I explained. "Brother Luke tells me you harbored refugees in those years."

"We did indeed. None, however, did we notate in our journals."

"Why so?"

"The Nazis left our order alone. Still, should they have come, we wanted not to give them cause to line us up against the monastery walls."

"How did they find you? These refugees."

"Anton brought them. Always was it Anton."

"Anton?"

"Of the *Maquis*. From Ribeauville."

"Anton was the nom de guerre used by Thomas Thoreaux, of whom I spoke."

"A man of much courage."

"How did he come to know of you?"

Another had shown Thoreaux the way. From the village of Brother Theodore's youth, also from Ribeauville, who knew of the monastery. Though of debatable honor, he knew the brothers would never betray him.

"It could be he who rescued the little one whom you seek. Told the sisters he would bring her here as a ruse. A wily one he was."

"Is he still in Ribeauville?"

"News—when it reaches us at all—is very stale, but last I heard, he had sailed to America."

"America?"

"Yes. He worked the docks in Marseille before the war, so perhaps he does so still. In America."

A frigid wind whistling down the mountain drew from the slit cottage rocks a low, out-of-time moan.

"What is this man's name? Your former neighbor."

"Renard. His name is Erec Renard. Perhaps he took this girl with him when he sailed away to America."

That was when it came back, that which which would not quite come to me at the train depot in Ribeauville, and before that on the drizzly streets of Portland the night before Thoreaux's story broke. Back from a frosted Ohio morning after Thoreaux and Constable Durkin passed by us and out of the courtroom, my mother letting go my hand and pushing it aside, never to take hold of it again, and saying, "All right. All right if that's what you want. Go back to helping your grandfather after school, if that's what you've a mind to."

School by then had been in session for some weeks. My classmates for the most part left me alone, but not the older kids, for whom I was a scared rabbit in open season. Especially for Billy Stamets, whose family owned the plant where my dad worked before he dropped dead behind his desk. Why Billy had it in for me I never figured out. Never did anything to him. Maybe he thought of me as one of the family peons he could practice on until they put him in charge, but he provoked me. Called me Boxcar Willie and Little Harry Hobo, and since he was twenty pounds heavier, every afternoon I found myself lunching on a dirt sandwich.

It was after another fight as I trudged up the front steps of the *Oracle* with a split lip that a stranger stepped out of its twin front doors. While he held them open for me, he said nothing. I had been crying, and it was windy that day, so with the tears in my eyes his face was a blur, but from what little I made out he seemed to be sizing me up too, because his one eye followed me as I came up the steps. Only the one eye, though, for his other still looked to where I had been a moment before. As would, my Pentecostal grandmother prophesied, the all-seeing eye of the Evil One when he came to harvest my soul—which, like the souls of all sinners cast out by the Lord, now trod behind me like some penitent seeking a redemption never to be found. The stranger's look so rattled me I stopped sniveling and hurried past him, keeping my face turned away, and down into the basement where Grandfather Hardy set the type for our Thanksgiving edition coming out next morning.

"Oh, some fellow looking to talk to Cousin Thomas. Said he knew him from his newspaper days back in France."

"What'd you tell him, Grandpa?"

"Told him he'd best settle in for a good long wait. Oh, and your mama called. Asked for you to pick up a loaf of bread on your way home. How're you fixed in the way of coin?"

****

So there it was. My story. All of it. All of it except the most important part of it missing: What had happened to Thomasina? Missing and with no way I could see for me to find her.

Chapter 25

Upon getting back to Ribeauville late next afternoon, I found Father Paul stooped beneath a baking sun behind the cathedral, hoeing his tomatoes, a tall pile of weeds at his feet. He took off his broad-brimmed straw hat when he saw me round the corner and stood wiping his brow with the sleeve of his black shirt smudged with patches of dirt.

"I see in your face you learned something in your journeys. Perhaps something more than you wished?"

"Much more."

He sighed, putting on his hat.

"Pity, but such is the risk of seeking true knowledge. So has it ever been since woman handed man the tainted fruit. But come. Let us talk in the cool of my study."

****

I told him all Clem and I had learned since we left. All I had learned since Clem left to return to the States to tell a story only half true, its telling likely to be murderous.

"Oscar Wilde claimed to know two kinds of unhappy people, Father. Those who never get what they want and those who at long last do."

We sat once more at the table crafted centuries before from Bastogne walnut, his dimly lighted study as shadowy as my way forward.

"You are blessed to gain such insight so young in life. Most never do."

"I could live with fewer such blessings."

"Sometimes I think so too, but then I ask myself what sort of a life is one shrouded in shadow?"

"No, you're right. Not much of a life."

"So now you have your story. Though not the story you set out to find."

In the table's twist of wood grain my finger traced the turns of ages past. Their wisdom and follies. In seeking out my story, I had shed light on the twists of another's. A past when revealed to the world would complete the ruin of a life already in ruins.

"That's not why I became a reporter."

"Why did you?"

Because since Beth, I told him, I had pledged my heart to the stray dogs and lost cats of the world. Not every day and not in every story, but some days in some stories I gave voice to voices otherwise muted. Maybe setting right old wrongs.

"Somehow setting right those wrongs others suffered because of you?"

"You see me too clearly, Father."

"An occupational hazard for men of the cloth. It comes from so many troubled souls bearing their troubled hearts."

Whispered steps stole past his study door.

"You wanted for your story to find for Thomas his own forgiveness, but you also hoped it would give you yours."

"Both he and I are in much need of forgiveness. For me a forgiveness not deserved."

"That is why it is called grace. But perhaps it is too

soon to give up hope. For either of you. What will you do now?"

"I've run into a dead end for finding Thomasina."

So return to America, I guessed. She might be there, but I was at a loss how I would find her, with Renard at large. What then? I had no clue. I had lost my wife. Thrown her away, truth be told, which is what reporters are supposed to do, so maybe now was a good time to start. Lost Helen through neglect. Abandoned my mother and my grandfather when they needed me. Clémence. Thoreaux in not finding for him his forgiveness. And in that lack I had lost the chance to find my own.

"Lost only to be found anew, perhaps, Jeremy. Life is nothing, Ecclesiastes teaches us, if not a circle. A tossed coin turning in the air. When will you return to America?"

"Tomorrow, I guess."

"You will come to see me before you leave?"

"It will be early."

"Not to worry. I begin my morning prayers while our Ortolans have yet to sing their first note."

"That early?"

"You are not the only one, bound by chains forged in the darkness of a past life, in need of the hammer and anvil of prayer. Each of us must seek out his forgiveness in his own way. Me in mine, your Thomas in his. You in yours. Seek and ye shall find."

****

Father Paul walked me out of his study, but as I crossed the cobblestone square on my way to the inn, I knew I had left unfinished business behind. I took an aisle seat in the shadows of the next to last pew, where I searched the deep well of my hands until the rusty-hinge creak of twin sentinel doors, followed by a rustle of coarse cloth on wood in the pew behind me.

"You have been the much busybody reporter, young Jeremy."

That sandpaper voice rasped of two packs a day for forty years.

"I would have thought France the last place you'd run to, Renard."

"As would the police."

"When you called me that afternoon, on the night we saw each other again after twenty years, you knew of his knighthood. Spun me your yarn of longshoremen corruption to keep me occupied there so I wouldn't return to Hanna."

"I listen to Radio France on my shortwave."

Often, Renard said, they broadcast the news of the day some hours ahead. Most useful for the fox who must keep ahead of the hounds. As was reading newspapers in the public library on Sundays. Especially French newspapers.

"Faced with the doggedness of the hounds baying at his heels, the clever fox needs every advantage, does he not?"

The conceited bastard. But like all true narcissists, he had a need to brag about his exploits. Needed someone to listen. Father Paul stepped out of his sacristy, oblong wooden box in hand. He seemed not to notice us as he inserted candles of honey and beeswax into their sconces for next morning's prayers. Maybe, with some coaxing, Renard would be the answer to mine.

"You remembered me even before you first

called."

"Some months before, your paper ran one of its human-interest stories."

The one, Renard said, on the thirty-fifth anniversary of the shooting down of the notorious American gangster Clay Turner. He remembered one rainy winter night when, to pass the long hours, Anton told them of how it was his big break. Renard had connected my byline. Filed it away. Knew someday it could be of use. Depending on how the casino dice rolled. When he heard Father Connor making his rounds on the docks, he had already considered calling me about the Local. About Rago. The release about Anton hastened his call.

"You were the one who let air out of my tires back in Hanna. Landed a boot in my face. Left your note in our Paris pension. Tried to run us down."

"Only to frighten you home. When I truly want someone dead, I do not fail. No, they are dead."

"Gutted the cat in our room."

"What!"

"The gutted cat in our room."

"Some fiend gutted a cat in your room?"

"It wasn't you?"

"Never. What a barbarism."

Did I know during the Occupation there were many who sank so low as to eat cat? He never could bring himself to eat cat, no matter his hunger.

"An innocent cat. What comes of this world?"

"But it was you who stole my passport. Framed me for Julian's murder."

"The police, I thought, would engage you longer than they did. Then you scamper home. Tail between your legs." Renard sighed. They were so much more competent than in the old days. They even employed college graduates now. Once little better than the thieves they caught sometimes by accident. Much more worrisome for practitioners of the dark arts. But the best laid plans of mice and men. Of rats and snakes too, but so it goes. I should consider myself lucky. Some men he had framed stayed framed. "Like the father of your new friend Inspector Inman."

"But what about Julian? How could you murder an old man? A war comrade."

"Old men with their need to bare their souls pose a special risk to one's health. They are a cancer all unto themselves."

From the window of his Peugeot, Renard said he'd spotted me through the gates of the garden and took no chances on what Julian might reveal.

"Betrayed Gabrielle to the Gestapo."

They had, Renard claimed, traced him from Marseille to his mother's family there. A trade necessary if he wished not to board the Dachau Express, but he was happy to assist. Though his mother's family was French, his father's was German. He'd managed to skirt the trenches by serving aboard a French merchant ship—served until his oil freighter hit a mislaid British mine on its way back from Persia— but was not averse to passing along to the Abwehr any helpful information he chanced upon whenever they reached a neutral port. Or so his mother claimed. Summers she ridded herself of her son by sending him to spend half his summers in Ribeauville and half at the farm of his father's family in Bavaria, where unknown to her he attended youth camps run by the Nazis.

"Your betrayals leading to not a little profit. Your sack of German gold."

"A man must eat, no? Even in time of war. Especially if he wishes to abstain from cat."

"Fathered a child by Colette, whom you abandoned."

"A romance of convenience. Winters here are much colder than in Marseille. Good too for the odd piece of pillow talk."

"Blackmailed Gabrielle to travel to America to keep Thoreaux's story a secret. To dissuade others from digging up the past."

They held her first at Auschwitz, Renard said. Until the Gestapo colonel convinced Gabrielle's husband, Dominique, that his only hope for saving her was to betray Anton. Only after he agreed did they move her to Dachau. A less brutal camp as death camps went. The Gestapo colonel even arranged for Dominique to visit her. Visited on those days when their crematorium burned. Flakes of smoldered flesh falling from the soiled sky as does the sooted snow into the New York harbor.

That was how he learned of Thomasina. Renard had no choice but to send Gabrielle to America. Should compromising questions be asked revealing Thoreaux's past, they risked revealing hers and Dominique's also. Questions giving rise to more questions. Renard was at grave risk of extradition, and his chance at last to seize control of the Portland docks lost.

He revealed Thoreaux's secret, part of it anyway, to Clem because running some of it would deter others, now having lost their scoop, from digging up the rest. He failed, however, to foresee me entering her life.

"Speaking man to man, for your sake I hope she is not her mother's daughter. Such a fate deserves no man, though with the afternoon I was with her in Hanna I sensed they would not be so fortunate. But let us return to this business between us. What am I to do with you? Now, when all of my efforts have failed."

The twin front doors again creaked. A mother carrying a bundled infant passed down the aisle to the front of the cathedral, where she spoke to Father Paul.

"I asked, what am I to do with you?" A sharp metallic click at my ear—and his whiskey-stale breath warmed the back of my neck. "What I should do is slit your throat here and now and be done with you. Put an end to my worries."

The throat under discussion dried to ashes. I tried to keep my voice steady.

"On the contrary. Your worries would only begin."

"Begin? Begin how?"

Begin, I said, by sending Inspector Inman to Father Paul, who now knew Thoreaux's story. So what would he do, then? Slitting open the throat of an American reporter is bad enough form, but that of a priest as well? I could tell him from experience the judge here was what we in America called a hanging judge. Not for a single second would he hesitate to award Renard the seat of honor beneath the business end of the guillotine.

Only after a long minute did his whiskey-stale breath cease to warm my neck, followed by a second soft click, a rustling of coarse cloth, and I let go the breath I had been holding in for half of forever. Renard was proving to be a man who knew much more than he let on; he might also prove to be a man who knew how to hold onto what he knew until the right price tendered. A man who could be coaxed.

"Perhaps, Renard, there exists a resolution profitable for us both. Perhaps you and I can strike a deal to our mutual benefit."

"Deal? What kind of deal?"

"Thoreaux's child."

"What about her?"

"Is she alive?"

"Why should I tell you?"

"Do you know where she is?"

Renard did not answer. So had Clem yet run Thoreaux's story? Had the wire services picked it up? Would Renard have found time to read it?

"Here's my deal. You tell me where she can be found, I kill the story."

"How do I know you keep your word?"

"You don't. But it's the best offer you're going to get. One better than buying a front-row ticket to the coveted seat of honor."

We sat, Renard's whiskey-stale breath again at my ear. Not until the young woman cradling the infant turned to go did Father Paul notice us. I nodded to him and also to the mother, who smiled in passing.

"Then slitting open the throat of a mother with babe in arms would certainly get you your seat of honor."

The front doors creaked.

"All right, damn you. All right. You drive a harder bargain than those damn devils of the Gestapo. All right."

I had my deal, Renard said, but remember this. If I broke my word, if my damnable story ever ran, find me he would. He read newspapers. Lots and lots of newspapers. Nowhere could I run where he would not find me. No matter the time it took. I had borne witness to his tenacity, so rest assured—find me he would.

"Harbor no doubts, young Jeremy. None."

On this, I did not. Clem would run her story any day, if she had not already. Come morning, I could call Inspector Inman, but I lacked a smidgen of evidence tying Renard to Julian's murder. Maybe better to make a call to the Chief Assistant D.A. I was friendly with back in Portland. Had in fact written a Sunday feature about him after his roundup of the Chinese gangs who had run the East Coast Mafia out of the heroin trade in the Pacific Northwest and resulted in him receiving a big promotion. He was ambitious and hot for his boss's job. What better comeuppance for our trench-coat D.A. than for his chief assistant to claim the collar for Renard, rather than him?

"I'll remember. Now tell me where I can find her."

Renard chuckled.

"What's so funny?"

"You drive a bad bargain, young Jeremy. The sidewalk vendors of Paris would make a fortune from you. A most bad bargain indeed. "

"Bad how?"

"You know already where she can be found."

"Where?"

"Her housekeeper."

"Housekeeper? Gabrielle's?"

"Yes, of course."

Yes, of course. The photo tucked away in Thoreaux's stack of spider-webbed letters. Because it was in black and white, I'd missed the resemblance. But—

"But her housekeeper's name is Thérèse."

"Re-christened so they not guess her father."

At least, Renard said, not until she came of age. When he returned from Petershausen, he handed her over into the bereaved arms of their cook, who had lost her son in the first days of the war.

"Why go to the trouble? Why not leave her with the nuns?"

Too high a risk, Renard said. The sisters in their haste to get the child out of the convent might reveal too much of her history. A small risk, but when the risk was his neck, his back against the wall across the street, he was averse to even the smallest risk.

"This is why I still reside in the land of the living, when outside these doors the graveyard overflows."

Overflowed no thanks to him.

Having struck a deal, I stood and turned to face him. A face much aged from the one that had looked down from the steps of the *Oracle*. A face not to be trusted. Wisp of a weasel mustache darkening his upper lip. Lizard-green eye—the good one—weary and wary. Disconcerting glass left eye—the duplicitous eye of the Evil One—failing to keep symmetry. No, not a face to be trusted. But by no means was I out of the woods. Not yet.

"You have nothing to fear from me."

"Be certain I do not, young Jeremy."

"When will you go back to America?"

"Tomorrow, and glad to go. Much do I miss my Sunday papers. They are my only friends left who speak to me."

"There's a rumor they've got newspapers here."

"No time. You keep me much too busy. No more

than a few scraps. You?"

His indictment for the murder of Kid Twist was a local item. Maybe went out once over the A.P. wire, but there was no reason for it to travel outside the States.

"No. Nothing. Like you, too busy."

"Just as well."

Maybe I could yet salvage my longshoremen exposé.

"Tell me one thing more before we part."

"Maybe I will, maybe I won't."

"The night you and I took our walk. You told me about the troubles along the waterfront. The blackmailing and corruption. The killings."

"So what of it?"

"So that wasn't Doug Rago's doing. Not all of it. Some of it was you. Maybe even most of it."

"What do you want to hear, young Jeremy?" Renard smiled. "It can be a harsh world, yes? So should you ever consider reneging on our deal, remember the graveyard across the street. Heroes seldom succumb to old age."

Not likely I would forget. Not likely either he had kept all that many promises in his life. Perhaps there was a more permanent solution for my Renard problem than to call my friendly Chief Assistant D.A.

"Yes. A very harsh world."

"But harsh as it is, I cannot believe it."

"Believe what?"

"A cat. Some brute gutted an innocent cat."

He rose, shaking his head at the brutishness of the world, and for a moment we stood sizing each other up before I reached into my pocket.

"Here, Renard. Let us seal this bargain we made as

we did our first," and dropped into his hand, as he did into mine on the fog-ghosted streets of Portland, the Reichsmark coin.

Renard considered the Nazi coin, turned it over in his hand, before his good eye rose to consider mine.

"Seal our deal we make this night, young Jeremy? Or do you renege on our other?"

"As you wish."

I left him in the cathedral, walking out into the midsummer night, listening for the echo of footsteps following behind me that never came.

Chapter 26

Next morning after making my call home to Portland, I borrowed from Father Paul the parish's rattletrap Renault. When my bloody-knuckle knocking brought no answer, I walked around to the rear of Gabrielle's villa where I picked up the path that twisted down to her stone barn. An iron-slatted door leading into her cellar opened with a strangled groan, and for a minute I stood frozen at the top of the steps. A willowy shadow stretched across half the length of a pallid rock floor to the center of the cellar where a face contorted as any found in a medieval book of admonition stared up. Twenty feet above and one short step off to the side of a ladder, Gabrielle's body twisted in slow random patterns.

The ashen figure looking up seemed not to hear my footsteps, and only after some moments did he turn to me.

"When?"

"Last night." Dominique's words a whispered rasp, the rustling of leaves at autumn's end. "Early this morning maybe."

She had got out of bed. He thought perhaps to visit the Remembrance garden. Often she did when sleep failed to find her. When no sound of engine came from their garage, he got up. The phone call that evening had much upset her. A reporter from *Le Monde*. About

Clémence's story. Asking if Gabrielle had anything she wished to say. What was there to say? Other than at last it had come to its inevitable end. Other than to bid her adieu to the world. A world that didn't know all of it. Not yet, but now only a matter of time.

"About what we did. What I did."

While I had asked what harm our story might pose to Thoreaux, in my damnable blindness never did I ask what threat it posed to others.

"How long have you been here?"

"Still dark when I left the house. A half moon setting. So, close to three."

Whatever it was he had done, now he was only an old man whose past had at long last caught up with him. As had Thoreaux's. As in time it does with us all.

"Come up to the house. This isn't doing you any good."

But his eyes would not let her go. Good or no good, the final duty of a husband, he said, was to bear witness.

"Tables turned, she would be where I stand now."

So together we bore witness. Impossible not to stare. Head tilted a little to the right. Rope knotted behind her left ear. From its askew angle, it looked like the fall had cleanly snapped her neck. No small trick. Only the year before, I had interviewed the official executioner for the State of Nevada, a craftsman who took great pride in the details of his trade. He told me he had to take into account a host of factors. The weight of the condemned. How muscled his neck. No little matter to get it right, and his pride in his macabre calling required he get it exact. Too short a drop and the feet of the condemned would boogie the air for two minutes or more until his carotid artery cut off the flow of blood to his brain; too long a drop and he ran the risk of beheading the poor sod and, hacking a derisive brown wad of Mail Pouch spittle off to his side, give a field day to the damned death-penalty abolitionists. From her days in the Resistance, Gabrielle would know about getting the drop right.

"The American?"

"Please accept my deepest condolences, Monsieur Mercier, but come on up to the house with me."

"Truly am I sorry for the cat, Monsieur Michaels."

From the shadows of the street corner, Gabrielle spied Clémence had grown quite attached to it. After our visit, they grew desperate to discourage us from asking any more questions. They feared too what Renard might do, a man not known for self-restraint.

"You saw our monument to the Maquis?"

"I was much moved."

Then I must understand, he said, there were many who would be moved to violence. Many whose hearts still burned with the fire of vengeance. Gabrielle was right. Only a matter of time.

"Hours. Days. Weeks. But come the truth will. It always does. Its sequela not far behind."

"Please come up to the house."

But he only gazed up at the figure hanging above us. The stretched neck. Face discolored to garish purple. Her bulging eyes falling on the figure who bore witness. Eyes seeing and not seeing the eternal and endless black below. The first sight of what was or was not. I tugged at his elbow.

"Please, Monsieur Mercier. Come up to the house. I'll brew some hot coffee. We can talk."

He lowered his eyes to me. Cups red rimmed. Sullen. Depthless.

"What of Gabrielle?"

"I will call into the village."

"All right, but do not go. Not yet. There is much you must know. Much you must understand."

Yes. Much to understand. Much to understand what I had done in pursuit of truth. What Dominique had called, using the Church-Latin word, its *sequela*.

****

I dialed down to my innkeeper, who said he would ring Inspector Inman, and after Dominique told me where to look, I set our coffees on the kitchen table. For some minutes, as he searched its depths, a dark countenance curved in the porcelain ring of his cup. Throughout the gloomy house, silence save for the hollow ding of his gold band tapping the brown-stained rim as steam clouded a ragged face. At last he looked up.

For well over an hour I listened to the long list of Renard's myriad treacheries. Of Dominique's own betrayals. All to save the life of the one who was the love of his own.

"Dachau. Gabrielle. Adèle. Our thirty-eight. Thomas. For much does the criminal Renard have to pay. May he find rest only in the darkest depths of the deepest ocean."

I laid my hand on his.

"This morning your prayer may well be answered. Have faith."

Outside the kitchen window, Thomasina hopped off her bicycle. In the doorway her glance darted from one to the other of us, a wicker basket of fresh-cut lilacs in hand.

"What is wrong?"

I explained Dominique needed a moment and asked her to step out to the patio. Beneath the shade of the olive tree, she heard all I had learned of the betrayal of her until-now-nameless mother by her now-named father.

"I do not know," she said, shaking her head. "I do not know. To leave here, I mean."

This was, she told me, all the home she knew. Never had she traveled farther away than into the village on Sundays. Never had she even been to Paris, but to go—to fly—to America? She did not know, and now she was with child. Her time upon her in only three months... "This not so very long."

Her face reddened when she noticed me staring at her finger absent of ring.

"He's gone away, hasn't he?"

"Yes," she whispered.

She said she had been telling herself—deceiving herself—he had not, but she should salvage what remained of her dignity and accept the truth of her situation.

"So, yes. He has abandoned me." She touched her swollenness. "Us."

"Do you know where? Perhaps I can find him."

He claimed he would go to look for work in Paris, but more likely he had fled to the deserts of Africa. Joined a transient brother who worked oil field to oil field. What did we call them in America?

"A roughneck? Libya, likely."

A smile of bitter remembrance thinned her lips. Even as a little girl she'd promised never to be trapped in so precarious a position. Never to be like those older girls who worked there only to go away when they grew plump. Never to return. Yet there she sat. Her time drawing near.

"Why is it we are doomed to repeat our mistakes? Over and over. Generation to generation."

She turned away, looking down to the stone barn, her father's ice-pond eyes melting a little at their corners.

"He swore he loved me."

When they met in the hayloft, she thought him special. Different. She was fool enough to believe him because he told her all she longed to hear. Because she saw him as her path to a life not as a servant girl, but he had only used her. Had his pleasure. His fun. Then left her to pay the garçon when their bill came due.

"Now here I sit. So much I wanted to leave here. This house of death."

Death she heard in their whispers. Gabrielle not able to find sleep. Often leaving the house at odd hours. Not returning until dawn. Could not sleep even with the many pills spread across her nightstand. Sometimes she took too many. Twice Dominique rushed her to the clinic. Even when sleep found her, her screams woke the house.

"Screams only growing worse after you came."

"Were they cruel to you?"

She shook her head.

"Never did they beat me."

Even after the cook who adopted her died of cholera, she did not go to bed hungry. Even in those years with shortages of everything. Save a shortage of misery. No, they were not cruel. Just a distant coldness.

As in winter. As though she was not worthy of their love.

"Do you know how that feels to a child?"

I nodded.

"And now. To go to this man in America."

A man who betrayed her mother. Betrayed as she had been betrayed. She did not know if she could, though there was nowhere else for her to go now. Though it was only a matter of time before Dominique would ask her to leave.

"Then where will I go?"

I reached a hand to the linen sleeve of her blouse.

"Listen to me, Thérèse. Listen to what I have learned in my own life."

Sometime in hers, I told her, she too would betray one whom she loved and who loved her. We all had done so. We all will do so again. She might say now as Peter said in the garden she will not, but she will. We all will. And then she will cry for forgiveness. Want it as a drowning woman gasps for air. It might be from the child she carried. From the husband I knew she would find and who would love her.

"We have all walked down that road, dark as it is, but if we want to be forgiven, we must be willing to forgive."

She shook her head.

"I do not know."

"Once you hear him out, perhaps you will understand. Then, perhaps, you will find it in your heart to forgive. Because only you can lift that burden from your father's heart, Thérèse."

We sat. Ortolans fluttered in and out of the doubtful sunshine of a summer morning until, with the first screams of a siren far down the lane, they rose as one.

"All right," she whispered, a finger to her lips lest she speak in haste. "All right. But call me by the name my mother christened me. I hate that other. Call me Thomasina."

Chapter 27

The three of us sat in the oppressive shadows of his study, the mantel clock above Thoreaux's head ticking in precise one-second idylls. Ticked as it had for each endless hour of each endless day since his return thirty years before while he listened to the heartache history's follies had wrought upon the world.

Thomasina and I, an hour before, had driven our Hertz rental down Thoreaux's lane through the leaf-shrouded gloom of a late afternoon. We stopped before the rickety steps of his front porch and stepped out, me scanning the upstairs windows as Thomasina turned in a slow circle.

"He must be lonely. A very lonely man indeed."

"Lonely and alone. Alone by choice."

"That is the worst. The worst and the most desperate of those who choose a life of aloneness."

"So it is."

"We are not too late? From what you told me on the plane. That he has not…chosen to follow the path of Madam Mercier?"

"I don't know. I hope not, but I don't know."

She nodded at his weather-scoured barn.

"Should we not look there first? Where you found the rope when you were a little boy?"

A silhouette behind one of the black-paned windows of his study. Then gone. Or perhaps only a trick of light.

"Let's try the house first."

We hurried up the steps, my fist raised when the door flew open, Thoreaux stood before us, gallows-faced. His ice-pond eyes darted from Thomasina to me, then back again to her.

"I knew, knew always, when my time came, it would be you who came. On how many nights have I dreamed it just so."

****

He sat for a long time before his hands fell from his face and he looked across the dust-laden desk.

"You deserve an accounting, child."

"No." Vulpine-red hair swept her shoulders. Little wonder night after night a candle lighted Thoreaux's black-paned window. "No accounting demanded. The harshness of those years has ringed my life. The horror. A thousand times have I asked how I would have accounted for myself."

"You are very kind."

But he said, even if she was willing to unknot the rope slipped over his neck, he was not. She merited an accounting for why her father betrayed a mother who suffered so much so her child might live. An account and an accounting.

"I have much need to confess. This rot of soul has too long festered inside me."

"All right. If it will give you peace."

"Too late, I fear, child, but where to begin?"

My chair at the far corner of Thoreaux's desk faced his bay window that mirrored in its black panes a man near the end of his days in search for how to come to terms with a life he had struggled with so long and not yet come to terms with. His eyes drifted a moment before lighting on Thomasina, who sat holding her folded hands in the swollen lap of a sky-blue frock speckled with mustard-colored buttercups.

"Maybe begin with that spring morning when gray German tanks rolled across Flemish meadows, which found me within the hour barreling north in my doorless carcass of a Citroen on my way to hook up with the failing French and British forces."

Not ten minutes after he kissed Gabrielle goodbye on the patio, Thoreaux drove up on Adèle, sheet-wrapped bundle tucked under her arm and a ten-gauge Gastinne shotgun, bequeathed by her grandfather, with which he had taught her to shoot partridge, strapped over the opposite shoulder. Even from far down the road his heart skipped a beat, the steering wheel under his hands wet when he pulled up. She eyed him over, accepted his offer. They talked. Or rather she talked. Ranted, really. Face as aflame as her red hair. Vowed she would shoot every goddamn *Boche* dimwitted enough to venture into her gun sights. If the idiot French would not recruit her, she would find some other means to make the Germans pay, but by hook or by crook, a crop of blond-haired corpses would soon sprout from French soil. Oh, such a spitfire, her mother. How could he not but fall in love with her beauty and more so her passion? She sucked the breath out of him, as does the kick of a French army mule to the gut.

"My soul along with it." His smile beamed across the desk at Thomasina. "Still does."

"It shows."

After her ranting ceased—her anger abated hours later—Thoreaux said he convinced her she could do far more good for France as his assistant in getting word of their plight out to the world than if she managed to enlist. She did not have the time to learn soldiering, but she already had the true passion of a patriot. Together they did much. Told a cynical world of refugees crowding into an ever-shrinking sliver of Free France. Their lack of food. The rampaging epidemics of typhoid. Cholera. Their agony to get out no matter the cost. Called into question the wisdom of the isolationist policies being promoted back here by Ford and a still-grieving Lindberg.

While she did not assist him often at the front—he had to costume her as a French private, which proved to be quite the sorcerer's sleight of hand—getting their stories out required even more wizardry. The military had hijacked all lines out. She, though, needed only to flash those emerald eyes to beguile some homesick radio operator. He since had wondered if any fell subject to court martial for their seduction, and if they accepted with a smile the price paid as not too steep. Thoreaux winked at me.

"You see, Jeremy. I too know what it is to sacrifice all for a story, No matter the cost. But Thomasina, she was marvelous, your mother. Simply marvelous."

"Until one day you two had to get out."

"Yes. Then she grew even more marvelous."

The two of them, Thoreaux said, almost did not make it out, but they managed to hitch a ride across the Channel on the sloop of Lord Somebody-or-Other. His third trip or so, he claimed, but Thoreaux thought he may have been a bit mad in addition to being eccentric. His was one of the last boats to cast off from the beaches. One of the last at Adèle's insistence. Much more important for as many real soldiers to make it across so they could come back to slaughter the bastard *Boche* than for a couple of scrum reporters easily replaced. He warned her if captured they would be hanged as spies, but she seemed to think such a fate romantic and not too unfair a price to pay.

Thoreaux said he could not remember his ever spending a night so cold and so wet, and he was so very, very terrified. Adèle, on the other hand, seemed put out not at all. Charmed as well as peppered his lordship for hours on end with all manner of meticulous questions concerning the science of nighttime navigation at sea. Once landed, they covered the Blitz. The preparations for an invasion certain to be only days if not hours away. Managed to catch the notice of the authorities with all their questions in their very distinct and not very English accents, though even to the most tin ear they should have hardly sounded Teutonic, but such can be the vagaries of war. A frightening time. Public wary of all foreigners. They were held in Pentonville.

"Don't visit there if you can avoid it. Ghastly. A simply ghastly place."

Even before they took tea their first morning, the English raised the black flag after hanging a man housed only four cells down from his. Landed to radio back on their beach defenses. Walked him past Thoreaux's cell on the way to the gallows.

"Baby-faced lad of a mere nineteen, I'd say. Pity is, I suppose Jerry gave him about as much choice about going over to the other side as the English did. Rotten fortunes of war. A most rotten business."

"How long did they keep you and my mother

locked up?"

Two days, Thoreaux said. Only as long as it took for the transcripts of their interrogations to find their way into the hands of a Major Mason. An MI6 officer with whom he shared more than a few drinks at the British embassy in Berlin.

"Mason?" I said. "Mason? Mason?"

"Yes, that Mason."

Now Secretary of State for Defense, Thoreaux told us. Seemed as if every week now his name landed in the *Economist*. Likely the one who planted a bug about the knighthood in Her Majesty's ear. Talked her into overlooking his prison stint. Asked if he and Adèle cared to go back. Entertain Jerry with a bit of hijinks until he and his lads could come join them.

"Obviously you said yes."

"Your mother said yes. Demanded, in fact, he put us on a plane that very evening."

Thoreaux had been flabbergasted but not about to let this one out of his sight. Not for a second. He may have lost hold of his senses, but he was not crazy. They agreed.

"Me with less enthusiasm than your mother, but me insisting he send us back as a team."

Mason handed them off to SOE. Kept an eye out until after it all, when they flew him back. Thoreaux saw him late one boozy night at his club. As he wrestled Thoreaux into a cab, Mason promised he would receive recognition in due course, but right then they had some rather awkward issues needing settled with the Bolshies. Some had worked with Thoreaux in France. War not even over and whispers already up and down Piccadilly of moles in Whitehall and what not.

"He was, I think, smitten with your mother, as well. Half hoped she'd be the one to come back. A hope I wish had been granted."

SOE flew them in. A black moonless night, and they set about their bedevilment. The cells they set up met with initial success, but less than a week after Gabrielle's arrest, her cover suspiciously blown, the Germans reported her liquidated at Auschwitz. His newshound nose should have sniffed something terribly wrong then and there. Never did the Germans publish the names of those executed. Waited a month before they knocked on Dominique's door one midnight. Told him if he wished for her truly to escape the fate of the ovens, he had better start handing over names. Raids ensued up and down the cells of their circuit. They dropped like flies. First five. Then seven. Then twelve. He knew they succored a traitor somewhere in their midst, but not once did he suspect Dominique, who played so well his role of frothing-mouth husband rabid for revenge. Thoreaux spoke with him often about ferreting out their traitor. So often Dominique must have thought he suspected him and felt forced to play his trump card.

"My mother's family."

"Shipped off to Auschwitz as well."

Marched half frozen from cattle car straight to the gas chamber, Thoreaux said. Dominique claimed, however, an Auschwitz guard who passed through his cell on his way to Spain after he deserted his post told him that, because of the special treatment Adèle's family received, the SS surely must be holding them hostage in exchange for information. Dominique insisted to Thoreaux she had to be their traitor.

Thoreaux considered him deranged by grief, but Dominique had her tailed by his handler. Not five minutes after she left their last safe house, the Germans swooped in. While devastated at her supposed betrayal, Thoreaux lacked the heart to hold a Walther to her temple. He could not, however, keep her in the cell. Made himself believe if they only banished her the Gestapo would know they had blown her cover. Send her home because she was of no more use to them. If he thought of it at all, he did not think they would murder her. What would be the point? But he was too distraught to think with clarity. At the loss of so many of his family due to his blindness. The loss of the great love of his life.

"If only she had not kept it secret she was with child. Would my decision have been different?" Thoreaux studied the Delphic dust patterns swirling his desk. "They kept Gabrielle alive. Dominique continued to report back. But there was nothing to report back. We were finished. I was soon gone."

Time's pendulum arced above his head, unforgiving in its precision and absent of error, its immutable journey predestined. Thomasina at last let go a long breath.

"Papa. May I call you Papa?"

Thoreaux would not look up.

"After listening to what you heard, child, of that iniquity I must lay claim to and call my life, I do not see why you'd want to."

"Because I do not see your sin as so vile you are not deserving of forgiveness. Or that you sinned at all. A man of weakness trapped within a web of evil extricated himself by betraying a man of honor." She glanced back at me over her shoulder. "All of us are betrayed in our lives by those we trust. Betray those who have honored us with their trust. Such is the price we pay for living. But we must forgive so we in turn are deserving to receive forgiveness."

"What you say is all too true, child." For if loving and being loved are one side of life's coin, Thoreaux said, betrayal and being betrayed are its other. Charon's specie of the realm all must render. Allowing himself to be betrayed, though, while an act of folly, was not the sin that damned him. No, he had doubted her. A sin for which there is no absolution. "None."

Despair darkened Thomasina's face, she at wit's end without entreaty. I rose from my chair, but as his eyes refused to meet mine, I stooped to one knee.

"Perhaps, sir, it is by your daughter you receive your absolution."

"How?" Eyes awash in tears and shame rose only to fall again. "I fail to see how."

"By seeing not only was Adèle a woman of courage, she was also a woman of wisdom. Of faith." The courage of wisdom on a snow-drifted road to know her life neared its end, I told him, but also faith to believe their child's would not. A child their love brought into this world. Faith to believe. Despite with no mother it would be a journey impossibly long. A father years away. Yet faith to believe.

"Yes, of much faith. Of much heart, too."

"As are you. Only a man of much heart would suffer as you do."

"You are much too kind, Jeremy, but I know myself far too well." His glance swept over the study. Its shelves upon shelves of books. "Thirty years here imprisoned. Long hours alone. The one crime I cannot be judged harshly for is to have lived a life unexamined. She, on the other hand, was everything I am not."

"Yet she forgave you. Your child with your name is Adèle's message of forgiveness."

A child, I told him, so christened so he would know she knew he did what he did out of his duty to those who trusted their lives into his imperfect hands. Just as the work of all our hands in this life is imperfect.

"Look before you. Your daughter is the forgiveness you have sought for half your life. Look at her."

The tick of the mantel clock filled the room.

"Papa?"

Red-rimmed eyes rose, fell.

"Your daughter is Adèle's message telling you your way forward is not cut off. She is not cut off. Not even in death. For her sake, for the sake of your child, you must hear her message of forgiveness. Otherwise all her suffering went for naught. All in vain."

I raised my hand to a knee that trembled under it.

"Yes, in your unknowing, you betrayed Adèle. Betrayed your child not yet born."

But so had I, I said, and I did so not having his unknowing. Knew full well I betrayed Beth even as I betrayed her. Betrayed our child never to be born. Betrayed before conception.

"What worse sin can there be than to betray one's own child not yet conceived?"

Eyes I could not read shifted from her father to me.

Betrayed, I told him, by taking advantage of a lonely girl I did not love. Not at first. Lied to myself I could walk away. She could get rid of it. Yet she did not—could not—because at last she would hold a love she had never held. A love she lost.

"You need not rebuke yourself, Jeremy." The back of his frayed shirt cuff rose to a corner of each eye. "It is a common sin of youth. One shared by many of us."

"Though it be a sin common to youth in no way lessens the sin. Worse than my sin of betrayal was my sin to drive her away. As if would she disappear, so would the sin. Its consequences. At first."

Her commitment, I told him, despite my callowness—a steadfastness she saw I had yearned for since my mother went away—in time revealed me to be the fool I was.

"That you saw at all speaks volumes of your goodness."

"But seen by me only after it was too late. The damage done. She was dead."

A hand blued by time and by the veins that bound it to his heart found mine.

"You ask me to forgive myself, Jeremy, but can you not forgive yourself?"

After she died, I said, I thought I would find my way forward in saving the lost dogs and stray cats of this world. Its Beths. But I did not. The way forward for me I feared had been lost. Thrown away by my own hand. My own betrayals.

"You are once more too harsh on yourself, Jeremy."

Thoreaux said he could not tell me why we betray, but he knew if we are to come to terms with our betrayals we must move beyond a shattered trust to commence anew. Hope would reveal itself when we reaffirmed those bonds of commitment. My forgiveness was to be found in my finding a way forward. If he had now found his through his namesake, as I said, perhaps I had found mine in bringing her to him.

"Found your way by showing the way to another."

I glanced to Thomasina, dappled in darkness. But also in light. Six months expectant with the child of another's betrayal. As was Beth on that summer morning when she stumbled down the steps.

"Perhaps, Jeremy, the way forward for us can be found in our selfless giving of self. In our commitment of self to another."

Was this indeed my way forward? Was this what I had failed to see? What I had withheld? Failed to make that commitment of self to another because I could not forgive myself? Would I find my forgiveness only if I again risked making that commitment?

Having no reply, I returned to the chair beside Thomasina. She reached across and, with a look I again could not read, took my hand into hers for a moment before she let go.

We sat, Thoreaux regarding the dark visage mirrored in his desk, his face a sea of remorse. Of remembrance. Then the bittersweet smile of a man on the cusp of a reckoning, long sought and however imperfect, stole across his face. He pushed back his chair and crossed to the stack of once spider-webbed letters yellowing in the bay of the black-tinted window.

"I have some photographs. Only a few, and only in black-and-white. They don't do your mother justice. Impossible to get color film in those years. Taken in the countryside on one of those rare holidays our task masters bestowed upon us, but would you like to have a look?"

"Very much." She turned to me, her look I could not read now gone. "Would you like to see them too, Jeremy?"

"Oh, no need to ask Jeremy." A mischievous eye winked. "He's already sneaked a peek, haven't you, Jeremy?"

My cheeks warmed, but I laughed. "Found me out, did you?"

Thoreaux sat in the bay window, shuffling through letters now leavened to the same color of wild mustard as dotted Thomasina's frock, smiling to himself until he looked up, his face suddenly clouded.

"Are you in a hurry to get back, Thomasina? I mean, could you stay on for a few days?"

"I would like that. Very much. More, if you wish."

"Give me a chance to be something of a father. If you can see your way clear to indulge an old man."

"A father?"

"Or am I being presumptuous?"

"Not at all. I would like that very much, Papa. I have always wanted a father. A real father." She looked over at me. "Can you stay on too, Jeremy?"

Chapter 28

They had a lifetime to catch up on. Two lifetimes, truth be told, which is what Grandfather Hardy taught me newspapermen are supposed to do. Then again, some stories are better buried six feet under.

I said I needed to grab some air and walked out to the front porch. Noony last shoved an *Oracle* into the rusted newspaper holder affixed beneath the mailbox three days before. On its front page, beneath big block headlines, the story behind Thoreaux's refusal. As the village had not tarred and feathered him, only one other victim remained to scapegoat, which would explain why the most recent edition was three days old.

****

The brass tinker bell jingled as I pushed open the nouveau doors of stained glass, but instead of Clem I found Jess Walters sitting back in my grandfather's old office, at loggerheads with the telephone.

"Now, see here, Jensen. You and that hardware store of your'n have seen fit to advertise in our pages for nigh on thirty years. In ever' one of them years we've given you a free puff piece. Front page. Sometimes twice a year, even. Maybe promoting you when you had some sale going on and maybe when business got slowed up some. Suspect we saved your bacon more than once."

Good old Make-'Em-Sweat-Jess had stepped up.

Swinging at all pitches anywhere near to crossing the plate. Not until he hung up did he see me standing up front and waved me on back, his smile wide and broad.

"Decided to sneak back into town on us, did you?"

"Yes, sir. Looks like Clem managed to drag you out of the basement and into the front office."

"Worse than that, I'm afraid."

"Worse how?"

"Why, the quitter. Went and dropped her keys off in my mailbox last night."

"She's quit?"

"Sure did."

"She's handed the *Oracle* over to you?"

"Thought that's what I said."

"What happened?"

What happened, Jess said, was she went and ran her story about the real reason Thoreaux refused his knighthood. Or what she said was the real reason. Didn't read quite right to Jess. He gave her fair warning not to run it. Wouldn't listen to him. Typical woman. More mule-headed than Samuel ever was, which was saying some. Village twice as tizzied up over her sequel as they ever got on the original. By noon next day, she'd lost every advertiser she had left except for Corey, and almost all of her remaining subscribers to boot.

"She still around?"

"Not for long, I reckon."

"Where's she at?"

"Packing, I suspect. Heard footsteps going up and down the back stairs all afternoon."

Jess said Colette had stopped him yesterday on the courthouse steps. None too happy. Told him Clem and

Aimée were heading out for the cesspools of California.

"So what are you doing here?"

"Trying to run a newspaper."

Retirement, he told me, hadn't sat with him all that well on his first fling with her, so he figured what the hey. Since he had them in hand, might as well roll the dice. What did he have to lose at his age? Had picked up most everything he knew about running a newspaper from Samuel. Been on the phone since seven that morning. Managed so far to snare back about half of their old advertisers and a couple of new ones to boot. Once they heard Clem was packing up and packing it in.

"Might make it. Might. Oh, and Henry called this morning."

"What's up with Henry?"

"Wanted for you to know about this Renard."

"What about him?"

"Salmon boat come across him floating in the river."

"Accident?"

"Not hardly."

Not, Jess said, with his feet bound with his belt and both hands hacksawed off at the wrist. Likely right before he dove in for his swim. Police got to checking out his room for clues as to who might have done him in. One of them noticed the plastering on his one wall looked a might fresh. Over six hundred thousand stashed away.

"Six hundred thousand after they confiscated their finder's fee. Still, a lot of bills for a lowly labor lackey."

"Police got them a Doug Rago locked up on

suspicion of murder."

"Seems like a more than likely suspect."

"Henry said with Renard dead and Rago dead to rights, you was looking right prescient. Your publisher's been asking when you were going to be back walking your beat."

Sounded like Henry's job was safe.

Footsteps trod overhead. I glanced up at the ceiling.

"Suppose I should go up and make my goodbyes."

"I suppose." Jess had picked up the telephone receiver again. "Worst kind of business you can leave behind is business you let go unsettled."

****

I knocked on the open door to her upstairs apartment.

"Back here!"

She glanced up from an almost-full suitcase when I came to the doorway of her bedroom where she stood folding the red dress she wore the morning we drove up to Cleveland Hopkins after she hammered the taillight of my Hertz rental.

"Jess told me, Clem. I'm sorry. Anything I can do?"

"No. Nothing anyone can do. Should've listened to what you told me at the railway station would happen."

"I was guessing. You didn't know. Not for sure. Like Jess says, sometimes you need to roll the dice to find out."

"Except sometimes when you roll them they come up snake eyes and leave you busted."

"Yeah. Sometimes they do. I'm sorry." I looked around. "So where's Aimée?"

"With her grandmother."

"Colette will miss her."

"They'll miss each other."

She snapped her suitcase shut.

"I'm sorry too, Jeremy. For what I said at the train station. None of it's true."

"No. Most of it was. You heard about your Aunt Gabby?"

"Late last night. Right before I dropped off my keys with Jess. What have I done, Jeremy?"

"No. What did we do?"

"I've been pissed off at the world and looking for someone to get even with ever since Corey pulled Chris and Charlotte out of fifty feet of water. Look at what I did. To Aunt Gabby. Thoreaux. You. Me. Us."

"We both have much to make right. To somehow find a way forward."

"That's why I need to get out of here."

"Running away was no solution for me, Clem."

"Well, maybe for me it is. Like you said. Sometimes you have to roll those dice to find out."

"I hope you do find out. Will you be back?"

"Not without reason."

"I'm sorry it didn't work out between us."

"It's what we both needed, but timing is everything. I have this poison inside me. It poisoned us. Until I flush it out, it will poison anyone who comes near me."

"Give yourself time."

She looked around her bedroom. "All packed. Time for this girl to boogie."

I reached for her suitcase. "May I?"

"You're so sweet. I'll miss that."

****

After I slid the suitcase into her trunk, I half hoped Clem would let me kiss her goodbye, so we could be certain, but as I slammed it shut she was already opening her door. So I guessed we really were finished. She put one foot inside, then turned back to me, coal-black eyes smoldering.

"I was in your grandfather's office, wrapping up some business this morning, when your editor spoke to Jess. It was you, wasn't it?"

"He's not someone you'd want in your life, Clem."

"Wasn't your decision to make. Even someone is better than no one."

What could I say? What could I say that the poison would let her hear?

"Another reason not to come back," and she climbed in behind the wheel. I watched her drive away—watched as I had Helen—until she turned out of the alley and up Union Street.

****

Jess was hanging up the phone, smiling as he penciled a checkmark next to a name on his notepad.

"You maybe need an extra hand dialing?"

"Wouldn't turn one down, if it got offered. You thinking maybe of sticking around to be of any real use?"

From the doorway I took in the old newsroom. Inhaled the comfortable smell of seasoned wood. The memory of hot lead steaming through floorboards on frosted mornings while an antique Mergenthaler Linotype clanged in the basement. A girl with vulpine-red hair sweeping her waist. As was Beth when she stumbled downstairs, six months expectant with child.

Maybe she was a chance to right my past. For even here there were tales worth telling, for in them their words had power. The stories they told had consequences. Consequences tolling on for years. For decades. This is one of those stories.

"Might stick around, Jess. Might just roll the dice one more time."

A word about the author...

Scott Kauffman is an attorney in Irvine, California, where his practice focuses upon white-collar crime.

He is the author of the coming-of-age novel *Revenants, The Odyssey Home* (Moonshine Cove Publishing) and the legal-suspense novel *In Deepest Consequences* (Medallion Press).

Learn more at:

www.scottkauffman.net